D1149957

TOMMY Parker

First Edition
- 2014 -

Published by
Candy Jar Books
113-116 Bute Street,
Cardiff Bay, CF10 5EQ
www.candyjarbooks.co.uk

A catalogue record of this book is available
from the British Library

ISBN: 978-0-9928607-1-4

Cover illustration
Copyright © Nathan Hudson 2014

Edited by Shaun Russell

Printed and bound in the UK by
CPI Group (UK) Ltd, Croydon, CR0 4YY

For Helen

— PROLOGUE —

A dozen of the King's Guard had chased him to the end of a long stone corridor. He was cornered now in passages deep beneath the Houses of Parliament; the building that he'd come to destroy. There was nowhere left to run.

Breathless, he turned to face his pursuers, sizing up each of them and searching for a weak link, weighing up whether there was any way that he could fight his way out. The guards, each of them protected by their leather coats and iron breastplates, stood four across and three deep, cutting off any hope of escape. They held half-pikes that were thrust menacingly towards him. He didn't stand a chance.

He thought about his partners in this scheme and wondered whether they would have more luck. It was certainly a great shame that they'd no longer be able to see their mission through.

And all because of that strange little old man.

He recalled the last few moments, considering where it had all gone wrong.

Their plan had been simple, but the effect would have been devastating; a blast that would have been heard around the world. He'd hidden in these cellars for days with little water and even less food, but none of that had bothered him as such small sacrifices would be worth it in the end. And he'd come so close too; today was to be the day. He had gone through his final checks: examining each wooden barrel, each fuse, and making sure that nothing could go wrong. Through their connections they had managed to secure the ideal location: a huge disused cellar located directly beneath the House of Lords. Right where they needed to be! The planning had taken months, years even, with thousands of pounds spent and countless favours called in, all of which would have soon borne fruit. They wouldn't have known what had hit them.

His surroundings had been filthy; his dust-covered cloak shrouded his scruffy clothes, and his normally smart boots had been made dull with dirt. Scraps of food were lodged in his moustache and his bushy, reddish-brown beard.

When he checked the contents of the last barrel, his cloak had fallen from his shoulder, exposing a thick, powerful arm. On his forearm was the scar he'd been given in a knife-fight but above that scar was a more intriguing sight altogether; a mark that he always kept hidden, unless in certain and familiar company – it was the inky tattoo of a quill, a mark that each of his co-conspirators also boasted. The mark of the Brotherhood.

He had examined the fuse one final time, thinking with pride how it was him who had been chosen to complete this, the most important of tasks. Those thirty-six barrels, filled to the brim with gunpowder, which would change history. And it was he who had been chosen to light the fuse. A single match that would illuminate the city and bring with it a new beginning. This King hadn't understood them. It had fallen upon his brethren to make a change.

He remembered looking at his pocket watch. The time had come. So much firepower would not just demolish Parliament but also most of central London. The blaze would light up the night and burn for a year. People would long remember this day and sing songs about it. And him? Well, they were sure to make effigies of him and chant his name. He would have been a hero.

If only it wasn't for that old man.

He recalled how, in his final moments of preparation, he had been startled by a voice from the darkness. He'd thought he had been alone.

'Penny for them, Guy?' the voice had said.

'Huh? Who's there?' he'd replied as he recoiled in fright, shocked that someone had been lurking in the shadows.

'Your thoughts, Guido,' the invisible voice replied, 'a penny for them?'

An old face had then moved towards him out of the darkness. The face belonged to a man, a rather pleasant looking old man, who was only just taller than the wooden barrel that he'd hidden behind.

'I don't know who you are,' Guy replied. He felt calmer as he realised that the stranger carried no threat. 'But you can't stop this. You're too late. This is my destiny!'

He had taken a match then and, kneeling by the slow-burn fuse, had deliberately, poignantly, struck the match and watched as the bright flame threw the cellar into light.

'I'm afraid, Mr Fawkes,' the old man had said, 'that there will be no fire in the sky tonight. I cannot let you succeed again. Not this time.' He'd then swiftly blown out the match before adding, 'But you *are* right about one thing: the world *will* remember you.'

Dumbfounded, Guy had done nothing but stare blankly at where the wrinkled face had been, holding the spent match as it had smouldered in his fingers. Coming to his senses, he'd then reached out, snatching at nothing but a handful of darkness. The figure had vanished. It was then that dozens of heavy footsteps clattered on the stone outside the door. Then a loud crash as the doors had burst open and sent shards of wood flying across the room as the King's Guard charged through. He'd run for all he was worth, but there was no way out. His escape route was blocked by a bolted door. He evaluated the scene again. *This wasn't how it was supposed to happen.* Who was that old man? And how had he vanished so impossibly into thin air?

Deciding that he'd rather go down fighting, Guy pulled a dagger from his belt and braced himself for the fight that he knew would end his life. He steeled himself to charge but stalled as the wall of soldiers parted suddenly. *Were they really going to let him through?* His optimism was short-lived. A heavy rattling was followed by the emergence of two soldiers rolling a small cannon into the gap that they had created. Clearly they were taking no chances with him. Then, reminiscent of himself only moments before, one of the Guards knelt and struck a match, lighting the fuse.

Seconds later there was a loud bang.

Guy Fawkes saw it all in slow motion. The dagger fell from his hand as the cannonball flew through the air towards him. This was it. His time had come.

The football flew through the air towards him. This was it. The time had come. If Tommy could save this then it meant that he would have made five world-class saves in a row. Not only that, but he'd also get bragging rights over his best mate. Ben had actually made pretty good contact with the ball this time, sending it shooting towards the top corner of their makeshift goal – a colossal concrete bus shelter almost ten feet high.

The ball rose high to Tommy's left, and he knew instantly that it wasn't even worth him moving for it; Ben had placed it well out of his reach. His friend looked on hopefully, willing the ball to find its target, hoping that he wouldn't miss yet another one. His hope soon turned to despair though, as the ball sailed past Tommy and finally settled on the roof of the shelter.

'YES!' Tommy cried. 'That's five in a row!'

'Technically, you didn't actually save that one,' a dejected Ben replied, disappointment plastered all over his face.

'Bet you wish I had though,' Tommy said with a knowing smile. 'Whoever kicks it gets it, remember? You'd best get climbing!'

— CHAPTER ONE —

Grandpa's House

Tommy Parker raced across Harbour View on his bike and came skidding to a halt outside the wall of number twelve. It was the last week of the summer holidays, and, as ever, he was spending it with his grandpa. This was something he had always done – often with so much enthusiasm from his parents that he was beginning to wonder whether the holiday was for him or for them. He had always enjoyed the visits, but since his nan had died the atmosphere had changed. It wasn't as fun. Grandpa wasn't the same either. He had changed too.

It was a clear morning with just a handful of wispy, white clouds adorning the light blue sky. Perfect conditions for riding his bike. And Tommy loved it! Football and riding his BMX. He couldn't think of two things he liked doing more. Football was the one thing he was *really* good at. In every other part of his life, he was average, he accepted that. Average height. Average build. He even had an average haircut – his brown hair cut short back and sides just like his dad's. He was also pretty average in school. Most teachers thought that he had at least a little bit of academic potential, but the general consensus was that he'd have to stop daydreaming in class. Maybe next year!

Hopping off his bike, Tommy wheeled it down the side path and into the back garden. As far as Tommy was concerned, Grandpa had lived in this house forever. He looked around the large, shabby garden, and his memories came flooding back.

Like the time Ben had slipped into the fishpond whilst trying to catch a tadpole. Tommy and his grandparents couldn't help but laugh as they watched Ben flap around on his back panicking, not realising just how shallow the water was.

Tommy leaned his bike against the side of the house and let himself in through the back door. 'Grandpa!' he shouted. 'It's only me.'

He moved through the kitchen – a room which was also full of happy memories.

Like the time his nan had baked every kind of cake Tommy could imagine. Cakes he'd never even heard of and ones which he often suspected she had invented just to amuse him: chocolate cakes, butterfly cakes, rock cakes, boulder cakes, fairy cakes and his personal favourite, furry cakes (invented when his nan had dropped most of the batch on the floor). But they had all tasted gorgeous!

They would spend hours simply enjoying each other's company, making up silly stories and singing songs until bedtime. The house was so full of life and laughter then, but those memories were now tainted with a generous pinch of sadness.

'Grandpa!' he shouted, louder this time.

Walking from the kitchen, Tommy entered the dining room, now mainly used as a study. There were two large bookcases dominating the back wall, each full to the brim with books of all sorts of shapes and sizes. He stood there for a few seconds, staring at the various titles. There were books on every topic you could imagine. His gaze was drawn, though, to a large, black book that was covered in dust and which was, as ever, just out of his reach on the top shelf. Tommy was just about to stand on tiptoes when he was startled by Grandpa's voice.

'Hello, stranger! I didn't hear you come in.'

Grandpa was stood at the door to the kitchen. He always used this familiar greeting. Regardless of whether he'd not seen him in weeks, or whether Tommy had just popped to the bathroom, he'd always say it. It was a catchphrase of his.

Leonard Parker, or Lenny to his friends, was in his seventies but had always looked good for his age, probably a result of the amount of time he spent in his garden. In the last few years though, the years since the death of Tommy's nan, he'd aged a great deal. From looking healthily filled out, he'd now lost too much weight, which gave him a gaunt, tired appearance. What had once been a generous head of hair had now diminished, leaving thin, grey strands on the top of his head. Most noticeably though, especially to those close to him, was the change in his eyes. When Nan was alive, Grandpa's eyes were full of mischievous energy. Now his eyes were tired and sad. Almost as if the spirit within them had died at the same time as Nan.

'Oh, hi, Grandpa!' Tommy said approaching him, extending his arm to shake his hand.

'What's this? You're not too old to give your Grandpa

a hug!' He leaned forward and squeezed Tommy briefly. 'Where's your mother?'

'Right behind me, bringing my stuff in the car. I beat her over,' he added proudly. Suddenly a loud bang emanated from the kitchen as the back door was thrown open. Both Tommy and Grandpa entered to find his mother stood in the doorway, her top half obscured by three large boxes, a battered old rucksack dangling from her arm.

'Tommy! Are you in here?!' a voice barked from behind the boxes. 'Give me a hand with these!'

He ran over to her, grabbing his rucksack from her grasp and taking the top box from the stack in her arms. As he did so, the head of his mum, Brenda Parker, became visible. And boy did she look flustered!

'How do I always end up carrying your stuff?' she asked, still struggling not to drop the remaining boxes.

'Hi, Dad', she said, placing the boxes onto the table, 'I've made you some Welsh cakes; they're in the top box.'

She kissed Grandpa on the cheek and then turned to Tommy, whose hand was already delving into the box of cakes.

'I saw Ben cycling up the road as I pulled in. I did beep to him but he was in a world of his own as usual.' Tommy headed towards the back door, grabbing his helmet from the table as he passed.

His mum followed and, with Grandpa distracted by the kettle, whispered. 'Don't stay out *all* day with Ben, spend some time with your Grandpa too. He doesn't see that much of you anymore, and you know how much he loves your company.'

'I know Mum, I won't be long. I'll just pop out for an hour or so,' he replied, thinking about how much more fun he'd have with Ben. Grandpa never wanted to mess around anymore.

'Well make sure that's all it is,' she said, ruffling his hair. 'I'm only staying for a cup of tea, so I'll call you tonight. Have a nice week...' Wheeling his bike along the side of the house, Tommy pretended not to hear as she shouted after him, '...and don't forget to do your homework!'

Tommy closed the side gate at the same time as his best friend, Ben Campbell, skidded to a halt by the path. They'd met when they were four, when Ben's family moved to Little Millbrook, and they'd been inseparable ever since. They were about the same height but, if truth be told, Ben carried too much weight for a boy of their age. His mother kept saying he was just 'big boned', but he hadn't always been this chubby, and Tommy knew that it got him down. He'd always been as fit and active as Tommy; in fact, Ben had been one of the fastest boys in junior school. But that was all before the accident two summers ago.

Ben had broken his right ankle when his skateboard had collided head on with Mr Wally Barnes, but what made it worse was that Mr Barnes just happened to be driving his Ford Cortina at the time. The break had been a bad one, never quite healing properly and, ever since, Ben had walked with a slight limp. As a result, their once regular adventures into the woods became more and more infrequent and Ben was certainly a long way off starring for the school running team.

In truth, Tommy blamed himself for Ben's accident, and the guilt he felt was sometimes unbearable. They had been spending one of their usual Saturday afternoons playing on their skateboards, taking it in turns to race down the hill. One would lay flat on his skateboard and roll down as fast as possible whilst the other would stand halfway down the hill and act as a lookout for oncoming cars. On one of Ben's turns though, Tommy had been distracted by something in the bushes on the opposite side of the road – and the distraction had proved disastrous. It was weird. He could have sworn that he'd seen his grandpa's old neighbour Mr Wiseman in the woods. But it couldn't have been him. There was no reason for Mr Wiseman to have been there. Anyway, Tommy had failed to notice Mr Barnes driving up the hill in his battered Cortina, and he couldn't shout until it was too late. The noise was sickening. Ben had collided feet first with the bumper of the car, his right ankle taking the worst of the impact, breaking in three places. Tommy would have done anything to prevent the accident. But it was all in the past, and the past couldn't be changed.

Ben sat proudly upon his brother's bike, which was obviously too big for him, his good leg stretched to its limit and his toes barely touching the pavement as he struggled to keep his balance.

'I had to grab the bike early before Richie got up,' he said. 'He'd have killed me if he'd caught me.'

Together they pedalled away from Grandpa's, across

the patch of grass and towards the road leading out of Harbour View.

'What d'ya fancy doing?' Tommy asked.

'Don't mind really, but I've gotta be back by five. Wanna sneak this back in when Richie's still out.'

'We could go up to the fort for a few hours then?'

'Nah, it's uphill all the way.'

Ben was never too keen about going up to the fort, not since he'd had a nasty fall there a few months back. Tommy on the other hand quite liked it; there was so much history to the place.

'What about down the docks?' Ben suggested. 'We could throw stones at some of the boats again?' he added enthusiastically.

'No way! My parents found out about that the last time – they grounded me remember? I swear they know *everyone* in this town.'

Then a shout came from behind them.

'Tommy! Hold up! Where're you going? OK if I come?'

Tommy stopped his bike and swivelled around as Ben, who had apparently gone deaf all of a sudden, continued along the road.

Running across the grass towards them, with a heavy looking satchel over his shoulders was Arthur Ford. Arthur, or Art as he was called by everyone in school, was the same age as Tommy. In fact, they were in some of the same classes. Tommy really liked him and knew him well from the summers he'd spent at Grandpa's. Most of Tommy's friends however, Ben included, didn't have a lot of time for

Art. Put simply, they thought he was a geek. There were many times when Tommy and Ben had argued over some of the flippant yet nonetheless mean comments that Ben had made about him.

Art struggled for breath as he ran excitedly to where Tommy waited. Ben, accepting defeat, slowly circled back towards them. Art was a fair bit shorter than Tommy and wore thick-rimmed glasses which made the messy brown hair that fell over his ears stick out in little tufts. He somehow looked out of place in a pair of shorts and T-shirt and was probably the only pupil who would have preferred to have worn his school uniform all year round.

'Well? Where're you going?' Art asked, finally catching his breath.

Ben spoke before Tommy could answer.

'We're going up the fort. I'd expect it's too far for you to come, y'know, if you haven't got a bike...'

A familiar look of rejection flashed over Art's face. He looked down at the double-knots in his laces. 'Oh. Never mind then. I'll just hang around here.' Tommy shot Ben a scalding look.

'I don't fancy going up to the fort anymore,' he said, 'it's too far. *And* it's uphill,' he added, making sure that Ben didn't miss his mocking tone.

'Oh fine,' Ben replied. 'Let's race down to the docks instead then. I can't be beaten on this thing!' He began to cycle hard down the pavement towards the main road.

'Nah, I'm happy to stay here', Tommy shouted after him, 'let's just kick a football around or something'.

Ben braked sharply, wobbling to a stop. Art's head rose along with his spirits.

'You don't have to hang around here for me,' he said, checking that he wasn't being a burden. 'I've got plenty to do. Mrs Smith gave me a few extra assignments for English.'

'Ooh, bad luck,' Tommy commented. 'How come?'

'I asked her for them. I wanted to get ahead.'

Art's enthusiasm for homework was baffling, but Tommy didn't want to dwell on the matter for too long because Ben, who would no doubt have a go at Art for asking for extra work, was now pedalling back to them.

'Anyway,' Tommy said, 'I'd rather just hang about here; it's too hot to cycle all over town. You're up for that aren't you, Ben?'

Ben, circling lazily around them on his bike, replied with an air of resignation, 'If we *must*…'

All three boys started over the grass back towards Grandpa's, Ben riding in big circles around them. Tommy noticed the edge of a large book protruding out of Art's satchel.

'What you reading?' he asked, keen to make him feel more welcome after Ben's frosty reception.

'Oh that? It's just a history book. I've got another assignment to do. You should have it too.'

Tommy did have that project to do over the summer, something about the Second World War. He'd completely forgotten about it.

'What book did you get?' Tommy asked, hoping for tips.

'*World War Two – Were there really any winners?* I'm

writing it from a humanitarian angle y'know, about the consequences and perils of war.'

'Sounds good,' Tommy said, genuinely impressed.

'Sounds *boring!*' Ben chipped in, still circling around them, a proud look on his face. His moment of glory was short-lived however, as he turned the handles too sharply on his over-sized bike, causing the front wheel to turn in at an awkward angle and him to collapse to the ground on top of it. Both Tommy and Art laughed and pointed hysterically.

'Ben... you OK?' Tommy finally managed to say between guffaws.

'Yeah, I'm fine! Just thought I'd plonk the bike down here and use it as a goalpost. Anyway, that topic *does* sound boring,' he added, getting up slowly and trying to shift the attention back to Art. But nothing could ruin the moment and Art continued to laugh uncontrollably. 'You're right, Ben', he managed to say, taking a few more seconds to wipe the tears from his eyes. 'It probably would be boring for you. It's an awfully complicated subject – some of the words even have as many as *three* syllables.'

'What's that supposed to mean?!' Ben demanded, stung by the comment.

'Oh, come on, Ben,' Tommy said, hoping to lighten the mood, 'you've never been the best with words. Remember that time at my Grandpa's? When we were playing that quiz?'

Ben's initial look of confusion was soon replaced by terrible realisation – he knew what was coming next.

'When he asked you, "*What L is commonly known as the*

King of the Jungle", and you replied... *elephant!'*

This was too much for Art, who had only just recovered from his previous fit of laughter. He doubled over onto his knees, his body shaking violently but no noise coming out. Ben, his face crimson, looked helplessly to Tommy with a mixture of embarrassment and anger. They continued to chuckle as Ben dusted himself off and pulled his bike back to a standing position. He appeared just about ready to storm off when a look of utter terror appeared on his face.

'Ssshh! Hush a minute!' he said urgently.

Art's moment of bliss was cut short. The sudden change in Ben's mood concerned them, and they both stopped laughing and looked at him. Ben was staring beyond them into the distance, his eyes transfixed on something, settling on a house at the other side of the street. He nodded his head slightly, too afraid to point with his finger, afraid of drawing attention to them.

'What is it?' Tommy asked, turning around cautiously.

'There. See?' Ben replied, nodding again. 'Old Mr Wiseman in his window.'

Tommy looked towards Mr Wiseman's place. The house had an eerie feel about it, even on this bright summer's day. The outside, originally painted a bright cream, was now a grubby shade of fawn with patches of mould and vine sprawling up the wall. Whatever the weather, every curtain in every window was always drawn. A household in constant mourning. All of the curtains were drawn, that is, except for today. For the first time in Tommy's memory, the curtains of the ground floor window were parted, and in that parting stood the unmistakeable silhouette of the homeowner. It was his presence that had caught the eye of Ben, and it was his presence which now drew the undivided attention of all three boys.

'Spooky...' Ben whispered.

None could avert their gaze from the window, each one fascinated by the short and more-than-slightly tubby frame of Mr Wiseman. He stood motionless in the window, appearing to stare in their direction.

Tommy finally broke the silence, 'C'mon guys, stop gawping at him! It's rude.' But even as he said it he couldn't take his own eyes off the house. Finally, and with great effort, he swung his body around to face Ben and Art. 'Seriously, let's go.' They struggled against the hypnotic stare of Mr Wiseman before they managed, as if coming out of a trance, to turn away from him and follow Tommy over the grass towards Grandpa's, Ben now pushing his bike and his limp even more pronounced since his earlier fall.

'Does he *ever* leave his house?' Art asked. 'I've lived here for years, and I've not once seen him outside. Come to think of it, I've never seen him have any visitors either.'

Ben stopped suddenly, his eyebrows furrowed into a frown. 'Are you joking? You don't know about him? He *never* leaves. Not since he killed all those people years ago. If he were to step outside his house, he'd get arrested. Or worse. He'd kill again...'

'Oh shut up, Ben! He's not killed anyone, Art,' Tommy said, aware of the increasingly worried look on Art's face. 'Grandpa says he's just an old guy who likes to keep himself to himself, that's all.'

'What? Like a hobbit?' Ben asked. Tommy and Art looked at each other, confused.

'You know,' Ben continued, 'those people that never like going out.'

'Oh… I think you mean *hermit,*' Art suggested, shaking his head in disbelief.

'Yeah, I think hobbits actually like the fresh air,' Tommy added.

'Well, you know what I mean,' Ben said. 'I just think it's creepy that's all – that he never goes out and never talks to anyone and stuff.'

'Besides,' Tommy said, 'I've seen him outside anyway. Remember Ben… when you had your accident?'

Ben rolled his eyes.

'Oh, for the last time, you *didn't* see Wiseman. It couldn't have been. I mean, he doesn't even go into his front garden – what on Earth would he have been doing in the woods over by us?'

'I'm telling you, it was him.'

'Nope, you're way off. I've told you before. You were probably just in shock from witnessing the *worst* accident ever.'

Art stood between them, his head bouncing from one to the other as they argued, as if he were watching a riveting tennis rally.

'What's this?' he asked.

'Oh, it was when I had my accident,' Ben said. 'I went head on with a car at about a hundred miles an hour and lived to tell the tale. Tommy reckons he saw Mr Wiseman watch it all from the woods.'

'Really?' Art asked, a look of wonder on his face. He glanced back towards Mr Wiseman's place, but the old man was no longer in the window, and the curtains were drawn again.

'I swear boys, it was him,' Tommy confirmed.

'Face it, Tom, you were seeing things. If he had been there, even *he* would have helped me – I was in a right mess, blood everywhere! You know I'm right,' Ben said and with a quick change of subject he awkwardly clambered onto his bike and began pedalling towards Grandpa's.

'Tom... did your mum happen to bring any Welsh cakes?'

Tommy had been waiting for that question.

The last days of the summer holidays were rapidly running out, and Tommy still had homework to do. He hated doing essays, always leaving them right until the last minute, and this particular one was no different. He'd wasted the last few days playing with Ben and Art but he now sat at Grandpa's dining table with his blank writing pad and a school book open before him, determined to make a start on his History essay. He was trying, without much success, to understand the rationing system employed by Britain during the war years. He'd put this particular essay off for as long as possible, and it was fair to say that he was totally stumped. He'd left it until as late as yesterday to cycle over to the library, where his mum worked, explaining to her that he'd 'just needed to add a few finishing touches' to it, and search for a suitable history book. It was clear from the empty shelves in the history section that he had left it too late. He had hoped to find a book about the London Blitz, or even the D-Day Landings that Grandpa always talked about. Something with a bit of action. But no, all he was left with was a book about rationing.

Tommy was sat quietly making notes when something sharp hit him on the cheek, making him jump.

'Oww! Hey! What was that?'

On the table by his pencil case lay the offending object. A rolled-up sweet wrapper.

'Grandpa, I'm trying to concentrate!' Tommy couldn't help but smile as he looked through the doorway into the lounge, over at Grandpa. He was sitting in his armchair by the fireplace reading, or at least *pretending* to read, the newspaper. Tommy was also a little surprised; Grandpa wasn't up for a laugh much nowadays, which Tommy put down to him getting older and, of course, Nan.

'What?' Grandpa replied, a slight grin showing at the corners of his mouth. 'It wasn't me.' *As if it could be anyone else.*

'What are you doing there?' he added, hobbling over to the table.

'Oh, just a History project I've gotta do,' Tommy replied, 'but I've left it so late I'm stuck doing it on rationing during the war – boring huh?'

'Not so boring when you were actually living it my boy. They were tough times.'

'Well I'll probably fail it anyway,' Tommy moaned.

'I'm useless at History.'

'Now that's not the attitude is it? You can accomplish anything if you apply your mind to it. Remember what your nan used to say? "Always shoot for the stars, even if you miss, you'll hit the tops of the trees".'

Grandpa picked up the library book and examined it quickly, before shaking his head and tutting.

'No wonder you're struggling. I think I can do a bit better than this.'

He walked over to his bookcase and pulled a tatty paperback book from the shelf.

'Here, you can use this. *World War II: A History.* The most accurate book about the second war, believe me – I was there. You should find some interesting things to put in your project.'

'Thanks, Grandpa.'

Tommy began flicking through the well-read and dog-eared pages of the book, pausing only when an interesting photograph caught his eye: battle-fatigued British soldiers, huge bomber planes and monstrous-looking tanks. The realities of war.

'You know,' Tommy said after a while, 'I'd have loved to have got my hands on some of them – the Germans I mean – looking at all the damage they caused.'

'Oh, they weren't all bad, Tom, most were just young men fighting their cause, doing what they thought was right for their country, just like we were. Many of them didn't have a choice. They wanted to be there as little as we did. Most of them anyway.'

Tommy had never thought about it like that. As Grandpa walked back to his armchair. Tommy couldn't resist blurting out his next question, 'Grandpa, you know Mr Wiseman?'

Grandpa paused and turned back towards him, 'Yes, Tommy, I do. Why do you ask?'

He hoped Grandpa could answer some of the questions he and his friends had about his mysterious neighbour. He walked back over to him and sat down. Tommy could hear the rasps as Grandpa stroked his chin, letting out a sigh.

'Tommy, you and your friends haven't been bothering Mr Wiseman again have you?'

'No,' he replied a little too quickly. 'No, not at all.'

Grandpa's raised eyebrows suggested that he wasn't convinced.

'Honestly, Grandpa! He was at his window this afternoon and we were just wondering about him.'

'Now take my advice,' Grandpa said sternly, 'you boys just leave Mr Wiseman alone, he's not harming anybody. I'd wager that there's more to him than just the lonely old man that you boys see. He's probably got some very interesting stories to tell.'

Grandpa stood up from the table and reached into the inside pocket of his tweed blazer.

'Right, I'm going up to my room to write a few letters.'

Tommy's eyes moved to Grandpa's hand. From his pocket he had produced an old fountain pen. A pen that, since Nan had died, never seemed to leave his side. It was almost like it provided him with some sort of comfort.

Tommy would often see him sitting quietly in his armchair scribbling something on a piece of paper with it, or maybe just rotating it in his fingers, lost in some deep and distant thought.

Grandpa made his way out of the dining room, stopping at the bookcase to pick up a photo album from one of its shelves. At the door he turned slightly and looked to Tommy with a smile, tapping the photo album as he spoke.

'I'm going to spend some time with your nan.'

And with that he left the room and made his way upstairs. Tommy realised how much harder it must be for Grandpa since Nan had died. No wonder he didn't have much energy or verve for life anymore; he'd lost his sweetheart. Tommy couldn't even begin to imagine what that must be like. He couldn't help but wonder just how many days and nights Grandpa had spent looking through that old photo album, wishing that he could spend just one more hour with her.

Upstairs, Grandpa sat at the dressing table in his bedroom, the photo album open in front of him and a blank piece of paper next to it at the ready. Sifting through the photographs, he finally came upon the one he wanted – a black and white picture of himself and Nan. He chuckled to himself, fondly remembering every detail of that day. Gently placing the picture next to the paper, Grandpa unscrewed the cap of his fountain pen and excitedly began to write, his words greedily eating up the page. He then closed his eyes and smiled.

— CHAPTER TWO —

Borrowing the Pen

The following morning, Tommy bounded down the stairs two at a time. As he entered the kitchen, he was welcomed by the smell of warm toast and the sight of Grandpa by the back door, a pair of gardening gloves in one hand and a trowel in the other. He looked an odd sight with a ragged old baseball cap on his head and a white string vest covering his equally white arms. Navy corduroy shorts showed off a pair of pale, knobbly knees.

'Morning, Grandpa,' Tommy said enthusiastically, grabbing a slice of toast from the inviting pile on the table, 'cool shorts.'

'Morning, Tom,' came the slightly distracted reply.

The flat response caused Tommy to slow the furious chewing of his toast.

'Everything OK, Grandpa?'

The question was met with silence.

'Grandpa?'

'Huh? Oh, sorry, Tommy. Yes I'm fine,' he said, forcing an awkward sort of smile. 'I'm just going to do some gardening. It's time I tidied up out there, it's a right mess.'

'Need a hand?'

'No, it's alright, I can manage.'

Tommy was slightly relieved that he didn't take him up on his offer. He couldn't quite put his finger on it, but conversation with Grandpa had proven a little awkward over the last few days. There was definitely something bothering him. Even more so than usual.

'Anyway,' Grandpa continued, 'you still have homework to do, don't you? Your mum telephoned last night to remind me.'

'Yeah, it's OK,' Tommy replied. 'I know what I'm doing my English essay on, so it won't take me long.'

'Get started then. You can make your old Grandpa a lemon squash in an hour or so. I think I'm going to need it in this heat.'

'OK, well don't overdo it out there.'

'Oh I've dug more than my fair share of trenches in my time, Tommy, I'm sure I can handle a few flowerbeds,' he replied, the smile on his face a little more natural this time.

After polishing off three rounds of toast and two cups of tea, Tommy finally sat himself down at Grandpa's dining table, intent on doing his essay. He'd purposely left this particular bit of homework until last, simply because he knew that it would be the easiest. The essay title was: *My Worst Summer Holiday*. He'd be able to write pages and pages on this one. He wasted no time in opening his writing pad and writing the title of the project at the top of the page. Underneath he wrote the date of his worst ever summer holiday: *Saturday 23rd July 1994*. Now he was ready to write his masterpiece.

Well, almost ready. In starting the first paragraph the

ink in his pen began to fail. He shook it repeatedly, but even that didn't help. It was empty. Searching through his pencil case, he found nothing that he could use. He then scanned the dining room for a pen, and his attention was caught by the sunlight reflecting off something on the sideboard. Getting up to look, he was surprised to find that it was Grandpa's old fountain pen. Forget surprised, he was shocked – Grandpa never left it lying around. He felt a sudden urge of temptation. He knew he shouldn't use it without Grandpa's permission, but he just couldn't resist. He'd never even have to know.

The pen itself was one of the grandest things Tommy had ever seen. From a distance it looked like any other type of fountain pen. But dozens of swirling designs could be seen along the length of its body. He studied the patterns carefully. What at first glance looked like random swirls was, upon closer inspection, actually an intricate design made up of many small symbols that resembled the inner workings of a clock. He picked it up. It felt heavier than it looked.

He then studied its main feature, undoubtedly the inscription down its side. It was written very neatly but was in a language that Tommy could not understand. One that he couldn't even identify. It certainly wasn't English and from what he could tell it didn't look like French either. He assumed that it was written in Latin or Greek or something else that he couldn't read. Even more frustrating, though, was that whenever he asked Grandpa what the inscription said, he had always told him, 'When the time is right you'll find out'. What a tease.

He looked again at the inscription:

ᎩᎷᏟ ᎢᏚ ᎠᏅ ᏬᎪ ᏠᎣᏛᎢ╱ᒪ

He really had to find out what it meant.

Sitting down at the table, he unscrewed the pen's golden top, and placing the nib of the fountain pen onto the paper, he began to write. Nothing happened. He changed the angle of the pen but, again, nothing.

Tommy examined it more closely, unscrewing it to check how much ink was in the cartridge. At first the pen wouldn't separate. It felt as though it hadn't been unscrewed in years, but it finally came apart.

No wonder it didn't work, Tommy thought. It was empty. No cartridge at all, not even an empty one. Grandpa must have left it on the sideboard to remind himself to get a new one. He screwed it back together and cursed his luck, disappointed that he couldn't use it after all.

Despite it being empty Tommy scribbled his name on the blank page, admiring how smoothly the pen flowed across the paper. To his surprise, on his third or fourth signature, ink came out. Only a bit at first, just enough to spell out the last few letters of his surname, but upon trying it again more ink flowed, coming out much more freely than before. It must have been ink left over near the nib, there was no other explanation for it. So not to waste it, Tommy turned a fresh page and began his essay again.

Beneath its title he wrote: *Saturday 23rd July 1994 – Ben's accident.*

What happened next Tommy would remember forever. No sooner had he finished writing, a strange sensation engulfed him. He experienced a sudden jolt and, for an instant, felt as though he were being pulled forwards. The dining room around him was a blur of colour, almost as if he were in a dream. He felt as though he was falling from a great height – the ground below him getting closer and closer. He was blinded by a sudden flash of light.

Tommy looked around him, blinking rapidly, trying hard to focus on his new surroundings. Then realisation dawned. He took a sharp intake of breath, shocked by what he saw, a scene all too familiar...

This is impossible! he thought. *He couldn't be here. Not now...*

'WHAT DO YOU THINK YOU'RE DOING, BOY?!'

Tommy was snapped back to his senses and to the surroundings of the dining room by a booming voice. He turned his head towards it just in time to see the blur of white and navy that was Grandpa storming across to the table, his face red with fury. He snatched the pen from Tommy's grasp.

'How DARE you use this without my permission!'

Grandpa's reaction only served to compound Tommy's confusion. He'd never heard him shout like that before, had never seen him so angry. He opened his mouth to apologise but failed to form the words. Before he could try again Grandpa had left the room as quickly as he'd appeared, taking the pen with him.

Tommy sat alone at the dining table, confused by what had happened. When he looked down at his writing pad he became even more bewildered. The page he was staring at was blank – the writing had vanished.

It had been more than three hours since Grandpa had shouted at him, and Tommy hadn't thought about anything else since. He'd phoned Ben and asked him to call over in the afternoon. He *had* to talk to someone about it, and he could definitely do with the distraction. He now lay on the sofa in the lounge, flicking through Grandpa's old history book, asking himself over and over why Grandpa had got so upset. For the life of him he couldn't think of a rational answer – it was only a stupid pen.

But of course there was that *other* matter. The thing that had happened to him before Grandpa had taken the pen from him. He'd had time to rationalise a little now – *surely* that couldn't have really happened? Most likely he'd dozed off and dreamt it. But it had all felt too real to have been a dream.

Tommy's thoughts were interrupted by the sound of Grandpa's bedroom door opening. He sat up slightly on the sofa, keeping the history book open on his lap. He tried to read a chapter about D-Day as Grandpa descended the stairs and entered the room, but he failed to get past the first sentence. He just couldn't concentrate.

'Tommy,' Grandpa said softly. 'Can I have a word with you please?'

Tommy, determined to avoid another telling off, tried to head it off.

'Yes, Grandpa. I wanted to say something anyway. I'm sorry for using your pen earlier. I just thought...'

'No, Tom, you don't need to apologise. It's my fault, I overreacted. You see Tommy, that pen... well, it's very important to me. It holds some very precious memories of your nan and I and, yes, you should have asked before using it, but still I'm sorry for shouting at you the way I did.'

An awkward silence followed as Grandpa picked up the newspaper from the coffee table and Tommy re-opened his history book. Neither could concentrate on what they were reading.

Tommy broke the silence.

'I'm surprised it worked anyway... the pen... there wasn't even ink in it.'

Grandpa replied without looking at him.

'Oh, you'll find out soon enough Tommy, that nothing is ever quite as it seems.'

He looked over to Grandpa, who was in the process of unwrapping a boiled sweet, but he decided against questioning him further. They could talk about it all later, once they'd got back to normal.

He settled back down on the sofa and continued to flick through the history book, turning page after page, ignoring the text and pausing only when certain pictures caught his eye. He stopped at one particular black and white photograph showing half a dozen men in suits standing around a familiar looking barrel-shaped man smoking a cigar. Tommy thought he recognised him, and his suspicions were confirmed by the writing beneath the picture. It was Winston Churchill, Prime Minister of Britain during World War Two. As he looked at the picture something else caught his eye. He leaned forward and stared closely at it. There was a very familiar item protruding from his jacket pocket. It was unmistakable.

'Hey, Grandpa!' he shouted excitedly, jumping off the sofa and running to him with the book. 'Grandpa, look!'

'What is it?' Grandpa asked, confused by the sudden burst of excitement.

Tommy thrust the book under his nose.

'There, look!' he said, pointing frantically at it. 'In his top pocket! His pen! It looks exactly like yours. With the twirls and everything!'

Grandpa lowered the book slowly before turning his head to face Tommy. As their eyes met Tommy was surprised to find that Grandpa displayed a calm look of realisation. He also saw that the once familiar sparkle of mischief had returned to his eyes.

'Tommy,' he said, 'that doesn't just *look* like my pen. That *is* my pen.'

CHAPTER THREE

The Mischievous Ice Cream

Tommy stared at Grandpa in utter disbelief, waiting for him to laugh. He was pulling his leg, wasn't he? But Grandpa just sat there with that mischievous expression on his face.

'What?' Tommy finally asked him. 'You're joking...'

'I most certainly am not!' Grandpa replied. 'I never fib about such things.'

He walked over to the dining table. Tommy followed him, looking again at the photograph in the book.

'You can't just leave it like that, Grandpa. What do you mean it's *your* pen? How could you have the Prime Minister's pen?' Tommy did the math in his head. 'That would mean it's about sixty years old.'

Grandpa's eyebrows rose in amusement.

'Oh, it's far older than that.'

Grandpa crossed over to the bookcase and reached up to its highest shelf. A flutter of excitement rose in Tommy's stomach as Grandpa's hand found the old, dust-covered book that had always proved just out of his reach. He blew off a layer of dust and placed it onto the table.

'Pass me my reading glasses would you?'

He didn't need asking twice, grabbing Grandpa's glasses

from the living room and rushing back, eager for him to begin. Grandpa opened the book, which was a huge scrap book of sorts, with hundreds of photographs, pictures and newspaper clippings sticking out at all angles. Some had been glued down but most sat loosely between the pages.

His eyes widened in disbelief as he recognised a photograph on the first page. It was the one of Winston Churchill that he had just seen in Grandpa's history book. On this one, though, a circle had been drawn in red ink around the pen in Churchill's pocket. Tommy pointed to it.

'You *really* think that's your pen, Grandpa?'

'I know it is. There's no doubt in my mind. I've had that pen a long time, Tommy, long before your father was even born. But as far as I can tell, I've only owned it for a very short chapter in its life. There's a lot more history to that little thing. More than I'll ever know.'

He flicked through the book, displaying the many more pictures, articles and handwritten notes that he'd assembled over the years.

'I've been trying to understand where it came from. That's why I started collecting all of these clippings. But I still haven't been able to put my finger on exactly how old it is. I've found it impossible. It's a mystery.'

Grandpa turned over a few more pages, searching for a particular image. When he found it he turned the book to Tommy.

'Do you know who that is?'

Tommy looked at the picture, a portrait of a man whose face again seemed familiar.

'I'm not sure, I think so.'

'That, Tommy, is Leonardo Da Vinci. And look,' Grandpa pointed at the picture, to a table beside Da Vinci. In particular, he pointed at a small object. Tommy couldn't believe his eyes. On the table was a small pot that had numerous sized quills, pens and pencils. At the front, in clear view, was the very same pen. Grandpa's pen. The detail on the picture was so good you could almost make out the pen's inscription and its unique design.

'It can't be.'

'That's what I first thought,' Grandpa replied, 'but it gets even more intriguing.' He flicked through a few more pages. 'Look at this one.'

Grandpa found another picture, again a portrait, this time of a man with a moustache, small beard and a frilly little scarf around his neck.

'Surely you recognise him?'

And Tommy did.

'That's Shakespeare, isn't it?'

'Spot on,' Grandpa replied, 'and look what's in his hand.'

Sure enough, in the hand of William Shakespeare was Grandpa's pen. Tommy was speechless. These were three of history's most famous names – Da Vinci, Shakespeare and Churchill! And each one of them had, according to Grandpa, owned his pen.

'And if you find *that* hard to believe,' Grandpa continued, taking his cue from the dumbstruck expression on Tommy's face, 'just look at this…' Grandpa turned page after page of his scrapbook.

'In all the years I've had this pen, I've searched and I've searched, trying to find out more about it. I'm confident that it's at least eight *hundred* years old, if not a thousand!' He paused for effect. 'But, only last year, I had to revise my estimation when I came across this...' Grandpa had stopped turning the pages and had now placed the book before Tommy's eager eyes. He found himself looking at a tattered piece of parchment that had turned yellow with age. On the parchment was a rather basic drawing of an important looking man. It was someone that Tommy didn't recognise. What he noticed instantly, though, was the small object that the man held over his head, raising it as if in victory. The pen.

'Another former owner of my pen, Tommy. Julius Caesar.'

Grandpa paused for a moment, allowing the information to sink in. He had, of course, recognised the name instantly.

'But this is what really baffles me, Tommy. Caesar was born in the year 100 BC. Which means if that *is* my pen, if Caesar really *did* have it, then this pen is over *two thousand years old* – older than Jesus Christ himself!'

Tommy didn't know *what* to think. On any other day, at any other time, he'd simply dismiss all this as a joke, a fairytale, something he'd expect to have heard coming from Ben. But surely Grandpa wouldn't be making it all up? And, of course, there was that weird feeling he'd had earlier, after using the pen. What was all that about? It really had all felt too real to have been a dream.

'Where did you get it from?' Tommy asked, his thoughts slowing long enough to ask just one of the hundred questions he had buzzing around his head like a swarm of angry bees.

Grandpa considered his answer for a moment before continuing. 'I found it. Or rather, *it* found me. Many years ago, Tommy, when I was a young man, only a few years older than you are now in fact, it came into my possession in a rather curious way. And you know, in all of the years I've had that pen, I still don't fully understand it. As you've seen from my scrapbook, it always seems to find itself right in the middle of key points in history. Owned by important figures, people who've had a major influence on world events. It appears destined to be a part of great things... that is, of course, until it found it's way to little old me.'

Grandpa chuckled to himself. Tommy simply sat mesmerised. This really was beginning to sound like something Ben would come out with. He simply refused to believe it was the same pen that all those people had. Common sense told him that it couldn't be.

'But how, Grandpa? How could it have lasted so long? Surely it would have got broken by now or something?'

Grandpa turned the pen slowly in his hands, examining it carefully.

'On the contrary, there isn't a scratch on it.'

He handed it to Tommy, who, in turn, began to inspect it.

'And what's even more amazing,' Grandpa continued,

'is that I've not once had to put any ink in it. It seems to have its own endless supply.'

The fact that Tommy *didn't* look too surprised by this drew a look of understanding from Grandpa. 'But of course,' he said, 'having used it earlier you probably know that already.'

'Actually, Grandpa, when I used it...'

'Something else happened?' Grandpa finished for him. 'Something... *strange*. Am I right?' he asked excitedly.

Tommy nodded.

'Yeah, but I can't explain it.'

'Well maybe I can, Tom. Now that I've begun to tell you, I'd better start from the beginning and tell you *all* about it.'

No sooner had Grandpa spoken than there was a loud knock on the front door. It was Ben's secret knock, one that he insisted on doing each time he called and that he could never get quite right. *Great*, Tommy thought. His timing was perfect as usual.

'Now who could that be?' Grandpa asked. 'I'm not expecting anybody.'

'It's probably just Ben,' Tommy replied. 'I asked him to pop over for a bit.'

A wave of disappointment washed over Grandpa's face.

'Oh don't worry,' Tommy assured him. 'It's nothing important. I'll just tell him we're busy.'

'You can't do that,' Grandpa said, 'not if you've asked him to call.' But in spite of that, a glimmer of hope returned to his eyes.

'Are you kidding?' Tommy said enthusiastically. 'I'm not going out now. There's no way I'm missing out on this!'

And with that, he jumped up and darted out into the hall.

He opened the door just as Ben, giving up on his secret knock, had started to work the doorbell, pressing it impatiently.

'There you are! What took you so long?' Ben asked. He looked a funny sight with one finger still pressed on the doorbell and his other arm struggling to balance a variety of sweets and chocolates, a bag of popcorn grasped tightly under his chin. 'Thought we could watch a film?'

Tommy blocked him off as Ben's leading foot quickly made for the doorway.

'Sorry mate, I can't. Not right now. Me and Grandpa are… uh… a little busy with something.'

Ben pulled up, both surprised and hurt. They stood in silence for a second, just looking at each other, until the bag of popcorn fell noisily to the floor. It was followed by a box of Maltesers which proceeded to burst open, spilling dozens of the small chocolates balls onto the ground at his feet.

'But I brought popcorn,' he offered hopefully, eyeing the fallen items.

'Sorry, Ben, I really can't. Why don't you try Art? He'll watch a film with you.'

Ben looked deeply offended at the suggestion.

'What? Are you kidding me? Last time we went round his to watch TV he made us watch a documentary on insects. No thanks, I'd rather be on my own!'

Tommy watched as Ben then chased the Maltesers about the place, shoving as many as he could into his mouth as he tried to storm off, only managing to drop another item for every one that he managed to pick up.

'See you tomorrow then!' Tommy called after him. 'And sorry again!'

With his best friend well and truly offended, he raced back to where Grandpa sat, eager to pick up where they'd left off. Ben would get over it; he had the hide of a rhino.

'Sorry about that, Grandpa. Now where were we?'

They sat at the dining table with two steaming cups in front of them. It was a story that Grandpa had said 'demanded a cup of tea.' Tommy didn't doubt it one bit. In the time it had taken Tommy to make it, Grandpa had gone to his bedroom and returned with a battered old wooden box. Sensing Tommy's anticipation and enjoying every second of the moment, Grandpa took his time in slowly opening the lid. Not once did he take his eyes off his excited grandson's face. The box was full to the brim with photographs. Grandpa lifted out a handful and carefully laid them on the table.

Tommy picked up a few of them for a closer look, realising that he'd seen most of them before. There was the picture of his dad as a toddler at the beach, holding his bucket and spade and giggling at the camera. One of his grandparents on their wedding day. And there was the one of himself, just about to blow out the candles on his 5th birthday cake (just before Ben had run past and knocked it onto the floor).

He turned his attention to something he hadn't noticed initially, a piece of crumpled scrap paper hidden amongst the photographs. He picked it up and turned it over in his hands. It was blank on both sides, but its texture gave it the feel of having been well-used.

'What's this, Grandpa?' he asked.

Grandpa took the piece of paper from him and looked at it thoughtfully.

'That, Tommy, is my blank canvas.'

Grandpa seemed to be making a hobby out of confusing him.

'What?'

'This is the piece of paper I use whenever I'm feeling a little low. Particularly when I'm missing your nan. You see, Tommy, this pen enables me to relive some of my... better days. There will come a time, hopefully many years from now, when all of your good times are behind you. When all your happy memories begin to fade into the past. Especially when you lose those closest to you.'

A tear began to well in Grandpa's eye.

'And then, well, then you'd give anything to relive those times again. That's why this little thing has become very important to me over these last few years.'

Grandpa sniffed loudly, composing himself before passing the pen to Tommy.

'Answer me this. Have you ever written a person's name on a birthday card or an address on an envelope and instantly been reminded of a specific memory? Or even just looked at a photograph and then replayed that moment over again in your head? Reliving the memory as if you were actually there?'

'I suppose...' Tommy replied tentatively.

'Well this pen allows you to do just that *and* more. It physically *transports* you into your memories! You noticed something special about it, didn't you? After using it? Tommy, you weren't just *thinking* about your memory when you wrote it earlier, or even *dreaming* about it. You were actually *in* it!'

Tommy nodded; his mouth wide open.

'All you have to do,' Grandpa continued, ignoring Tommy's impression of a hungry goldfish, 'is write down one of your memories, any occasion that you've experienced, and you get to relive it. This pen gives you the ability to travel within it!'

Tommy felt like a butterfly collection had just been let loose in his tummy. He thought back to when he'd used the pen earlier, when he had written the heading of his project. Is Grandpa saying that he *hadn't* just imagined it? That it had *actually* happened?

'I had hoped to tell you in my own time,' Grandpa said, 'but you always did have trouble suppressing your curious side. It worked for you too though, didn't it?'

'I'm not sure,' he replied hesitantly, struggling to keep up with the pace of his own thoughts. 'I felt *something*, but it was strange.'

The truth was Tommy didn't know what had happened. He could have sworn that, for just a few seconds, he was back there.

'Just before you took the pen off me, I thought I was back when Ben had his accident,' he said. 'Y'know, on the hill. I know it sounds crazy, but it seemed so real.' Grandpa's face beamed, and he shouted again, this time in excitement.

'I knew it! I knew it would work for you too! Shocking isn't it?! I remember how strange it felt that first time that I used it.'

He'd never seen Grandpa so animated. The excitement in his voice rose as he took the pen again and thrust it into the air between Tommy's face and his own.

'You asked me earlier where I got it from, well I'll tell you. I'll tell you all about it. I've had this pen since World War Two – yes, all those years ago – when I was a young man in France. It was given to me by a stranger, a German man. I didn't even get to know his name.'

Grandpa shook his head and chuckled, taking a sip of his tea.

'Our paths crossed a few days after my unit had landed on the beaches. We'd come across a small village, most of it destroyed. I went off for a walk; it was dark and cold and before I knew it I'd found myself inside a ruined church.' He took another sip from his tea, this time making a slurping noise.

'I can still smell the musty damp inside of that church. That and the smell of gunpowder. Those memories will stay with me forever, and they are not ones that I've ever chosen to revisit.'

Grandpa paused, lost in his thoughts, before continuing.

'It was when inside that church that I heard footsteps, someone running on the gravel outside. The front doors burst open and a man appeared, running for all he was worth, right at me. As he neared me I could see just how frightened he was. He was out of breath, sweating, and his eyes as wide as two saucers. He ran straight up to me and then thrust his hand out to mine, grabbing it firmly. Looking me in the eyes he said words I'll never forget: "Keep it safe. Dangerous people will look for it!" He then pulled me towards the choir stalls, and we hid there for a while, as men I couldn't see searched the church. And then he was gone, his pursuers close behind him, leaving me alone again. When I came out of my hiding place, I looked into my hand and I saw this...'

He raised the pen.

'Before I could even think, my unit had found me. They'd come looking after hearing all the commotion. I told them what had happened, all of it apart from the bit about the pen. I don't know why, but I decided to keep that part a secret.'

Tommy looked down and noticed that a layer of skin had formed on top of his tea. He was so engrossed in Grandpa's tale that he'd forgotten all about it.

'So, I hid it away from them and kept it safe all throughout the rest of the war. When I finally came home, I packed up all of my army gear and put it in the darkest corner of the attic – including the pen – which is where it remained for years. It was only after your nan passed away, when I was sorting through a load of our old belongings, that I happened across it. In truth, after all of those years I'd forgotten about it. Think about it son – that wonderful pen had just lay there, in my attic, unused for years. I feel rather bad about it now, now that I've done all of this research and discovered who its former owners were. And, of course, had I known about what it *does*, then I'd have used it regularly right from the off!'

Tommy opened his mouth to talk but Grandpa raised a hand to silence him.

'No, let me go on, I've wanted to share this secret for such a long time. A few days after I'd found it again, I started using it. Just a few notes here and there about my time during the war and adventures shared with your nan. And when I used it something wonderful happened. I found myself transported back into the very time that I'd been writing about. Clearer than the most vivid dream – I was actually *living* the memory again! You see, Tom, I'd only just lost your nan, but then, with the pen, I was able to spend time with her all over again. It was like I was watching memories as if they were films, seeing myself in them as clearly as I could see the other people. And the curious thing about it is that once you've experienced the memory, when you return to the present, the ink disappears from the page. Like some sort of invisible ink. Perhaps it goes to show that the whole experience is just temporary.'

Tommy stared at Grandpa open-mouthed, his chin almost hitting the dining table.

'So since your nan left us,' Grandpa continued,

thumbing his way through the photographs, 'whenever I was feeling a little nostalgic, I'd use the pen. You know, just to pay her a little visit from time to time. Recently, though, it's become something of an obsession. I spent every day with your nan for almost sixty years, and when she died the best part of me died too. I miss her terribly, Tom, but I've come to realise that I've been using the pen far too much. Most nights I spend in my memories, re-living every spare moment I can with her. Our wedding day, anniversaries. And now I've come to realise I can't go on like this.'

Grandpa took a moment to compose himself, hurriedly wiping away a tear that had trickled down his cheek.

'It's too painful living in the past. That's why I was a little grumpy this morning. I wasn't grumpy with you, I was grumpy with me. Annoyed at how reliant I've become on it. I decided last night that I was no longer going to use it, that it was time to let it go, and that means letting her go too. It's not right to live in the past, Tommy; you have to live for today, I understand that now. I hope you will come to understand that too, and not use it too much.'

Tommy studied him carefully.

'What do you mean?'

Grandpa held the pen out towards him until he finally took it. The new-found knowledge of the pen's magic made it feel even heavier than before.

'I can't have this, Grandpa, you keep it. Keep using it to see Nan.'

'No. I've thought about it long and hard. I intend to spend the rest of my days in the present. I've been blessed with a wonderful family, and I'm going to make the most of that now. It's time for someone else to enjoy it.'

'But why me, Grandpa? Don't you want Dad to have it? Or one of my uncles.'

In truth, having seen the effect that it had had on Grandpa recently, Tommy really didn't know whether he wanted it or not.

Grandpa shook his head dismissively.

'Twenty years ago maybe, but not now. They'd laugh me out of the room as soon as I'd begin to explain it. No, I'm sure you must have it. This is something that only someone with an imagination like yours could even begin to comprehend.'

Grandpa leaned in so that the tip of his nose almost touched Tommy's.

'There's only one thing I ask of you, Tommy. Keep it a secret. I ask that for two reasons.'

He raised his index finger. 'First, if word of the pen's power got out, then it would be a very sought after item. I'd rather it be kept by someone who respects what it does and uses it for the right reasons.' Grandpa then raised a second finger. 'And second, I've not forgotten the words of that German man. He seemed deadly serious when he told me that people would look for it. I know that doesn't seem likely now, not after all this time, but its best to err on the side of caution wouldn't you say? Is that OK?'

'Yeah, that's fine, Grandpa,' Tommy replied.

But even as he replied he thought instantly about how difficult it would be to keep it secret from Ben – they told each other everything. Grandpa must have read his mind.

'*Promise* me, Tommy. It means a lot.'

'Grandpa, I promise.' And Tommy decided at that moment that he would keep it a secret. Not because he was worried about his safety, he was sure that nobody would be looking for it now, but because it was what Grandpa wanted.

'Can I ask you something else?' said Tommy, looking at the pen more closely. 'What *does* the inscription mean? You said you'd tell me when I was ready, well, surely now's the time?'

'Actually, Tommy, I'm afraid that I can't keep my word on that one. I've never been able to figure that part out; it's why I've delayed telling you. At first I thought it was Latin, maybe even Ancient Greek, but everywhere I've looked I've found nothing. It doesn't translate into any language that I've come across. I think it will just have to remain one of the pen's many mysteries. Unless, of course, you have more luck.'

Tommy had a thousand more questions about the pen, but there was one glaringly obvious one that he was dying to ask.

'You know when you use it to go back into your memories? What happens to you? Do you like... disappear or something?'

Grandpa scratched his head and looked baffled. Then he laughed loudly and, not for the first time today, did an uncanny impression of an over-excited schoolboy.

'Do you know I'm not sure!' he declared, 'I've only ever used it when I've been on my own. But I guess there's one easy way to find out. Go on... try it,' Grandpa encouraged.

Tommy looked at the pen, his hands now slick with sweat, his stomach doing involuntary somersaults.

'Nah, maybe later,' Tommy dismissed, nervous all of a sudden.

'Go on, don't be worried,' Grandpa continued. 'I'll be here.'

What the heck, Tommy thought; *he'd have found it hard to wait anyway*. 'OK, I'll do it,' he said in as brave a voice as he could muster.

'Good lad.' Grandpa flicked through the photographs from the box. 'Now, can I recommend that you start with something quite simple, nothing too emotional? I don't want you visiting any memories that may upset you. It's a wonderful thing to experience your memories again, but it can also be rather upsetting if you're not ready for it.'

He selected a photograph and handed it to Tommy. 'Here, try this one.'

The picture was of Tommy as a five-year-old, sat upon his nan's knee. Behind them was a beautiful view of green grass and a clear blue sky, overlooking a range of hillside that went on for as far as the eye could see. Grandpa had taken that picture when they had gone on a picnic to the top of the Preseli Mountains. On the back of the photograph, written in pencil, was the date it had been taken.

'Just write down that date,' Grandpa said, 'and then alongside it write something like picnic with Nan & Grandpa.'

Tommy took the crumpled piece of paper and smoothed

it out in front of him. Then, removing the pen's cap, he took a deep breath.

'Well, here goes...'

He wrote: *Picnic with Nan & Grandpa: May 28th 1989.*

As soon as he finished writing Tommy felt the exact same sensation he'd experienced earlier. First, a sudden jolt to his midriff, as if being pulled backwards by an invisible rope, then both the dining table and Grandpa began to fade into the distance. His entire surroundings became a blur, and he had that feeling of falling from a great height. Then a blinding flash of light...

Tommy blinked rapidly, looking around him, anxious to see whether it had worked. To his amazement, he felt the warmth of a summer's day upon his face and a gentle breeze rustling his hair. *It must have worked!* Turning in a circle where he stood, he took in his new surroundings – the familiar landscape visible from the top of the Preseli Mountains. He couldn't believe it had worked – he definitely wasn't dreaming this time! He wanted to go and explore the area, to check that it was all real, but he was startled by Grandpa's voice.

'Tommy! Look what I've got...'

He turned to where the voice had come from and saw Grandpa walking towards him, carrying three large ice cream cones, each with a chocolate flake sticking out the top. Tommy went to reply but was cut short as Grandpa drew level with him, ignored him completely and then walked straight past, towards two people sitting a short distance away. It was as if Grandpa hadn't even seen him, as if he wasn't even there.

And there was something else. Grandpa looked different somehow. Tommy walked after him, catching him up until he was level and then looked closely at his face. He definitely looked younger than he had a few moments ago in the dining room. Now, walking along with him, he could see that he had more hair and was slightly chubbier. There was also more of a spring in his step.

As they neared the two other people, Tommy suddenly stopped in his tracks, realising what he was about to witness. He stared for almost a full minute at the three people, forgetting even to blink. He looked on as Grandpa handed a cone to Nan who took it from him and laughed at the vanilla ice cream that had melted and trickled down his hand. Tommy beamed upon seeing her. She looked so happy, just as he remembered her. His heart ached and he had to restrain himself from running over to give her a big hug. Grandpa then leaned over and handed the other cone to the third person in their group. This smaller person was sat down with his back to Tommy, and he took the ice cream hungrily, sounding an appreciative giggle. He was dressed in shorts and T-shirt and had a little cap on his head that shielded his eyes from the sun.

Tommy walked around them to get a better view of the child's face, preparing himself for the shock. *It couldn't be, could it?* As he rounded upon the little person, his eyes almost popped out of his head. It was! Tommy found himself looking at himself! Not his reflection in a mirror, not himself as he was now, but himself as a five-year-old boy, complete with ice cream smeared around his mouth and chin.

Feeling light headed, Tommy made a concerted effort to breathe. This was certainly something he'd never dreamed of experiencing – coming face-to-face with *himself!*

Then, just too late, he heard Grandpa say to the five-year-old Tommy, 'Watch out now, hold it with two hands', before the ice cream, held at a dangerous angle, fell straight into his lap. Tommy remembered that happening too! How upset he'd been when he'd dropped it, and if he remembered correctly, yes, he watched as Nan gave him her own ice cream. His younger self walked over to her and gave her a cuddle before proceeding to drop his new ice cream right down the back of her dress. Both Tommy's gasped. The young Tommy looked at her silently, uncertain whether she was going to tell him off. But then both his nan and grandpa burst into laughter at the youngster, who, satisfied that he wasn't in trouble, began to giggle and jump around excitedly.

Watching his memory unfold, Tommy's nose began to tingle. He had to do his best to fight back a tear. He realised now what Grandpa had meant about choosing memories carefully. This was a happy memory, one that he was fond of; he never thought it would affect him like it had. He supposed it was the sight of seeing Nan again that had upset him. He missed her so much.

Tommy wandered away from the group and closed his eyes, shaking his head, struggling to comprehend what he'd just seen. He was startled by a hand on his shoulder, a phantom hand that didn't belong to anybody in the memory.

Then came the familiar feeling of falling. He screwed his eyes shut and waited for the imminent flash of light. When it came he opened them, looked around and found himself sitting back at Grandpa's dining table. He jumped with a start at the closeness of Grandpa, who, now looking as old as ever, was eager to find out what had happened.

'Well?' he asked. 'Did it work?'

'Umm, yeah. I... I saw, Nan. And you. And I was there too, but I was young. It was really weird!'

Tommy stood and paced around the dining room, running his hands through his hair, his mind still trying to process the whole experience.

'What did *you* see, Grandpa? I must have been gone for at least ten minutes.'

'No, Tom, nothing,' Grandpa replied excitedly. 'I didn't see anything. You used the pen, closed your eyes for a second or two, and then I touched your shoulder. Next thing you were back looking at me. It was all over in a second. Now how's *that* for magical?'

'Wow,' Tommy said, almost under his breath. 'So, if you hadn't been here, if you hadn't brought me back, then how would I have come out?'

Grandpa pondered the question for a moment.

'I've always found that when you no longer want to be there it lets you leave. I think the pen can sense how you feel. It's always looked after me anyway.'

Grandpa began to collect the photographs from the table, placing them back into the box.

'Its magic has always amazed me,' he said, 'and there's

a story behind every photograph, y'know, every picture, even the seemingly boring ones. I've found precious moments in memories that I missed the first time around. It's been a pleasure visiting all of those times again. Remember though,' Grandpa continued, 'it's not a toy, so please don't misuse it. I trust that you won't.'

Grandpa, with the teacups in one hand, closed the box of photographs and picked it up.

'I'm sure you've got a lot of questions, but this last hour has exhausted me. I'm going upstairs to have a nap and then do us some dinner. We can talk more about it then. Discretion is the key, Tom. Keep it between us.'

And with that Grandpa hobbled into the kitchen, swilled out the cups in the sink and headed upstairs with his box of memories.

Tommy's bike ride home at the end of the week took him a lot longer than it did on the way over. He had a lot to digest. He'd quizzed Grandpa for as long as he could about the pen, about the memories he'd visited and how often he'd used it. Tommy would have happily stayed up all night talking about it had it not been for the rather insistent call from his mum to get home. It was, after all, time for the new school year to begin.

Now, with the pen tucked safely in a balled-up sock in his rucksack, he cycled lazily across the docks of Little Millbrook, letting his mind wander, thinking about all of the memories he could revisit. He had so many options, so many football games that he wanted to replay. His head was exploding with ideas.

He'd certainly had the strangest summer holiday of his life, and he had a strong feeling that things would never be quite the same again. The only downside to it all was having to keep it a secret from Ben. That would be hard. But he had to; he'd promised Grandpa. And that was one promise he didn't want to break.

— CHAPTER FOUR —

The Hinton Brothers

The first day back at school went better than Tommy could have hoped. He had never been one to dread the start of the new term; in fact he enjoyed going back and meeting up with his friends again, and this year the new timetable had presented an unexpected delight – double Games first thing on a Monday morning. He and Ben couldn't believe their luck! Today, the rather relaxed lesson saw Mr Fender leaning against the fence of the Astroturf, his head in a magazine, while all the boys were left to kick a football about, something that suited Tommy perfectly.

It meant that he and his friends were able to catch up on what they'd done over the summer. Ben had insisted that Tommy go along with his story that he'd gone to the North Pole fishing with an uncle, and that they'd accidentally managed to catch a colony of penguins in their net. Thankfully, Tommy didn't have to keep up with the charade for too long though. In the science corridor later that morning, Art helpfully pointed out (in front of a rather large audience) that it must have been a pretty big net, as there weren't any penguins in the North Pole. That certainly subdued Ben's storytelling for a while. Unfortunately, it also served to heighten the tension between him and Art, something that Tommy didn't want. He was hoping they'd start getting on a little better this year and that Ben would finally welcome him into their group. If the two of them kept trying to show each other up at every turn, then that certainly wasn't going to happen.

By far the most difficult thing for Tommy on his first morning back at school was keeping the pen a secret. He'd had, without question, the most exciting summer holiday out of everybody at school, but he couldn't breathe a word of it to anyone. He'd had to sit through a whole host of mediocre summer holiday anecdotes, and he couldn't so much as mention the pen. It was torture. It was especially difficult when one of the other boys in the year, Gareth Savage, had asked him what he'd got up to. Now Savage was a boy who certainly lived up to his name – he was huge! And he had a temper to match. He was easily twice Tommy's size, and he had all of the characteristics of early-man. Word in the locker room was that he had even started shaving. It was when Savage teased Tommy brutishly about having a *boring summer holiday at his Grandpa's* that he almost broke his silence; he wanted to scream out loud and tell anyone who would listen about what he'd really got up to. But, true to his word, Tommy managed to hold his tongue.

Soon all of the usual school rituals were resumed. The most important of which came at the end of Science and was signalled by the dinner bell. Lunch heralded the execution of Tommy and Ben's own little military operation, one which they'd managed to perfect last year.

It worked like clockwork. Ben would take possession of their school bags and would head directly to the Dutch Barn to start the mandatory lunchtime football match. Tommy, meanwhile, would dart straight to the canteen, knocking over whoever stood in his way, so he could get to the front of the dinner queue. It was imperative to get a good place in the dinner queue for two reasons. For one, there was no way that Tommy and Ben were going to waste half of the break queuing up when they could be playing football. The second reason was slightly more complicated: Martyn Button. Or rather, Martyn Button's mum. He was a boy in their year, and she was a dinner lady and the bane of their school dinner lives, always hoarding the good stuff for her son. She always made sure he got what he wanted. Many times Tommy had eyed the last turkey burger only to be disappointed to see it whisked from under his nose at the last minute. Later he would see it, slightly squashed but still perfectly edible, stuffed under Mrs Button's till (rumour had it that she once managed to cram a whole gravy dinner under there).

Tommy made an excellent time on this, the first dinner run of the year, and not even Mrs Button could deprive him of picking up a couple of hot turkey burgers for him and Ben. He then joined Ben at the Dutch Barn, where a game of football was already well under way and, after making short work of his burger, Tommy was soon in his element. He loved football, could play it all day long and, if truth be told, he was one of, if not *the* best player in the year. Most couldn't keep up with him, and in no time at all he found himself skipping past tackles and firing shots through the barn's large pillars which made up the goalposts. Ben was on Tommy's team, of course, and had taken up his now familiar position as goalkeeper, a position he'd reluctantly become accustomed to since his accident. All the practice had turned him into a pretty decent 'keeper, and he'd made a few brilliant saves today already, stopping a couple of certain goals.

Instead of revelling in the game right up to the end of lunch as he normally would, Tommy grabbed his bag and left a good fifteen minutes before the end, the unusual move distracting Ben, and causing him to drop a pretty easy save. If Ben knew where Tommy was headed he'd have been even more confused, for Tommy was going somewhere he'd never before dreamt of going during lunchtime – the school library. But it was something he *had* to do. Since getting the pen from Grandpa, he'd thought of nothing else. If he could just discover something new about it then Grandpa was bound to be impressed.

So, Tommy spent the last few hurried minutes of lunch frantically flicking through any sort of history book he could lay his hands on, targeting mainly the old, tattered-looking ones. Sadly though it was all in vain. There wasn't a sign of the pen anywhere.

His lack of success in the library seemed to be a sign of things to come; the afternoon was nowhere near as enjoyable as the morning had been. They were even given homework – on their first day! The only saving grace about that particular lesson was that he was sat with Art. It wasn't quite like sitting next to Ben; Art was nowhere near as chatty, but he had his own sense of humour which Tommy liked. He always knew the answer to everything too – an attribute that Ben *certainly* couldn't bring to the table.

'Hey, Tom, did I see you in the library earlier?' Art asked him, as they packed away their books at the end of the lesson.

His lunchtime adventure had been rumbled.

'What? Oh yeah...' he replied evasively. 'Just popped in there for a minute to look something up.'

Art's look of astonishment made Tommy slightly uneasy, and he fully expected a barrage of questions to follow. Fortunately, though, they were interrupted in the corridor by Ben. He would be sure to change the subject.

'Alright, Tom!' he shouted. 'Oh, hello, Fart.'

Ben approached them, his limp slightly more pronounced than usual, the exertions of the football match at lunch obviously taking its toll.

'Tom, what on Earth were you doing in the library at lunch?' he added.

So much for Ben changing the subject.

'How'd you know I was in there?'

'I've got spies everywhere. I think there's something you need to tell me isn't there?' he continued. 'Come on, you know you can't keep a secret that big from your best mate. I know exactly what it is anyway.'

Tommy began to panic. His face grew warm as it flushed a deep crimson. *How could he have found out? He'd not told a soul.*

'Well...' Tommy started.

'Come on, Tom, you can't hide it any longer,' Ben said. 'I'll say it if you're afraid to: you're turning into a *nerd* aren't you? I knew it! It's from hanging around with Mr Bookworm here.'

Tommy laughed nervously, breathing a sigh of relief. That was a close one.

'Yeah, that's it,' he said. 'I'm a nerd. Look, I was just finding out something for class, you should try it sometime.'

'Research? You should've said! Research is my middle name! I could've done it for you in no time.'

'Yeah, if he was researching how to be an idiot,' Art said scathingly. 'Tommy, I'm going back to form class, is it still OK if I walk home with you?'

'Yeah sure, meet you at the front gates.'

Ben waited until Art had disappeared around the corner before looking at Tommy in pure disbelief, his eyebrows closely resembling the shape of two hairy question marks.

'*What*?!' Ben exclaimed.

'What?'

'What do you mean? "What?!" He thinks we're walking home with him!'

'That's 'cos we are. And I'd prefer it if you didn't call him names. Just make an effort to get along with him will you? He's nice. A good laugh too.'

'You are joking? He's probably the most boring kid in school!'

'Well then,' Tommy said, walking along the corridor, now bustling with students. 'If that's right, then you're either gonna have a very *boring* or a very *lonely* walk home.'

*

'Well?' Tommy asked Ben again, 'what would you choose?'

Having finally persuaded Art not to stay late to finish his homework, the three of them walked home together, Ben a few paces in front of them kicking about a crushed can of pop. He was clearly deep in thought.

'Don't rush me,' he replied. 'I'm thinking.'

A further minute or so of silence passed by before Tommy lost patience and changed the subject.

'So, Art, seen any more of Mr Wiseman lately?'

'Nope, not since…'

'INVISIBILITY!' Ben shouted excitedly, interrupting Art mid-sentence.

'What?' Art said, slightly annoyed.

'Invisibility,' Ben said again. 'I'd choose invisibility, you know, as my superpower.'

'Finally!' Tommy said. 'Took you long enough.'

'Oh hang on, actually I'd choose strength… or flight… or… oh, I don't know!' Ben seemed to be genuinely struggling with his decision, his frustration visible.

'What did you choose again?' Ben asked Art.

'I went for super speed,' Art replied matter-of-factly. 'That way I could finish all my homework in one night.'

'That's *sad*,' Ben said. 'Anyway, you do all your homework in one night already.'

Hoping to avoid another argument, Tommy quickly diverted the attention back to Ben. 'Come on, it's not *that* hard, you've just gotta choose one.'

'Oh, OK then clever-clogs. If it's so easy, what would your superpower be?'

Tommy took a few seconds before he answered, pressing his hand against his trouser pocket, feeling the outline of the pen.

'I think I'd choose time travel.'

Ben and Art looked at him for a moment without saying anything before Ben burst out laughing.

'What? That's *it*?!' he said. 'You were giving me all that stick about my choices, and the best you can come up with is *time travel*?! It's not even a superpower!'

'Yes it is,' Tommy replied defensively.

'No it ain't.'

'Yes it is.'

'It ain't.'

'Well actually,' Art intervened, 'superpowers are normally defined as supernatural or paranormal ability. So if someone travelling through time is considered out of the ordinary, and I would say that it is, then it could probably be called a superpower. Unless Ben, you know a lot of people that travel through time?'

'Thank you!' Tommy said, a look of satisfaction on his face.

Ben scoffed loudly and kicked the can a few more metres in front of him.

'And,' Art continued, 'having superpowers can cover objects as well. Y'know, like Iron Man with his suit or Batman with his gadgets. They're both ordinary guys, just with super objects. So if you didn't actually have any powers yourself and you had to rely on a time machine to travel through time, then that would still count too.'

Tommy was happier now that Art had made his point for him.

'So, like a car or a... I dunno, a *pen* or something?' Tommy asked tentatively.

Art looked puzzled. 'Well, yeah I suppose. Although I can't quite see how a pen would help you travel through time.'

Tommy looked from Art to Ben and then felt for the pen again. Surely Grandpa would understand if he told them? They were his best friends. He placed his hand into his pocket, gripped the pen and was just about to take it out when Ben interrupted him. They had reached the part of the walk home which took them past the town's fire station, where Tommy's dad worked. Every single time they passed it, Ben had asked him the same question and today was no different.

'Tom, is your dad working today?'

'No, he's off for a few days.'

Tommy knew what was coming next.

'Oh,' Ben said with a hint of disappointment, 'I was just wondering if he'd let us have a go on the pole...'

Ever since Ben had been invited to a Christmas party there a few years ago, he'd become obsessed with the fireman's pole. All of the children had been allowed to have a go on it, and Ben had become infatuated, so much so that he'd had to be physically dragged away from it.

'I've told you,' Tommy said. 'They won't let us go on it anymore.'

'It was just a thought,' Ben said, sounding a little put

out. He kicked his can out in front of him again, passing the large double doors of the fire station and reaching the pavement on the other side. He then stopped in front of the building next to the fire station and turned to face them.

'Hey, Art, bet you didn't know Tommy's dad is friends with the ghosts that haunt this place,' he said, casually flicking his thumb over his shoulder.

Ben was now enveloped by the huge shadow being cast by the towering structure of the old Central School. Now long closed and boarded up, it was the school that both of Tommy's parents had attended. Before the new comprehensive had been built the Central was one of two schools in the town and generally the one where most of the naughty children seemed to end up (a fact Tommy kept reminding his parents of). Only the main building now remained, standing four storeys high, derelict and burnt-out, having been ravaged by a fire that had resulted in its closure over thirty years ago. The most tragic part was that it had claimed the lives of two local teenage brothers, the Hinton boys. Numerous theories existed about how the blaze had been started and how the brothers had come to be in there at the time. Many thought that they'd simply suffered the misfortune of being there when a gas main exploded; others believed it to have been started after they'd crept inside to smoke cigarettes.

But what Tommy, Ben and the rest of the local kids knew for an absolute fact was that the ghosts of the Hinton brothers now haunted the school. Terrifying sounds could be heard by those who walked past the school at night, and shadowy figures could be seen to move about inside, with ghoulish noises echoing through the deserted hallways. For years the people of the town, young and old, had reported the spooky goings on, with each new generation of curious children daring each other to investigate the source of the chilling noises. Only twice before had Tommy and Ben plucked up enough courage to enter the school, and that was in broad daylight with a group of at least a dozen others. Even then they only got as far as poking their heads through one of the broken windows.

Now, though, Tommy stood at the front wall of the school and looked to the sky in exasperation. Once again, Ben had managed to exaggerate a story.

'What's he on about?' Art asked.

Tommy threw his bag against the wall.

'Well, he's sorta right,' he said, jumping up and sitting on the railings of the pavement facing the school. 'My dad *did* know them *before* they died. He went to school with them; I think they were in some of his classes actually. Dad doesn't like to talk about it much though, whenever I try to bring it up he just says that they were in the wrong place at the wrong time, that it was a burst gas pipe that started the fire and they were just unlucky enough to get caught in the middle of it.'

'What were they like? The Hinton brothers?' Art asked.

Ben jumped in before Tommy could answer.

'Oh, I hear they were really mean and cruel. They used to bully all the younger kids when they were alive, and what's worse, they're even meaner now as ghosts. That's why they still haunt the school – they're waiting for it to re-open so they can possess all the children and come back to life again.'

Both Tommy and Art stared Ben into silence. Art, however, appeared slightly more anxious than before.

'And that,' Tommy said calmly, 'is what annoys my dad about it all. People keep making up stories about them. You know people used to think that they were twins too.'

'That's cos they were,' Ben interrupted.

'They weren't.'

'Were.'

'They weren't.'

Ben finally accepted defeat and went back to kicking his can.

'They weren't even the same age,' Tommy continued, 'they just looked really similar. And, 'cos they were inseparable people just assumed they were twins. Dad reckons they were nice boys, a little mischievous, but generally pretty OK. The best stone-throwers of his generation apparently.'

'How old were they when they died then?' Art asked, captivated now.

'I think one was fourteen, and the other was a couple of years younger.'

'About our age then,' Art said vacantly, staring at the school as he spoke. 'What did they look like?'

'I'm not too sure really. Pretty similar obviously and they were about the same height. Dad says the only real difference between them was that the younger one had really big front teeth, kinda goofy looking.'

'But no-one *really* knows how they died, do they, Tom?' Ben contributed. 'You know, how the fire started? I mean, people *say* it was a burst gas main, but who really knows?'

'Ben, look around you,' Tommy said, pointing at the run down building. 'I think it's safe to say that they died in the fire. It was just a terrible accident.'

'Yeah, I know that,' Ben said, 'but *how* did it start? I've heard that they were setting off fireworks and smoking in there and all sorts.'

'Yeah, we've all heard the rumours, but Dad says neither of them smoked. He just doesn't believe in all the gossip.'

'Why were they in there so late?' Art asked.

'I don't know. That's the one thing people have never figured out. Y'know, just what drew them in there?'

Tommy cast his eyes over the main building, looking up at a large double window just below the roof – the window to the attic. It was dark and dingy and impossible to make out anything on the inside. But then something suddenly made him jump. In truth, it had scared the life out of him. Something had moved in the attic window. He hopped down from the railings to get a better look. The bright sun behind the school made it very difficult to see properly, but the more he looked, the more he was sure that he could see the shape of something moving up there. Or *someone*. Whatever it was, it was big. It moved again, he was sure of it this time. He was positive that a large figure had just stood back from the window, moving back into the shadows.

'Did you see that?' Tommy shouted to the other two,

panic rising in his voice. 'Up there in the window!'

'See what?' Art asked, slightly concerned by his behaviour. Ben however, didn't seem too bothered.

'Yeah, yeah,' he chuckled, 'lemme guess. You just saw the Hinton ghosts up there? Were they waving? They probably heard us talking about them and just wanted to say hello.'

Tommy pointed at the window.

'I'm serious! Look!'

Art and Ben moved to where Tommy was standing and looked up at it.

'Nope. I can't see anything,' Art said.

'Me neither,' added Ben.

They stared up in silence for a moment, Tommy with the unnerving feeling that they were being watched.

The silence was finally broken by Ben. 'Hey Tom, if you *had* to, where would you rather spend the night – here, or at Mr Wiseman's?'

What a question. Didn't he take *anything* seriously? Tommy had just seen something moving in the window, and it was very likely that it *had* been one of the Hinton ghosts! He didn't fancy spending a single minute in the school, let alone a whole night.

'Come on, I'm outta here,' he said, grabbing his bag and quickly walking away from the school. 'It's almost tea time.'

The answer to Ben's question was still a much closer call than he dared to admit. There was something about Grandpa's neighbour Mr Wiseman that gave him the creeps. He'd never want to enter *either* place if he could help it.

— CHAPTER FIVE —

The Hairy Toffee Apple

A ll that talk about super powers with Ben and Art had got Tommy's mind racing. He couldn't wait to use the pen; he couldn't deny himself any longer. He knew he'd told Grandpa that he'd take it seriously and not use it all of the time, but the lure of it was too great. That magical sensation he'd experienced was amazing! He just had to try it out one more time.

In his bedroom he gathered together everything he needed, momentarily considering the memory he should revisit. It was an important decision, and he wanted to get it right. There was that football match last year where he'd scored a hat-trick; that would be good to see. Or that Geography field-trip where Mr Haynes had lost his footing on the riverbank and fallen into the stream; that would be worth another look too.

When it came to it though, the choice was a pretty simple one. Last year, when the funfair had come to town, he and Ben had been chased by a gang of older boys, and, when they'd been caught, they had both suffered pretty nasty dead arms and legs. Now, Ben had always protested his innocence, maintaining that he hadn't done anything to start the chase, but Tommy wasn't so sure. He knew that Ben could be too cheeky for his own good sometimes, plus he was a rubbish liar. In fact, Tommy was positive that there was more to it, and now, with the pen, he could find out if his hunch was right. He could go back and see what *really* happened.

With the memory decided, he lay down on the bed and placed a notepad in front of him. He then took the cap off the pen, unable to resist marvelling at its mysterious inscription as he readied himself to write.

Realising the enormity of the step he was about to take, he took a deep breath and wrote: *Little Millbrook Carnival – Saturday 19th August 1995.*

Next came the earth-shaking sensation he'd experienced at Grandpa's – the feeling of disorientation and the sensation of falling. Then came the blinding white light and the magical change of scenery. As Tommy acclimatised to his new surroundings, he could see that the pen had worked again, transporting him from the cosy security of his bedroom and out into the street, albeit only a hundred yards from where he'd just been laying on his bed. He now found himself at the entrance to the field behind his house. The one where the funfair always sets up – at the topmost end of the football pitch.

He looked at the pen in his hand, struggling to accept the miraculous things that it could do. He stuffed it into his pocket for safe-keeping; there was no way he was losing this thing!

Tommy glanced back to his house. It looked pretty much the same as it had when he'd got home a few minutes ago, with one obvious difference though, one obvious sign that the pen had moved him through both time as well as space: the car outside his house was their *old* car. The one that they'd sold months ago. Absolute concrete evidence that he'd been taken out of the present and into the past. Well, *his* past anyway. He was inside his memory after all.

There was another clear sign that he was now exactly where he wanted to be. Although he couldn't see it, he could hear the unmistakable sounds of the funfair. A joyous noise he'd recognise anywhere. He followed it around the corner and through the gate of the field, greeted by the familiar sight of the fair. He breathed it all in; the wonderful aroma of hotdogs and fried onions mixed with candy floss, honeycomb and nougat. His stomach ached at the thought of all that delicious food which, to him of course, was so far out of reach. He wouldn't be able to eat it if he tried. Before him, stretched across one end of the field, were an abundance of carnival stalls, tents and rides with a beehive of excited children running about, all haggling with their parents for an advance on their pocket-money.

Towering before him was the Helter Skelter, its slide made to look like a giant tongue that snaked around the exterior of the conical structure, spiralling upwards until it reached the open mouth of an enormous, painted clown face that looked more menacing than good humoured. Child after child slid down the corkscrew slide on their mats, bumping painfully to the ground at the bottom before running as quickly as they could to the steps to do it all over again. In the space where the football posts would normally be, stood a large structure housing the Dodgem Cars, and next to that were the Waltzers (on which Ben had thrown up last year, plastering both himself and Tommy in puke as they continued to spin round and round).

He approached the main thoroughfare of stalls with some caution, still unsure of the idea that, although actually inside his memory, he couldn't be seen or heard by those around him. He watched a nearby father trying to win a cuddly toy for his daughter at the coconut shy, loudly offering his condolences with every near miss in order to test his invisibility.

'Ooh! Unlucky!' Tommy said loudly as the man's ball whistled past one of the coconuts.

'Wow! Nearly had it with that one!' he shouted again as the father missed with his final throw.

Tommy watched him closely for any type of reaction, any sign that he'd been heard, but there was nothing. Feeling slightly braver, he then walked up to the man and waved his hand in front of his face. Again, nothing. He couldn't be seen. *Invisibility!* Ben *would* be jealous! Feeling more confident in his surroundings, Tommy casually strolled around the stalls for a while, nosily listening in on some conversations (during which he discovered that one of the girls in his year had actually fancied Ben!) and looking longingly at the hotdog stand, which only served to remind him that it was almost time for supper.

It was while he was jealously watching a boy taking a bite out of a juicy cheeseburger that he saw something a little disconcerting. A sight that he had never before seen at the Little Millbrook funfair and a face that seemed to be cropping up a little too often for his liking; it was Mr Wiseman. Tommy noticed him, smiling pleasantly at a young girl as she leaned across the barrier of one of the stalls trying desperately to get closer to the rubber duck that she was trying to hook with her pole. Grandpa's old neighbour beamed happily as she succeeded in her quest and jumped with joy as the stall worker passed her a goldfish in a transparent plastic bag. Mr Wiseman cheered and clapped, happily looking around him at the crowd, his eyes settling for a moment on the place where Tommy stood. Tommy instinctively took a step back but then relaxed and laughed off his paranoia, remembering that there was no way on earth that the old man could see him.

His rumbling stomach told him to get a move on, so upping the pace, he walked around the fair with a bit more purpose, searching for the younger versions of himself and Ben. It didn't take him too long to find them, alerted to their presence by Ben's very loud commentary at the shooting gallery.

'This one's for my father!' he shouted, taking aim with the air rifle before firing a pellet at a pile of tin cans. He missed.

'And this one is for my mother!' he yelled, missing again and this time almost taking the stall-owner's eye out. Rambo could sleep safe.

Tommy remembered all of this. Not especially surprising as it had happened only a year ago, but it was still hard to get his head around. The detail of every part of the memory was perfect; just like watching a film of his life. And there *he* was too – his younger self. That was a sight he'd never get used to – seeing himself standing there, just a few feet away, like he were looking at some uncanny doppelgänger.

Young Tommy watched as Ben theatrically, and unsuccessfully, used up the remainder of his pellets.

'Better luck next time, kid,' the gruff carnival worker said, keenly grabbing the rifle from him.

'I ain't coming back here,' Ben replied. 'It's a rip off! Your sights must be off!' He then took the toffee apple that Young Tommy had been holding for him and began licking greedily at its red, sugary shell. 'C'mon, Tom, let's go to the arcade. I raided my piggy-bank for all the 2ps.'

Tommy followed behind as Ben and his younger self made their way across the fair, Ben walking gingerly as they battled through the throng of carnival-goers. It was only a year or so since his accident, and Ben had only just had the plaster taken off, so his limp was at its worst.

Entering the arcade, Tommy was greeted by the near-deafening noise of the gambling machines that beeped and flashed wildly at them, the variety of slot machines and video games designed to entice all of the children to spend their 'hard-earned' pocket money. He looked about the place and smiled as he saw boys that he knew from school staring hypnotised at computer-generated cars that they raced on the screens in front of them and another group who were busy blasting away an army of zombies with their plastic machine guns. This was his idea of heaven.

He shadowed the boys to the centre of the arcade, to the two-penny-push machine, where Ben began dropping his coins into the slot in an attempt to win the pile of 2ps that had gathered near the drop-tray. He must have been doing something right, because a few seconds later there was the welcome sound of a handful of coins dropping into the winner's tray. Ben shrieked excitedly, scrambling to collect his winnings with one hand, while holding on tightly to his toffee apple with the other. The win, despite only being a handful of coppers, hadn't gone unnoticed. A group of older boys who had been lingering by a motorbike simulator (and stopping the younger kids from having a go) had taken an interest in Ben's success.

Now this was what Tommy had come to see. It was why he had chosen this particular memory.

The ringleader of the group was one David 'Shakey' Waterston, a nasty piece of work if ever there was one. He'd earned his nickname due to his habit of bullying younger children, picking them up and shaking them violently until their dinner money fell out of their pockets. He was a few years older than Tommy and Ben, and so far they'd managed to stay under his radar. But Tommy knew that all that was about to change – he'd lived through all of this before. Young Tommy and Ben were about to experience Shakey at his worst. The only question Tommy needed answering now was 'why?'.

'Oi!' Shakey shouted over to Ben. 'Gimme some of that! Half of its mine anyway – I put loads in there today.'

The large boy, a mop of dark, curly hair on his head,

then stomped over and grabbed half of Ben's winnings before coolly strutting back to his gang of mates. Ben looked heartbroken.

Tommy sidled over to where Ben and his younger self stood, still cautious despite the fact that he knew it was impossible for him to be seen. He had an overwhelming sense of déjà vu as he eavesdropped on their conversation.

'He wouldn't be so quick to do that if Richie were here,' Ben told Young Tommy, looking at the few coins that remained on his palm.

And he wasn't wrong there, Tommy thought. Ben's big brother could certainly look after himself. He was a couple of years ahead of Shakey too, so in the schoolyard food chain he was above even him. Unfortunately, though, at this particular time in their lives, Ben and Young Tommy languished somewhere very much near the bottom.

'He's not always been so tough either,' Tommy heard Ben continue, still clearly agitated. 'They didn't always call him Shakey. Richie says that in junior school people used to call him 'Warty'.'

'What, 'cos of his last name?' Young Tommy ventured.

'Yeah, that. But also 'cos he had a huge wart in the middle of his chin. It's gone now, but I'd have loved to have seen that! Bet he wasn't so cocky then.' Ben daydreamed for a second before adding, 'he was in the school orchestra too – in the first year – his mum made him play the saxophone or something – such a loser!'

All three of them stole a glance over at Shakey. Young Tommy and Ben quickly averted their eyes in case they were seen, but Tommy, safe in the knowledge that he couldn't be, continued to stare. If he looked hard enough, he could just make out the faint scar on his chin where the wart had been.

By the time he'd returned his attention to them, Young Tommy had dragged Ben over to a nearby shoot-'em-up in order to distract him, but it still didn't stop him from grumbling.

'I oughta go over there and teach him a lesson,' Ben said aloud, still munching furiously on his toffee apple. 'I'd show him where he could shove his sax.'

Young Tommy turned his back and inserted a few coins into the game.

'Just leave it, Ben, or you'll get us both a hiding. C'mon, concentrate on this. I'll even pay for your go.'

Now came the important part, Tommy thought, watching the scene closely. If he remembered correctly, not long after this brief exchange Shakey and his thugs had begun to chase them – and he'd never really known why. Ben had always maintained that it was just because they were bullies and that was all there was to it, but Tommy wasn't so sure. He knew Ben better than anyone, and he was always confident about one thing: Ben was never as innocent as he made out. Now was the time to see whether he had been honest with him.

The truth revealed itself almost immediately. As Young Tommy was busying himself with the game, Ben turned and faced Shakey. Tommy watched in amazement as his idiotic friend then mouthed 'Warty' to him and pointed to his own chin, pulling an over-theatrical look of disgust. Shakey was dumbfounded at first, but as comprehension dawned his face flushed with anger. He began pounding his fist against his palm, just a taster of what Ben was going to experience in the near future.

So Ben had been fibbing all along! He *had* been the cause of their chase and subsequent beating. Tommy vowed to take it up with him as soon as he got back.

But Ben hadn't finished yet. He then did something that surprised even Tommy, and he'd come to expect pretty much *anything* from him. Ben drew his arm back, took aim and proceeded to launch his half-eaten toffee apple at Shakey. Tommy followed the flight of the missile as it travelled, the apple and stick twirling in a blurry haze of red and white, before seeing it land right on the top of Shakey's head, nestling itself deep into his curls. This, of course, sent Shakey over the edge. He ripped the sticky apple from his scalp (taking a fair chunk of hair out with it) and charged over to Ben in a rage, his mates in tow.

'Uh, Tom…' Ben said urgently.

'What?' Young Tommy responded, still concentrating on his game and oblivious to what had gone on behind him.

'Run.'

'Huh?' Young Tommy stole a glance at Ben, whose eyes were now wide with terror. He then clocked the approaching gang.

'I said RUN!'

Ben yanked Young Tommy from the game, and together they ran out of the arcade and through the bustling crowd of carnival-goers, dodging past a group of school mates queuing for candy floss and around a muscle-bound man impressing his girlfriend at the Test-Your-Strength game. Tommy jogged behind unseen, watching as Shakey's group gave chase, knowing full well how it was going to end. The pursuit took them past the Dodgems and round the back of the Helter Skelter, where Tommy knew they would finally be caught.

As always, Ben was captured first. It was inevitable really; his limp always slowed him down. You'd think he'd have known that and not wound Shakey up in the first place, but Ben was Ben after all. And this chase had ended exactly as the first one had. Tommy rounded the corner just as Ben had his legs kicked from under him, causing him to fall hard into the dirt. Young Tommy could have still got away if not for the second or two that he paused trying to help Ben. It had proved costly; the gang now had them surrounded, and they were both going to pay for Ben's cheek. Shakey stood over Ben, glared at him and then pulled him up from the floor by his upper arms. He started to shake him. Hard! He must have defaulted to his signature move out of habit, because he then suddenly realised that he hadn't chased Ben for his dinner money. He'd chased him for something else. For payback. For calling him by that horrible nickname he'd had to endure as a youngster and to avenge that large clump of missing hair that now coated the toffee apple. He threw him back to the ground and began punching his arms and legs as hard as he could. Following his lead, two of his friends then pushed Young Tommy to the floor and copied him.

Tommy watched on and winced, remembering the pounding like it was yesterday. They had been punched over and over until their arms and legs were numb – he hadn't walked right for a week. But not even the beating could silence Ben. It had to be said, he certainly had spirit. With every punch that Shakey threw at him he retaliated with an even more ferocious volley of insults.

'Gerroff me, Warty!' he grunted. 'Don't you know who my brother is? He's gonna smash your face in!'

Unfortunately, that was the last thing that Ben managed to say before Shakey shoved the remainder of the hairy toffee apple into his mouth, gagging him. Not that Shakey knew it yet, but Ben would be true to his word. Tommy knew that just a few days later in school, completely out of the blue, Shakey had approached them sheepishly in the playground sporting a whopper of a black eye. He proceeded to offer them an awkward apology, and it was only as he walked away from them that Tommy had noticed Ben's brother watching on with amused interest from the other side of the yard. The food chain at its best.

Tired of seeing himself and Ben getting beaten up, Tommy turned away and made his way back through the fair. He'd seen enough and had found out what he'd wanted. It was time for him to leave. Casually strolling through the stalls, he mused as to just how and when he'd leave the memory. He wandered aimlessly until he found that he'd strolled right up to the ghost train. It was the same old, tired train that they brought every year, but Tommy hated it now just as passionately as he did the very first time it had frightened the life out of him, when he was five or six. To this day he still had nightmares about it.

It was something else he saw that alarmed him even more than the ghost train. It was Mr Wiseman again and this time he seemed to be looking straight at him. He reminded himself that the old man was more likely looking through him, at the scene of Ben and Young Tommy getting beaten up – it *was* drawing a fair bit of attention after all. Tommy side-stepped a few yards to get out of his line of sight, but unbelievably the old man's gaze followed him. *This couldn't be.* He couldn't be looking at him; he shouldn't be able to even see him! Tommy was sure of it though; in fact he was positive. He moved a few more yards to the side – again, the old man followed him, staring at him quizzically. Tommy looked about him, hoping to see somebody else there that Mr Wiseman could have been looking at, but he was very much alone. And still the old man continued to stare. He should be looking at nothing but a hedge!

Now curious, Tommy took a couple of tentative steps towards him. As he did, Mr Wiseman swiftly turned his back and scuttled off, disappearing behind the ghost train. Tommy quickly followed, concerned at the thought that he could be seen by anybody when inside his own memory, let alone Grandpa's creepy neighbour. He rounded the corner expecting to see him walking off, but he saw no sign of him amongst the crowd. *Where had he got to?*

Tommy smiled to himself. The old man must be quicker

on his feet than he looked. His smile soon faded when, all of a sudden he felt light-headed and had to grab for the nearby railing to keep his balance. The fair became nothing more than a misty haze around him, and he felt like the world was spinning; he was forced to sit down just to avoid throwing up. He felt sure that he was about to leave the memory, the sensation being similar to last time, but, and he couldn't quite say how, it all felt different somehow. It felt wrong. He shut his eyes against the dizziness, expecting that the next sight he would see would be his bedroom, but when he opened them he was still at the fair. The carnival noise around him grew louder and louder as the joyful cries turned into painful screams that pounded harder and harder against his eardrums. He began to feel nauseous and had to put his head between his legs to avoid being sick. He sat there for what felt like an age, but then the feeling passed just as quickly as it had come. The spinning stopped and the sickness subsided - yet still he hadn't left his memory.

Before Tommy had the chance to grow worried about being trapped inside his memory, the disorientation was replaced by tiredness. An overwhelming fatigue like he'd been drugged. His eyes felt heavy and he struggled to stay awake, having to lay his head down to rest. He curled himself up on the step of the ghost train and closed his eyes, determined that sleep wouldn't take him – not in this strange place. He failed almost immediately and drifted into a deep and dream-filled sleep.

— CHAPTER SIX —

A Surprising Discovery

Tommy was disturbed from his uncomfortable sleep by a loud and all too familiar noise. He was lying on top of his bedcovers and was still fully dressed from the night before. The pen was at his side, and the paper he'd used was now stuck firmly to his cheek (no doubt glued there by a fair amount of dribble). His school uniform was now so creased that it looked like his dad had ironed it. He had a thumping headache, and it took him a few moments to realise where he was. He was absolutely exhausted, and, when he tried to raise his head from the pillow, it felt like there was somebody standing over him, pushing it back down.

'Get up, Tommy!' his mum boomed again. 'I won't tell you again! You'll be late for school!'

Ergh. School. The last thing he needed today.

With great effort he forced himself up to a sitting position and rubbed the blurriness from his eyes. He pulled the paper from his face and examined it. It was blank. He thought hard about the previous evening and his visit to the funfair, the trouble was that he'd had so many dreams that he couldn't figure out what was real and what wasn't. Had he even used the pen last night?

His answer came later that day when he saw Ben at

school. Tommy had accosted him after class, confronting him with the new information about their run-in with Shakey and demanding the truth. Tommy had assured him that he'd received new information from a reliable source and that if Ben didn't tell him everything then he'd tell his mum where he kept the magazine he'd stolen from his brother. It hadn't taken him long to break. Ben confessed fully to his part in causing the chase, admitting to calling Shakey 'Warty' and also to throwing the toffee apple at him. He told Tommy everything except that he was sorry – he was *never* in the wrong! So the pen *had* worked again. He hadn't dreamt it! Although pleased with his latest journey, it had also left Tommy with a slightly uneasy feeling. That sensation he'd experienced when leaving the memory this time had been so unpleasant that part of him had actually hoped that he *had* dreamt it.

After school he headed to the town library in the hope of finding out even more about the pen. Tommy's mum had worked there for most of her adult life, and she was pleased to see him when he called in to, as he put it, 'get ahead with some homework'. He was amazed that she had actually believed him. He sat at his favourite study table on the second floor; his favourite because it was right next to the library's collection of comic books. He'd spent countless hours in this particular section, taking advantage of the endless supply of Superman and Batman back issues. Today, though, he sat at the table not reading about superheroes but about something a little out of character for him... history. Ever since Grandpa had given him the pen he'd been able to think about little else but looking for clues.

So far he'd only managed to find the same old pictures that Grandpa had shown him in his scrapbook. Pictures of the pen with Da Vinci, Shakespeare and other famous faces from the past, but he'd uncovered nothing new.

His new passion for books had led his mum to believe that the new school year had brought with it a change in Tommy's attitude toward study, and she'd already passed numerous comments about what a good influence Art was on him: 'He's such a lovely boy, you should hang around with him more often,' was her current favourite. If only she knew the truth. The discovery of the pen had actually placed his homework further down his list of priorities, and it now languished somewhere between doing the washing up and mowing the lawn.

There was also another benefit to spending so much time in the library. He had found himself, on more than one occasion, sitting opposite Jennifer Fox. Yes, THE Jennifer Fox! Now Tommy wasn't normally one to pay much attention to girls, he preferred spending his time thinking about more worthwhile things like football or computer games, but for Jennifer Fox he was certainly prepared to make an exception. She was the prettiest girl in his year and was easily the most popular. Good at sport, she had loads of friends, and she even rivalled Art when it came to enthusiasm for homework. Tommy had had a crush on her since junior school. This warm and fuzzy feeling even culminated in him going so far as to cycle all over town looking for her house just to give her a Valentine's Day card.

By 'give her' he of course meant that he had posted it through her letterbox and run away as soon as the card hit the floor.

Despite fancying her for a few years, Tommy still hadn't plucked up the courage to speak to her directly, having to make do with showing off in front of her whenever the opportunity arose; flick-ups in the Dutch Barn, 'Knock-Knock' jokes in the corridor – you know, the usual. All of that was bound to impress her.

It was today, when Tommy had allowed himself a break from the history books and a sneaky five minutes with a Batman comic, that his attention was drawn to her as she appeared at the top of the stairs, taking a seat at the table opposite his. *Typical*, he fumed, quickly trying to hide his reading material; *she had to appear just when he was reading a comic!* He hid his embarrassed smile behind one of the tattered history books and hoped that she hadn't noticed. He took regular glances at her as she quietly took a book and writing pad out of her bag and placed them in an organised manner on the table. Tommy wouldn't normally look twice at most of the girls in school, but there was something about Jennifer that made him want to stare, something magnetic that drew his eyes to hers. She had the most beautiful blue eyes and golden blonde hair that fell just below her shoulders. He wasn't ashamed to admit that he rather liked her.

With his concentration beginning to waver, Tommy raised the history book so that it hid his face, positioning it so he could look over at Jennifer while still giving the impression of being deep in research. He watched her as she read her own book, her lips moving ever so slightly as she read. She had the habit of absent-mindedly twirling her hair around her forefinger before letting it fall again to her shoulders. He was captivated. So captivated that he didn't even notice as his own book slowly lowered, exposing his mouth which had fallen open, giving him the appearance of a love-sick goldfish. He clamped his mouth shut quickly and raised the book again as she glanced in his direction, briefly making eye contact with him. His face burned with embarrassment and his heart raced as he cautiously lowered his book again, hoping that she hadn't caught him staring. A heat wave coursed through his body as their eyes met again – she was still looking over! But then Jennifer's gaze moved slowly downward, toward his book. Clearly unimpressed, she raised her eyebrows in disapproval and then looked back down at her own work. Slightly confused, Tommy looked at the book and was horrified – the comic he'd been hiding inside it had poked out of the top and was now clearly visible. He felt totally deflated at the thought of her knowing that he still read comics. What *would* she think of him?

Stuffing it into his bag, he picked up a different history book from the pile and flicked through its pages impatiently, trying desperately to put Jennifer out of his mind. He'd become an expert at skim reading over the last few days and now had a well practised knack of being able to stop on the pages that had pictures. This particular book was about the United States of America. He paused at the pictures of former American Presidents, scanning their clothes and surroundings for any sign of the pen, but he found nothing.

Ten or fifteen minutes passed with him studying every picture he could find, his eyes beginning to tire from staring at each one. Losing patience with the book, he thumbed his way towards the last few pages and just as he was about to clap it shut his attention was caught by a picture at the back. A picture of Abraham Lincoln. It showed Lincoln, complete with his unmistakable beard and tall hat, sat at a table surrounded by a handful of other men. He was posing for a picture that showed him about to sign a document. Tommy was hit by a surge of excitement when he looked at the pen in Lincoln's hand. He sat up in his chair and leaned forward so he could examine it more closely. It was Grandpa's pen. *His* pen! He took it from his pocket and placed it next to the picture in the book. A perfect match! Finally, he'd found something new! He couldn't wait to go and tell Grandpa the news. Then, as he was about to close the book, something else in the picture caught his attention. He looked at it carefully, shaking his head in disbelief. *This was impossible*! It just couldn't be right. He had to see Grandpa, and quickly!

In a scrambled rush he closed the book and threw it into his bag. Then, jumping from his chair, he knocked it backwards onto the floor and ran towards the stairs. The sudden commotion gave rise to a chorus of 'Sshh!'s' from the handful of people in the library and yet another look of disapproval from Jennifer. But he didn't care. He didn't have time to worry about that now.

He passed his mum at the foot of the stairs, startling her with his manic behaviour. She shouted to him as he ran through the doors, reminding him not to be late for dinner, but dinner was the last thing on his mind. He didn't even have time to apologise to the man in the black overcoat that he bumped into on the pavement outside the library, almost knocking him over. No, this was *too* much of a coincidence. He was sure of it now – there *had* to be more to it. More to *him*. The only thing on his mind right now was how could Grandpa's old neighbour be in a photograph with Abraham Lincoln?

CHAPTER SEVEN

The Curious Visitor

Tommy arrived at Grandpa's in such a hurry that he even forgot to time himself. He was willing to bet that he'd broken the record though. He pressed his finger hard on the doorbell and impatiently hopped from foot to foot, not daring to look over his shoulder towards the house of Grandpa's neighbour – a man who had now become more mysterious than ever. He was positive that it was Mr Wiseman in that picture with Abraham Lincoln, but how could it be? It must have been taken hundreds of years ago, and the old man looked exactly the same as he did now. And that, coupled with the fact he seemed to be cropping up all over the place whenever the pen was used, made Tommy think that he had to be connected to it all somehow. It was time for him and Grandpa to confront him.

Tommy rang the bell again. He could hear it in the hallway but nothing else; no approaching footsteps, no doors opening or closing, nothing. Grandpa would normally have answered by now. Then it occurred to Tommy why he hadn't. He slapped his forehead in frustration. It was Tuesday night. Grandpa always played snooker on a Tuesday night, which meant he wouldn't be back for hours. Typical, this was urgent! He *had* to find a way to speak to him.

He wheeled his bike back up the garden path and made a decision. He'd go over to the club and ask to speak to Grandpa; there was no other thing for it. They probably wouldn't let him in, especially after Ben had got them thrown out last year when they'd been carol singing (Ben had a deeply offensive singing voice), but he had to at least try.

He pedalled across the grass towards the main road, keeping his head down, deliberately avoiding the need to look at Mr Wiseman's house. Reaching the pavement, though, he did allow himself a quick glance, and noticed that it somehow appeared even more creepy than usual. The setting sun, seemingly also afraid of the house, was hiding behind its chimney, throwing the front of it into near darkness. Then something happened that almost made his heart stop. The porch light came on! He gasped, causing the handlebars of his bike to wobble. He was in! Of course he was; he always was. Well, almost always. Tommy was no longer sure that he was the hermit that they all thought him to be.

What Tommy did next he would question for years to come. Maybe it was his curious nature getting the better of him, or maybe it was a force much more powerful at work, but he did something that he would never normally have contemplated. He decided to walk up Mr Wiseman's garden path, knock on the front door and ask him all about it. All about that picture of Abraham Lincoln and all about his connection to the pen. A simple plan, yes, but also a terrifying one.

In a determined effort that took all of the will power he could muster, Tommy hopped off his bike and began to push it slowly towards the termite-eaten front gate of Mr Wiseman's garden. With every step he took towards the house, the sun disappeared further behind it. Resting his bike against the unkempt hedge, he cautiously pushed the gate open, its age loudly announcing his presence with a lingering *creak*. He held his breath, sure that the noise had broadcast his arrival. He looked behind him. He could see Art's house and beyond that Grandpa's. The place looked completely different from this angle. Unfamiliar. Tommy longed now for the safety of Grandpa's front garden. It was only fifty yards away, but it might as well have been five thousand. He took one last look, positive that this would be the last time he would see it, and then he steadied himself and slowly walked up the path towards the door, like a prisoner taking his final few steps along death row.

As he neared the front of the house, Tommy could see the detail on the windows; the painted wooden frames peeling, cobwebs decorating each corner. Focusing on the front door and the light of the porch, he tried to convince himself that he had nothing to worry about. After all, Mr Wiseman was only a harmless old man. Or so he'd thought. He wasn't so sure anymore.

The sun had now all but totally abandoned Tommy, the house fully eclipsing the last of the evening's sunshine. He desperately wanted to run, but something inside made him stay. He gripped the shoulder strap on his rucksack tightly, placed the other hand over the outline of the pen in his pocket and took a deep breath, quickly striding the last few steps to the door. *There! He'd done it!* Now the only thing that stood between him and the most intriguing person he knew was a wooden door. It was now or never. He reached up to the knocker, but before he could release it the door swung open, and in front of him stood the little old man, a broad smile on his face.

'Hello, Master Parker,' Mr Wiseman said, 'I've been expecting you.'

Tommy was dumbstruck. He just stood there in silence, desperately trying to find something sensible to say, but words failed him. In contrast, Mr Wiseman looked completely at ease, a look of warm welcome on his face. They stood about two feet apart, their eyes at the same level despite Mr Wiseman standing on the step to his front door.

His appearance was almost comical; nearly as wide as he was tall. He had a rotund, tubby body (not too unlike a beer barrel) and an equally round face with red, chubby cheeks. On the top of his head sat a bushy mop of whitish-grey hair. His big, intelligent eyes and sharp nose made him look like a barn owl. Come to think of it, looking at him close up, Tommy was surprised at just how friendly Mr Wiseman looked.

'Well,' Mr Wiseman said, breaking the silence, 'are you going to come in?'

He turned, deftly for a man of his shape, and waddled down the hallway, leaning forward as he walked, as if walking into a strong wind. Tommy remained where he was, still unsure whether he should accept the invitation or just make a break for it. Against his better judgment, he took a bold step forward. A footstep he thought he'd never take. A footstep that would change his life forever.

— CHAPTER EIGHT —

The Guardian

The inside of Mr Wiseman's house wasn't anything like Tommy had expected. He thought it would have been dark, dingy and covered in cobwebs, with bats in the attic and rats in the cellar (where, of course, Mr Wiseman would have slept in a coffin). In reality, however, it was quite the opposite. Cosy almost. There was a beautiful grandfather clock in the hallway and a pleasant odour of furniture polish mixed with freshly baked bread.

He followed Mr Wiseman into a room just off the hallway, entering it just as his host was relaxing into a comfy looking armchair near the fire. Tommy struggled to take in his surroundings, quite simply because there was so much to see. There were books stacked up in tall piles on the floor, old charts and maps tacked to the walls and even a suit of armour leaning up against a bookcase. His eyes were drawn, not to the suit of armour, not even to the mysterious man, who was sat by the fire, but to a small item that stood alone in the centre of the mantelpiece. It was a small wooden cup with no handles, or any other discernible markings for that matter, but nevertheless it took pride of place.

'Ah, I see you've noticed that little item,' Mr Wiseman said, seeing where Tommy's attention lay. 'Enchanting, isn't it? Believe it or not, that chalice is almost two thousand years old, and it's been the subject of much interest over the years. Sparked many a *crusade*. If I had the time to tell you about it, I'm sure you'd be quite familiar with its story. But that is for another time. Please, take a seat.'

He motioned for him to sit.

Tommy perched himself on the arm of the nearest chair. The chair nearest to the door, just in case.

'So, Master Parker, how can I be of assistance?'

Again Tommy noticed how friendly the old man's eyes were.

'How do you know my name?' he asked. That was a good start. Begin with an easy one, then get to the good stuff.

'Let's just say that I'm an old acquaintance of your grandfather,' he replied, smiling.

Tommy steadied himself for a moment, carefully selecting his next words, trying to figure out how much information he could divulge about the pen without breaking his promise to Grandpa.

'OK,' Tommy said, deciding on his best approach, 'I was in the library earlier... and I saw this...'

He took the history book from his bag and opened it to the right page. Nervously walking across the room, he handed it to the old man and then hurried back to the chair by the door. Mr Wiseman looked at it with amusement, letting out a quiet chuckle. He appeared to recognise the picture immediately.

'Ahh, I see. Well, you *have* been busy, haven't you? Not

my favourite picture. I always thought it made me look like I have a double chin, don't you think?'

Tommy's jaw dropped. That wasn't the response he'd been expecting. He'd thought Mr Wiseman would deny having anything to do with the picture, telling him that it was merely someone who looked like him. Instead, all he seemed to care about was that the picture had captured his bad side!

'So you're saying that it *is* you?!' Tommy asked incredulously.

'Of course it is. Unless there's another handsome devil like me. I remember that like it was yesterday. I liked old Abe. I've always been sorry that I couldn't have done more for him. I would have saved him if I could. Got shot you know, very sad.'

Not for the first time in the last week, Tommy was lost for words. *How could this old man possibly think that he could have stopped a President from being assassinated?* And, of course, Tommy had known that Lincoln had been shot; everybody knew that! But it had happened ages ago – far too long for Mr Wiseman to have been there. He opened his mouth to say as much, but Mr Wiseman hadn't finished.

'Is it so hard to believe that I'm in that picture, Master Parker? I'm an old man; I've seen a lot of things. And we live in an incredible world – a world of being able to transmit images through the invention of television, of man travelling through air and space in large crafts. And, of course, a world where magical pens can transport you into your memories.'

Tommy's hand instinctively shot to his pocket. So he

knew.

'Oh yes,' Mr Wiseman said, his eyes following Tommy's hand. 'I know all about that pen of yours.'

'But how?'

'I know more than you'd dare think, Master Parker. You have barely scratched the surface.'

Tommy, despite his shock, still managed to take offence.

'No, actually, my grandpa told me all about it.'

'I don't doubt that he did young man; he thinks the world of you. I'm sure he told you everything. At least, everything *he* knows.'

'What do you mean?'

'I mean, Master Parker, that there's more to that pen than even your grandfather knows. And if you want to know more, I will tell you.'

He stood and approached Tommy, his eyes sparkling. He held out an old, frail hand.

'You have it with you don't you? Show it to me.'

Tommy was unsure. At the forefront of his mind was his promise to Grandpa. But Mr Wiseman seemed to know all about it, more even than Grandpa did. And there was something about this strange old man that made him want to trust him. Tommy dug his hand deep into his pocket, found the pen and, with some hesitancy, handed it to him. At the exact moment that Mr Wiseman's fingers grasped it, Tommy felt a small electric shock.

Taking possession of the pen, Mr Wiseman examined the markings down its side and smoothed his fingers along its length.

'It's been so long,' he said, caressing it like it were a beloved pet, 'and it's not changed a bit.'

He silently mouthed the words of its inscription. Tommy hoped he would explain what it meant, but he was to be disappointed.

'I must say, your grandfather has done a very good job safeguarding this. It came to him at a time of great peril.'

Tommy realised who he must be. It all fitted in perfectly with Grandpa's story and explained why he knew so much about it. Tommy jumped to his feet excitedly.

'I get it,' he said, '*you're* the man Grandpa told me about! The man in the church during the war. You gave Grandpa the pen, didn't you? It was *you* who told him to look after it.'

Mr Wiseman smiled broadly, entertained by Tommy's enthusiasm.

'No, Master Parker, that wasn't me. That was the pen's *former* owner. Somebody else with an interesting story, but again that is for another time. Oh no, my involvement with the pen runs far deeper.'

Tommy returned to his seat, frustrated. Just when he thought he was getting somewhere, the plot became even more confusing.

'Yes, a very good man your grandfather,' he continued. 'Very noble. Many have been less strong. Many have been seduced by its power, have become obsessed by it. But not him. I always knew that I'd made the right choice.'

Tommy looked at him, puzzled.

'But you just said you didn't give it to him?'

'That's right I didn't, at least, not directly. Anyway, never mind that now. Tell me what *you* think about the pen. About its... abilities.'

Where did he start? There was so much to say.

'Well it's certainly better than my other pens,' Tommy said. 'It's amazing. I couldn't believe it when I used it. I didn't think that kinda thing was possible. What is it? Some sort of time machine?'

The old man half shook and half nodded his head.

'A crude definition, but I suppose you could call it that. It certainly facilitates a time distortion of sorts. It allows time travel but *within* one's own memories. And there's much more to it than that. So much more.'

'You've experienced the fact that it can be used to *visit* memories, but it is important now that I tell you this: *the pen does have another use*. It is important, now more than ever, that you fully understand just what kind of power this pen has. Only then will you understand why it is so desired. Only then will you understand the importance of keeping it safe.'

Mr Wiseman unscrewed the pen, separating it into two parts.

'When you used it, you used it without ink, and the writing disappeared soon after. Is that correct?'

Tommy nodded, not having a clue how the old man knew all of this.

'And in so doing, it enabled you to visit your memory, to visit and *observe* only.'

'Well, yeah.'

'A passive participation, good for nostalgia but little else. Well, Master Parker, what if I was to tell you that it is possible not just to visit those memories but to also become *active* in them? To actually interact and *affect* your own memories? Imagine the possibilities. To have the opportunity to go back and change a course of events, to correct mistakes that you once made, or to do the things that you regret not having done. Or even affect the past actions of others. Imagine the power one would have in those circumstances.'

Mr Wiseman slowly screwed the two parts of the pen back together, not once breaking eye contact with his guest.

'Well, this pen,' he said, 'can allow you to do just that. This pen, Master Parker, is The Pen of Destiny.'

The Pen of Destiny? Changing history? Was he serious?!

'What? Well... How?' Tommy asked, trying not to sound too eager.

'It's quite simple really. Simple but ingenious. All you have to do is place a regular cartridge of ink inside it. It will then allow you to make a more *permanent* mark on events. A mark on history itself. Allowing you to become the author of your own destiny. Only in the most exceptional of circumstances should the Pen be used to alter what has already come to pass. I will give you an example: if it wasn't for this little item,' he said, with an element of pride in his voice, 'then Guy Fawkes would have won.'

'Huh?' Tommy cocked his head.

'You are aware of the Gunpowder Plot?' the old man asked him. 'Well, they actually succeeded the first time around, until I intervened of course. But only in these, the most extraordinary of situations, could the Pen have been used – and used, as it was – for the good of mankind. Events the first time around were just too unspeakable to allow. I had to correct things.'

Tommy couldn't believe what he was hearing.

'But be warned,' the old man continued, 'to use it in this way is dangerous, very dangerous indeed. To interfere with history, even in the most seemingly inconsequential manner, can have a catastrophic effect on mankind. Every action, no matter how small, has a consequence, that action itself beginning an irreversible chain of events. *The Butterfly Effect.* It can prove disastrous to interact with persons from the past. It is for that reason, Master Parker, that the Pen must never be used to change history.'

He held it out for him to take and Tommy, rather too keenly, grabbed it from him and shoved it into his pocket.

'But if it's so dangerous then why are you telling me all of this?'

'I'm telling you, Master Parker, because it *is* so dangerous. You need to know all of it before you can fully understand. Only when you understand can you truly be effective in guarding the Pen.'

'You see,' he said seriously, 'a war is brewing. We're not the only ones who know of its existence. It was only the good sense and discretion of your grandfather that has kept it safe for so long. There are others who would use this Pen for the wrong reasons. For power. For dominance. Imagine if you will, Master Parker, that for the last fifty years, rather than with your grandfather, the Pen was in the possession of someone less virtuous. Someone corrupt. Its story is far older than you can imagine. There has been a battle raging throughout time for this item. Sometimes it falls into the wrong hands, and when it does I and its current Guardian do everything in our power to retrieve it. For there is always a Guardian. One Guardian to ensure that the Pen does not fall into the clutches of evil. And now, Master Parker, that Guardian is *you*.'

Tommy shot up from the arm of the chair, running his hands through his hair. What had begun as an exciting new revelation had turned into something altogether more dangerous. To use it to alter the odd harmless memory sounded like it could be fun. But all this other stuff about affecting mankind, about a war brewing. He didn't like the sound of it one bit.

'I don't want to be Guardian!' he said, a little too curtly than he'd intended. 'I don't want that pressure on me. I didn't ask for any of this.' He walked over to Mr Wiseman, thrusting the Pen out for him to take. 'Here, you keep it. You seem to know all about it. It's better that you have it, cos I'll... well I'll probably just lose it anyway!'

The old man held up a hand to calm him.

'No. You must keep it safe now. You alone have been chosen.'

Although he didn't raise his voice, there was something very final in his tone. Tommy knew that it would be useless to argue.

'Who's after the Pen then? Who am I *guarding* it from? And just how old is this thing? As Guardian I think I deserve to know these things.' Tommy failed to keep the anxiety from his voice.

'You will know its full story by the end, you can be sure of that.' Mr Wiseman replied. 'As for *who* wants the Pen, well, that is a question that you certainly deserve to have answered.'

Good, Tommy thought, *at least I'll know who I'm supposed to be looking out for.*

'They are merciless, unforgiving people who will do anything to have that Pen in their possession again. And I do mean *anything*, Master Parker.'

Now he wished he hadn't asked. Tommy waited for him to elaborate. He had to wait a good half minute.

'Well?' he finally asked, unable to wait any longer.

'Well, what?' came the response.

'Well, who are they? What do they look like?' Tommy demanded. This guy was unbelievable.

'You'll certainly know them when you see them.'

'That's it? That's your insight? Thanks for the tip off, I feel safer already!'

'You'd do well to let me finish,' Mr Wiseman said quietly with all the patience of a Saint.

'You'll know them when you see them, for these three reasons: firstly, if you ever get close enough to them, and I pray that you don't, then you will see that each has the same tattoo. A tattoo of a quill. The symbol of their cult. Secondly, they will be dressed from head to toe in black.

For some reason they've always had a particular liking for long, black coats.'

That rang a bell with Tommy. He thought about earlier when he'd run out of the library. There was that guy he'd almost knocked over in the rush; *he* was dressed all in black. Was it just coincidence, or did that mean that they were here already? A shiver went down his spine. This was becoming very real all of a sudden.

'And the third?' Tommy asked.

'Pardon?'

'You said there were three ways of recognising this cult. What's the third?'

'Oh yes, the third,' said Mr Wiseman, suddenly remembering his final point. 'The third way is the easiest to spot. They'll be the ones trying to kill you.'

Tommy sat in stunned silence.

'I'd try to look out for the other two clues first if I were you,' he added helpfully.

'Yeah, thanks, I'll bear that in mind. So do they have a name, this 'cult'?'

'They call themselves *Secuutus Pluma. Followers of the Pen.* An ancient brotherhood whose goal is to locate the Pen and use it for one thing and one thing only: evil. They are led by a Grand Master, but even he serves a higher power. It is unfortunate that you are Guardian in the time of Nidas.'

'What's a nidas?' Tommy asked.

'Not what. *Who.* Nidas is the deadliest Grand Master of all. A particularly nasty piece of work who is obsessed with finding the Pen. He really will stop at nothing.'

Great, Tommy thought, *could this get any worse?*

'You said earlier that it's fallen into the wrong hands before,' Tommy pointed out. 'Does that mean they've got their hands on it in the past?'

'Yes, I'm afraid it does. And the history books you've been poring over these last few days have recorded all of their efforts. They've taken possession of it a number of times and each time they do there is always a common feature: humanity suffers. The Cult has managed, throughout the ages, to infiltrate society at every level. From the average man on the street to politicians, high powered business men, even royalty. In more modern times they've even developed a faction within the world's most influential of groups – celebrities. If you were to think of history's most destructive people, you can virtually guarantee that the Pen was at one time or another in their possession. Adolf Hitler, Judas...'

'What?!' Tommy interrupted. 'Judas?!'

'Oh yes, Master Parker, it's true. But that's where the Cult's greatest weakness lies. They always underestimate the inherent goodness and strength of humanity. For it was their betrayal of Jesus that ultimately led to the emergence of mankind's new faith. Just think... if it wasn't for *Secuutus Pluma* then we may not even be celebrating Christmas!' Mr Wiseman chuckled, his chest wheezing. 'How's that for irony? I bet they lose sleep over that one!'

'It is my purpose in this life,' he continued after he'd recovered, 'as it is now yours, to ensure that the Pen does not fall into the hands of this Cult again. That it remains with the pure of heart. With persons such as Abraham Lincoln and your grandfather. And now you. You may not realise it yet, but you are a very important young man. Very important indeed. You have a great future ahead of you. The Pen has found its way to you, Master Parker, for a reason. It is now your turn to guard it.'

That's some responsibility, Tommy thought. *He could barely look after himself, and now he was expected to look after the future safety of the whole world.*

'For a while now the Cult have been frustrated in their quest, and it is only in these recent times, since your grandfather had begun to use the Pen again, that they have been able to narrow their search. Had he been in any *immediate* danger, I would of course have intervened and shown myself earlier...'

Tommy nodded, satisfied that Mr Wiseman hadn't allowed Grandpa to be put at risk.

'...as I have with you now,' he finished.

It took a moment for those last words to sink in.

'What? Do you mean that *I'm* in immediate danger?'

Mr Wiseman nodded sadly.

'They are getting close, Master Parker. Too close. They have managed to track the Pen down to Little Millbrook. And not for the first time. They almost found it here thirty years ago, but I managed to confuse their search somewhat. Unfortunately, that confusion proved only temporary. Now they have returned, and they are positive that the Pen is within their reach. It is time. Every century or so a conflict occurs, good meeting evil as it always must. Only after these battles can the true balance of mankind be restored.'

Tommy was getting scared now.

'What should I do if I see one of them?' he asked, listening harder than ever, thinking again of the man at the library.

'Run.'

'Really? I hadn't thought of that,' he blurted.

Mr Wiseman continued, oblivious to Tommy's failings in tact.

'There are a number of things you need to bear in mind about that Pen, Master Parker.'

Tommy felt as though he should be writing all of this down.

'Firstly, avoid using it unless absolutely necessary, which considering these men are virtually knocking on your door, is never. Second, keep it safe. Don't let anyone else know that you have it. The more people aware of its existence, the more chance there is of it falling into the wrong hands. Thirdly, and most importantly, trust in your friends. Trust them with your life. They are good people; you will need them in the times ahead more than ever.'

Trust his friends with his life? Clearly, he'd never met Ben or Art. Ben couldn't take things seriously if his own life depended on it, let alone Tommy's. And neither of them were exactly bodyguard material.

'I will assist you where I can, Master Parker, but I cannot be everywhere at once. Above all else, trust in your own goodness. Don't ever doubt it, even when it seems that all hope is lost. It is that which will see you through in the end.'

Tommy was numb. He felt positive that if he pinched himself hard enough he'd wake up and all of this would have been a dream.

'So to sum up,' Tommy said, 'If I use the Pen then this violent group of men will find me, but they'll probably find me anyway, so when they do I'll just get my mate Ben to protect me. Got it! It all sounds so easy! In fact, have you got any other pens that you want me to look after whilst I'm at it?'

Mr Wiseman laughed out loud.

'That's the spirit!' he said, 'you're showing that you're a fighter already! I knew you wouldn't let all of this get you down.'

Tommy could only look at this curious man, puzzled, as he continued to chuckle to himself. He really didn't know what to make of him.

Mr Wiseman's laughter was drowned out by the chiming of the grandfather clock in the hall.

'Master Parker, it's getting late. I'd make my way home if I were you; the Cult always come out at night.'

'Do they really?' Tommy asked, concerned.

'I have no idea. But if I was a mob of scary pen-hunters I would, wouldn't you?' he replied, smiling.

'Umm, I suppose so,' Tommy said as he was ushered hurriedly out of the living room. A harbinger of doom with a sense of humour. *Great*. Just what he needed.

Before he left, Tommy had to ask the one question that had been nagging at him for ages, even before he'd known about what the Pen could do.

'One more thing,' he said, 'the inscription on the Pen, what does it mean?'

The old man smiled at him warmly as he opened the front door. 'Well, I often find that when you're trying to learn something new, it is often better that you first understand the past. Reflect on it some more, Master Parker. That should do the trick.'

And with that cryptic statement Mr Wiseman closed the door, leaving Tommy completely in the dark.

CHAPTER NINE

Secuutus Pluma

T he man sat behind a large wooden desk, his chair creaking every time he shifted his weight. He wore a crisp white shirt with long sleeves, a thin black tie and black braces. His considerable frame pulled the braces tightly over his shoulders, and the clasps attached to his trousers threatened to snap at any moment. On his cheek an ugly scar ran from his left eyebrow down to his chin.

Two other men stood across from him, arms by their sides, their postures those of well-trained soldiers awaiting inspection. They too wore white shirts and black ties, but they also sported matching black coats, leather gloves and each had a black fedora hat. Their faces were almost hidden in shadow, the room barely lit by the small desk lamp and the intermittent flickering of a broken light from the hallway.

Behind the men a rusted old boiler ran a plethora of pipes into the ceiling and walls, which, in times gone by, would have sent hot water to the dozens of radiators in far off rooms. Blackened smoke and scorch marks adorned the brickwork. It only served to give the place an even more sinister feel. The atmosphere was tense. Despite their military posture the heads of the two men were bowed slightly, neither wanting to make eye contact with their superior, neither wanting to be the bearer of bad news.

'I won't ask again,' the big man said, the reflected lamplight the only thing alive in his otherwise soulless eyes. 'We have returned to this wretched place, Brother Lethley, on your recommendation. Because of *your* enquiries.'

He stood slowly, raising himself to his full height. He towered over the others, standing as tall as a grizzly bear (but twice as ugly). They bowed their heads even further in shame. And, of course, fear. One of the men held his head distinctly lower than the other.

'I don't need to tell you how disappointed you've made me.' He emphasised his last word by hammering his fist angrily on the desk, causing a small crack to appear under his hand.

Lethley finally raised his head, cautiously looking towards his boss. 'But, sir, it was a reliable source,' he said nervously, 'I was guaranteed that it was here.'

'The only reason I agreed to indulge you and your *reliable source* was because it had brought us back to this place. I thought the coincidence too great to ignore. Yet it seems that we have both been made to look foolish. And I don't like being made to look foolish.'

Lethley hung his head again.

'When He discovers that we have again wasted valuable time and resources coming back here,' he continued, 'I expect that we will *both* feel His wrath. But not, Brother Lethley, before you feel mine.'

Lethley dared not look up. The colleague to his left took a step backwards, out of harm's way, as the big man walked menacingly around the desk, his hand reaching towards a pouch attached to his belt. Lethley didn't move. He knew it would be useless to run, they'd always find him. Nor would he dare fight back. He had to take the punishment that was coming to him, even if it was final. It was their code.

The man took a giant stride towards him and stood glaring at his prey. Lethley, with every ounce of effort that remained, forced his head upwards so that he could look into the eyes of his superior – a show of respect expected even in these circumstances. Then he saw the glint of steel in the man's hand. He knew what was coming next: he'd borne witness to it many times in the past. Time and again he'd stood and watched on with admiration as his superior had brutally eliminated weak links from their organisation. Survival of the fittest. It was because of that talent that he had so quickly reached the position of Grand Master.

In these last moments Lethley cursed the source who'd misled him and cost him his life. He looked up one final time to meet his fate head on. Fate. *How ironic*. The one thing that he and his brothers had committed their lives to and his was to be such a gruesome one. He closed his eyes and exhaled a long breath. This was it.

But a moment passed. Too long a moment for someone as clinical as the Grand Master to wait. Lethley then heard hurried footsteps in the hall and someone entered the room.

'Sir!' The new voice shouted, 'It's here! We've found it! At last we've found it!'

The big man's cold, deadly stare remained fixed upon

Lethley as he slowly returned the metallic item to the pouch on his belt. He turned to look at the newcomer. Lethley's body went so weak he could barely stand.

'Go on,' the big man said.

'It's with him. It's with Parker!'

A satisfied smile grew across the man's face, causing his scar to twist and crease, shining in the lamplight. Brother Lethley looked unmistakably relieved. He couldn't wait to give his source a big hug. The Grand Master turned and looked at him, his smile turning into a look of disdain. Nidas' next victim would have to wait.

— CHAPTER TEN —

A Decision Made Easy

Tommy hadn't slept much that night. In fact he'd barely slept a wink. His mind was a confused mess; all he could think about was the Pen. That and everything associated with it. About visiting his memories, about dark and dangerous strangers, but above all about him having the power to affect history itself. He lay there looking at his alarm clock, watching the minutes tick by, praying that sleep would finally come for him. He remembered looking at the clock at 3:24am before finally drifting off into what he thought was a long and deep sleep, during which he dreamt of large shadowy figures chasing him across the town. He managed to escape the dream just as they'd backed him into a corner of the Little Millbrook fort, and he faced the choice of surrendering to them or falling sixty feet onto the rocks below. He'd looked at his clock then and saw that it was 3:27am. The dream had lasted just three minutes! It had officially been the longest night ever.

The problem was that he'd got himself worked up on the bike ride home from Mr Wiseman's house. Everything he'd been told went round and round his head. He'd decided against waiting around Harbour View for Grandpa to get home. It was too dark, and the streets didn't seem as safe anymore, not after what the old man had told him. Instead he'd pedalled home as fast as he could, looking over his shoulder more times than ever before. Every shadow sent a tingle down his spine. Every dark corner potentially hid a member of the Cult who lay in wait, ready to jump out at him. And was it his imagination or did every single person in Little Millbrook wear a long, black coat? Maybe he was just being paranoid. After finally reaching the safety of his house, he'd spent the remainder of the night in his bedroom, locking the Pen securely in his keep-safe box and hiding it behind a stack of wrestling magazines under his bed. No-one would find it there.

School that day was a struggle. As a result of the appalling night's sleep, he drifted through the morning drowsy-eyed and stifling a yawn every minute. He was totally shattered. If it wasn't for Ben's constant chattering in Geography, he was sure he'd have fallen asleep. Yet despite his exhaustion there was still that underlying paranoia; a kind of fear that there were people out there, most probably in his own little town, who wanted to harm him.

But he couldn't help thinking about the other stuff too. The exciting stuff. About the Pen's *other* power. Being able to actually change the past – it presented so many possibilities. So many *wonderful* possibilities!

Looking at Ben, a thought suddenly occurred to him. So obvious that he was shocked he hadn't thought about it before. He could use the Pen to go back to when Ben had been hit by the car – he could stop it! He'd no longer have his limp, and he'd be just as he was before the accident. No sooner had the idea entered Tommy's head, though, he'd quickly put it out of his mind. Mr Wiseman had specifically warned him against using the Pen for that sort of thing. What had he called it again? *The Butterfly Effect?* Tommy daren't use it to do anything to interfere with history too much.

He was snapped sharply out of his daydream by the sound of the dinner bell. That and Ben glaring at him with a look of frustrated disappointment.

'What you playing at?' Ben said. 'Are you trying to ruin our chances of a decent lunch?'

Tommy jumped to his feet, realising his mistake. He should have been on his toes and chasing down their turkey burgers as soon as the bell had gone.

'Sorry, mate, I was miles away.'

'Just go.' Ben said dramatically, the thought of an empty stomach adding fuel to his annoyance.

Tommy, trying desperately to make up for lost time, burst out of the classroom, trampled over a couple of classmates and disappeared around the corner and out of sight.

Ben threw his and Tommy's bags over his shoulder and limped as quickly as he could out of the classroom, fighting his way through the crowds and beating a path towards the Dutch Barn where the game of football had already started. He dropped the bags behind one of the posts and shouted across to the nearest goalkeeper, the burly Gareth Savage, whose face was screwed up into a concentrated frown. That, along with his freckles and bright ginger hair, gave him the look of a confused orangutan.

'Alright, Sav? What's the teams?'

Savage, who was still a good foot taller than Ben despite being bent at the knees, didn't turn to look at him. His eyes were fixed on the ball, which was flying in his direction. Plucking it out of the air with one shovel-like hand, he shouted, 'It's our half of the year against theirs. Where's Parker?' he added, throwing the ball out effortlessly to a team mate. 'We're two nil down already. You're hardly gonna change the game with your dodgy leg, are you?' Savage pointed a large index finger at the other end of the barn. 'Just get up front out of the way until Parker gets here.'

Now Ben wasn't usually one to take such insults, especially about his leg. Normally, had someone offended him like that, he would have swung first and talked later. But Savage wasn't your ordinary schoolboy. He was one of the few boys in school that he and Tommy were wary of. He was a brute. Even most of the older boys gave him a wide berth, and it was for that reason that Ben ignored the uncomplimentary remarks and jogged gingerly over to the other end of the pitch, as far away from him as he could get.

After a few short minutes of playing outfield, Ben realised why he'd become so accustomed to playing in goal since the accident – he was completely off the pace. Twice he'd found himself with an opportunity to score only to be caught by a defender at the last minute. He just wasn't anywhere near as fast as he used to be. And if his confidence wasn't low enough, each time he made a mistake he had to put up with Savage shouting insults at him from the other end of the pitch. 'My nan coulda scored that one, Campbell' and 'You're kift, Campbell! You play like a girl!' And then, of course, there was his personal favourite, 'Well played, hop-a-long!' What an idiot. If he wasn't twice his size, Ben would have stopped and gone over to sort him out. If.

It was during one such barrage of abuse that Ben watched as Savage jogged back towards his goal, the opposition bearing down upon him. Ben crossed his fingers, hoping that his mistake wouldn't cost his team a goal. He watched on as Savage settled himself, preparing for the shot, but then he saw something to Savage's right that looked oddly out of place in a football match: Art. He was walking slowly across the field of play, his head down as he read a book. He was in his own little world, totally oblivious to the game going on around him. Ben had a horrible feeling that something was going to go terribly wrong.

It all seemed to happen in slow motion. The opposition took a shot at goal, and Savage leapt to his left, using every inch of his frame to stretch for the ball. Flying through the air, his hand edged closer and closer to it, but just as he was about to pluck it out of the sky, he dived straight into Art who had walked into his path. Both of them ended up in a heap on the floor leaving the ball to go sailing through the goalposts. The goal scorer wheeled away in celebration leaving Savage and Art on their backsides; Art rubbed his head, his glasses hanging at an angle from his ears. Savage jumped up in a flash, his face turned a deep shade of purple, making his head look like a giant beetroot.

'What the hell you doing, pip squeak?!' he yelled at Art, who still sat winded on the floor.

A crowd had begun to gather around them. Ben made his way over, fearing the worst, arriving at the outer circle of pupils in time to see Art heave himself up to his feet and dust himself down.

'Why don't you look where you're going nerd? Aren't four eyes enough for you?'

'I'm sorry,' Art replied calmly, straightening his glasses, 'I must have tripped over your knuckles.'

Thankfully, Savage had missed the insult. A witty comment like that would have to be broken down and explained to him at a later date.

Ben hoped Art would quit while he was ahead and just walk away, but his hopes were to be dashed.

'He's mocking you, Sav!' shouted a faceless voice from the crowd.

Great! It was too late for Art now; Savage would have to save his reputation. A fight between these two would be the biggest mismatch since David versus Goliath (ignoring of course the fact that David had won that one – there'd be no upset here).

'Is that right, four-eyes? Are you mocking me? You really are the weakest link, you know that?' Savage quipped, looking around the crowd for approval. He'd heard that put-down on a television show once and thought he'd use it to impress the onlookers. Only those smaller than him laughed. The noise was deafening.

Yet still Art stood his ground.

'Then I presume that would make you the *missing* link?' he responded instantly. Again, the insult was lost on Savage, but not even he could mistake its tone which suggested it wasn't intended as a compliment.

Ben slapped his forehead in anguish. Why Art? Why? Why couldn't he just walk away?

'Hit him, Sav!' a voice said.

'He just called you a monkey!' said another.

Savage didn't need much encouragement. The fuse had already been lit. All Ben could do now was wait and watch the explosion.

Art regretted it the second he opened his mouth. He vaguely heard someone from the crowd shouting something about hitting him and then he suddenly went numb, realising he was likely to experience an awful lot of pain. His arms and legs didn't want to move, the only part of his body that seemed to be responding was his stomach which was doing somersaults. He focused upon the huge figure before him as it took one large step towards him, the massive hand balling itself into a tight fist.

Frozen to the spot, Art could do nothing but stare at the fist as it grew larger and larger the closer it travelled to his nose. He flinched at the last moment, closing his eyes and waiting for the pain that would follow. Surprisingly, his last thought was for his glasses, hoping that they wouldn't break again; he'd only just got them fixed from the last time someone had picked on him.

He heard a slapping noise, flesh on flesh, followed by a painful yelp. But he was confused: he didn't feel any pain and he hadn't even said anything! So who had screamed? Art tentatively opened his eyes and saw that a different hand was now directly in front of his face. A hand that had caught Savage's fist, blocking his punch!

'Oww!' Ben shouted, 'Gerroff him!'

His hand was still stinging from the force of the punch, and for years to come he would ask himself why he'd done it. Maybe it was the fact he hated Savage's bullying ways. Maybe it was because Art was a friend of Tommy's. Only time would teach him that he had probably done it because, deep down, he actually liked Art, though he wasn't quite ready to admit that yet. Not today. Not with his hand hurting so much.

'Just leave him alone!' Ben shouted as forcefully as he could, surprised to find that he was still holding onto Savage's fist. He let go of it quickly and took a step back.

'Campbell! Did you just do what I think you did?' Savage asked him, part annoyed, part confused. This was all new to him. Nobody had ever been stupid enough to stand up to him before.

'Umm... I don't think so,' Ben replied. 'Why? What did you think I did?'

The reality of the situation now hit him hard. The crowd's silence was replaced by a low hum of whispers, and he could almost feel the electricity that the crowd's collective will power had created. All were desperate to see some violence, urging Savage to punish somebody, it didn't matter who.

'You've asked for this, Campbell,' Savage said menacingly, cracking his knuckles.

Like a well-rehearsed dance routine, Ben took one step back for every step that Savage took forwards. Retreating, Ben found that he was hampered not only by his bad leg but also by the wall of people who now prevented his escape, none satisfied until they saw blood. Amazing how a group of schoolchildren could suddenly turn into nothing more than barbaric revellers ready to witness the thrashing of a person who only thirty minutes before they'd probably sat next to in Maths.

Then it came. The familiar tune started at the rear of the crowd, quietly at first and then growing into a choral chanting that rumbled and echoed through the Dutch Barn.

'Fi-ght! Fi-ght!! Fi-ght!!!'

In the past it had always sounded like a harmless bit of fun, but now, out here on his own, it sounded as though they were announcing his death sentence.

With nowhere left to go Ben could do nothing more than try and reason with him.

'Come on, Sav, we don't need to do this.'

'Don't tell me what I can or can't do. I can do anything I want.'

And without further warning Savage leapt forwards and swung his arm towards him. Ben managed to dodge him at the last moment, the punch whistling past his left ear. Taking advantage of Savage being off balance, he then ran to the other side of the circle, but still there was no way out. He felt completely outnumbered. Scanning the crowd for a gap, he found nothing until... yes, a definite gap! A gap by the only friendly face in the crowd – Art. He'd managed to create a small parting for him and was desperately trying to hold it open.

Savage regained his balance and moved towards him again. There was no way he could keep dodging him; he wouldn't miss a second time. Savage stomped to within a few yards of him, his face even redder than before. Pounding his fist, he said through clenched teeth, 'Right, Campbell, you've got nowhere else to go, say goodnight!'

With that he took one almighty swing just as Ben sidestepped to his left, and made a dash for the gap. Had he moved a split second later, Savage, without a doubt, would have broken his face. As it was, though, for the second time in a minute, he had found himself swiping at nothing but thin air.

Ben ran for all he was worth towards Art. A few more yards and he would make it. But, just as he was about to dash through the gap, one of Savage's cronies threw a bag on the floor, right in his way. The bag itself wasn't that big, but it was certainly enough to throw Ben off his stride, especially with his limp. He shifted his stride in an attempt to hurdle the bag, jumping off his good leg to maximise his chances of clearing it. He jumped with every ounce of spring that he could muster but his trailing leg hadn't lifted high enough, and his foot caught on the bag's strap, causing him to tumble forwards and land in a crumpled heap on the floor. He was helped to his feet rather too quickly by Savage, who grabbed him by his jumper and hauled him skywards so that they came face-to-face. He was angry, *really* angry.

'Try to make a fool outta me?' he said, dropping Ben to the floor. Ben landed hard on his bad ankle, and it twisted from under him causing him to cry out.

'This'll teach you!' Savage shouted, taking a few steps back before running up and kicking him hard to the ribs.

The crowd groaned as one as Ben doubled up in pain and struggled for breath. Savage then grabbed him by the scruff of the neck and punched him straight on the nose. Ben's eyes watered freely and he could taste blood in his mouth. He closed his eyes, hoping it would end, but he wasn't that lucky. He felt another swift kick to his body, which hurt just as much as the first. Struggling to see through the tears he could just about make out Art as he was being held back by two of Savage's foot soldiers – then everything went fuzzy, and he couldn't focus properly.

It was then that he heard something. A voice that had managed to cut through the ringing in his ears. A voice that was audible even over the shouts of the baying crowd. A voice clearer and more welcome than any other sound he had heard before.

'SAVAGE!' it said. 'Leave him alone!'

Tommy's lunch run had ended in success, having managed to lay his hands on two fresh turkey burgers *and* two packets of bourbon biscuits – a pretty good haul. He'd hot-footed it to the Dutch Barn, keen not to miss too much of the game, but upon his arrival there wasn't a game of football anywhere in sight. Instead, he saw a large group of people gathered by one of the goal mouths. He could see the tall and unmistakable frame of Savage over all of the other heads, standing in the centre of the crowd and facing another person. A group like this, encircling someone like Savage, could only mean one thing – someone was about to get hurt. He walked over to the group, taking a bite from his burger and looking around for Ben so he could get the low down on who was involved, but he couldn't see him anywhere. Just as he reached the outside of the circle, he heard Savage shout, *'Right Campbell, you've got nowhere else to go, say goodnight!'*

A bit over-dramatic, Tommy thought, even for Savage, but then he did a double-take. Did he just say *Campbell?* Tommy stood on his tip-toes, looking again at the person facing Savage. It was. It was Ben! How on earth had he got himself into this? Tommy shouted his name, but he wasn't heard over the din of the group. He saw Savage swing a punch, a powerful one that Ben thankfully managed to avoid. He willed him on silently, praying he'd find a way out before Savage finally caught up with him. It was looking good, he'd almost got to a gap, but then Savage's mate, that idiot Bogeys, had thrown his bag right in Ben's way. His heart sank. He could do nothing but watch helplessly as Ben feebly tried to jump it but failed and fell to the floor. Tommy knew that he'd never have fallen over that bag before he'd had his accident. He'd have easily hopped over it and been a hundred metres away before Savage had even noticed he'd gone. But that was the old Ben.

Tommy fought his way through the crowd, continuing to struggle forwards, only able to look on helplessly as Savage rained kicks and punches down on his friend who lay helplessly on the floor. It was brutal. Finally, Tommy managed to force his way to the front of the group, just as Savage was lining up another damaging kick.

'SAVAGE! Leave him alone!' he shouted as courageously as he could.

The noise from the crowd seemed to stop instantly, silenced by Tommy's unexpected show of bravery. His body shook uncontrollably, but he was surprised to find that it wasn't through fear but through anger. Watching his best mate get beaten up like that made his blood boil. Savage stopped his attack and turned slowly, rage etched on his face.

'What did you say?' he spat.

Tommy stared right back at him, taking a firm stride forwards.

'I said leave him alone.'

'You wanna choose your friends better, Parker. This cripple has just got you into a hiding.'

Savage walked towards him, his fist cocked, its target now changed, but Tommy didn't move an inch. First Shakey, now Savage. *How many more times was Ben going to get him beaten up?*

As Savage approached, Tommy raised his arms to defend himself, just like the boxer's did. This was it.

'Quick!' a voice from the crowd shouted, interrupting

them. 'Haynes is coming. LEGGITT!'

Savage stopped in his tracks. Not even he was stupid enough to fight in front of this teacher. Mr Haynes was old school. The sort of teacher who wore socks *and* sandals and who'd bring back the cane quicker than you could say 'detention'.

Savage looked to Ben and then back to Tommy.

'It's your lucky day, Parker!'

He then ran off with a group of friends, away from the approaching teacher, the rest of the crowd dispersing in every direction. Ben was left on the floor holding his ribs, his face bloodied and tear-stained. Tommy ran over to him, Art doing likewise from the opposite direction.

'What happened here?' Mr Haynes demanded.

Silence.

'Campbell, look at me boy. Who did this to you?'

Ben remained slumped on the floor, wiping the blood from his nose with his sleeve.

'Huh? Oh, I just fell over, sir, playing football.'

'Really?' the teacher replied sceptically. 'Parker. Ford. Do you want to try telling me the truth?'

They looked at each other awkwardly, neither wanting to take the lead. Ben's eyes pleaded with them not to say anything.

To everyone's surprise, it was Art who spoke first.

'It's like Ben said, sir, I saw it all. He fell over the ball, it was quite funny really.'

Tommy nodded enthusiastically. This was the first time he'd heard Art lying to a teacher. He was so proud.

'Well it doesn't look too funny to me!' Mr Haynes snapped. 'Get him off to the nurse this instant and then straight to class!' he added, storming off in search of another pupil to harass.

Ben pulled himself gingerly to his knees, attempting to stand, but his bad ankle buckled under his weight. Tommy went to help him, but Art stood in his way.

'No. Let me do it,' he said, holding his hand out for Ben to take. 'Thanks, Ben,' he added.

Ben looked at him hesitantly, apparently deciding whether his pride would allow him to accept Art's offer of help. He then held his arm out, allowing himself to be pulled to his feet.

'Don't worry about it, Fart,' Ben said, 'it was nothing.'

'What's up with you two?' Tommy asked, confused by how friendly they were being all of a sudden.

'Nothing, mate,' Ben said, 'I'll explain later.'

Tommy and Art gave Ben their shoulders, and together they hobbled down to the nurse's room, Ben moaning constantly about the pain in his leg. Tommy couldn't help but feel guilty about it all. Ben would never have been caught before his accident. Savage wouldn't have got near him if not for his limp. He felt as if it was all his fault. Now more than ever, he felt to blame for Ben's condition, and he just wished that there was something he could do about it.

What was he thinking?! He *could* do something about it! Of course he could, he had the Pen; he could change anything he wanted. To hell with what Mr Wiseman had said. Surely it wouldn't hurt to change just one little bit of history? Besides, it would only affect Ben – what harm could it do really? As far as Tommy was concerned, this qualified as a pretty 'extraordinary situation' as Mr Wiseman had put it. And even though he could hardly say that it was for the 'good of mankind' it was certainly for the good of Benkind, and that was close enough for him.

It was at that point that he decided. He would use it as a one-off, just a little something to help his best mate. It was the least he could do to make him normal again.

In between dramatic groans Ben tugged on Tommy's arm and tried to mouth something to him.

'Tom... Tom...' he said, barely coherent.

'Yeah, Ben, what is it?'

'...did you get my turkey burger?'

— CHAPTER ELEVEN —

Something in the Trees

Tommy slammed his bedroom door shut, causing a photograph to fall off the wall and into a pile of dirty clothes on the floor. It was his favourite picture – the one of him and Ben after the final football match of last season: Tommy proudly holding a large trophy and Ben standing just behind him, smiling broadly. Beneath the photo was an inscription showing that he'd finished as the top goal scorer for that season.

He threw his school bag onto the bed and swiftly collapsed down after it, burying his head into his pillow and letting out a muffled grunt. He was *so* angry with Savage! What gave him the right to humiliate Ben like that? The only good thing to have come of it was that Ben and Art seemed to be getting on a bit better since, and, having heard the full story from Art, he had to admit that he was pretty proud of Ben for what he'd done. He had that limp and Tommy knew that he was to blame for it. He was sick and tired of watching Ben suffer because of him.

On the way home Tommy had called into the paper shop near his house and, with his remaining pocket money, had bought a pack of ink cartridges (and a ten pence mixture to calm his nerves). If Mr Wiseman was right, maybe he could do some good and help Ben in the only way he could think how.

Tommy dived under the bed and retrieved the Pen from its hiding place. He inserted an ink cartridge and stared at it for a long moment, giving one last thought to the words of his new mentor: *The Butterfly Effect*. Every action having a subsequent reaction. What harm could it do really, though? Even if he *did* manage to prevent Ben's accident, he was hardly going to change the world, was he? Besides, Mr Wiseman had also said he was going to need his friends around him. What good would Ben be with his current handicap?

Giving little thought to the unpleasantness of the previous journey into his memory, he grabbed a piece of plain paper from the pile on his desk and lay face down on his bed.

In big, bold letters he wrote a date that he would never forget: *Saturday 23rd July 1994 – Ben's accident.*

This was it. There was no turning back now.

As soon as he finished the sentence, he felt that same sensation. The sudden jolt as if being pulled backwards, and the feeling of falling even though he was lying on his bed. His surroundings seemed to blur before disappearing completely and then a blinding flash of light…

Waiting a few seconds for the green dots in his eyes to vanish, he tentatively opened them and was faced with a sight that told him that the Pen had worked. Gone were his wardrobe and the pile of dirty washing, and in their place was the scene he had visited ever so briefly when he'd first used the Pen at Grandpa's – Little Millbrook woods. He could even feel the warmth of a summer's day on his face and smell the freshness of the trees and woodland.

He took a moment to find his bearings and then ran through the undergrowth, fearing that he had no time to waste, dodging the trees and following the beaten path until he came to a clearing by the road. He hid behind a bramble bush and took it all in. It *had* worked! The Pen had brought him not only to the right date but to the right time too. In front of him was a sight that made his heart pound and the hair on the back of his neck stand on end. Just a few yards in front of him stood both himself and Ben, looking a couple of years younger and a few inches shorter – even more so than when he'd seen them at the funfair. His mum was right; he really *had* had a growth spurt this past year. Each were holding their skateboards and chatting to one another without a care in the world. It was surreal looking at them again, seeing them as even younger than when he'd seen them little more than a day or so ago. Ben looked much slimmer too, and as he watched them walking up the hill it was obvious that he showed no sign of his limp.

Tommy had to be more cautious now. With him using real ink it meant that he no longer had the benefit of invisibility; he was in danger of being seen. He had to figure out a way to stop Ben being hit by Mr Barnes' car without them noticing him. What he wanted to do was to rush out there and tell them both not to skate down the hill, but Mr Wiseman had warned him about interacting with people from the past. Plus, he'd seen loads of science fiction films about this kind of thing. He knew that if he went and spoke to them, one of two things was sure to happen. One, they'd all faint. Or two, the universe would explode. And he didn't want either. No, he'd have to come up with a much shrewder way of warning them.

His mind raced as he tried frantically to think of a plan. He watched Ben walk up the hill, skateboard under his arm and shout behind him, 'Don't blink, Tom! They don't call me Ben 'Bob-sleigh' Campbell for nothing!' before running effortlessly towards the top of the hill, around the bend and out of sight. Tommy's younger self took up a position on the opposite side of the road, just a few metres from where he now crouched behind the bush. He had rested his skateboard against his legs and shouted up to Ben, 'OK mate! All clear!'

He had to think of something and quickly. Any second now Ben would come hurtling round the bend, and he would have failed. He then heard a noise coming from the bottom of the hill; a car engine spluttering to life like the sound of an old man coughing. He knew exactly what it was; this was how it had happened before. It was Mr Barnes' car. Though there was still no sign of Ben, any second now he'd come flying round the corner and straight into the oncoming car. He felt like running to Young Tommy and shaking some sense into him. Rather than acting as look-out, he was just staring at his skateboard and spinning its wheels in a complete daydream. What an idiot!

Tommy cautiously stood from behind the bush, positioning himself behind a large tree. As he did so, Mr

Barnes' battered navy car appeared at the bottom of the hill, chugging its way slowly upwards, its owner sitting stiffly behind the wheel. His fingernails dug painfully into the bark of the tree, a surge of panic hitting him as he heard the exhilarated screams of Ben coming from the opposite direction. He could see Ben now, flat on his back, flying down the hill at maximum speed on a direct collision course with the car. Young Tommy casually watched and laughed as Ben hurtled downwards gathering more and more pace. Tommy had no other option; he had to act now. Throwing all caution to the wind, he shouted at the top of his voice,

'BEN! WATCH OUT! CAR!'

He could barely bring himself to watch. A startled Ben sat up on his board, a look of horror on his face, and emitted a high-pitched girlie scream which, in any other circumstance, would have made Tommy wet himself with laughter. Spotting the car in front of him, Ben planted his feet into the ground and raised the front of the board so its tail scraped against the road in an effort to brake. Sparks flew behind him, but he was travelling too fast, barely slowing at all. Tommy cursed himself for having left it too late. Young Tommy now also waved hysterically at both Ben and Mr Barnes, desperately trying to get the attention of the latter. But it was to no avail, the driver hadn't seen him.

They were close to impact now, twenty metres apart... fifteen... ten...

Then, just at the last moment, when it looked as though Tommy would have to witness the accident for a second time, Ben managed to swerve out of the car's path and into some bramble bushes at the side of the road. Mr Barnes, seeing Ben as he passed him, blasted a loud toot on his horn and shook his fist at him in annoyance before continuing his journey up the hill.

Finding himself anxiously hugging the tree, Tommy remained out of sight whilst his younger version dropped his skateboard and dashed into the path Ben had created through the thicket. A few moments later, the two of them appeared out of the undergrowth, Ben picking thorns and nettles from his clothes. Tommy was close enough to hear their conversation.

'Thanks for that, Tom,' Ben said breathlessly. 'I'd have been a goner if I hadn't swerved.'

Young Tommy looked at him puzzled.

'What you thanking *me* for?'

'For shouting. I didn't see the car...'

'I didn't shout.'

'Course you did. I heard you.'

'Seriously, Ben, I didn't. I heard something, but I thought it was you screaming.'

'C'mon, you think I wouldn't recognise my best mate's voice?' Ben said, clearly exhilarated about cheating death.

'Anyway,' he added defensively, 'I wasn't screaming.'

There was a pause as Ben considered something for a moment.

'Hang on a minute... I owe you my life!'

He threw his arms around Young Tommy and embraced him in a bear hug. Behind the tree Tommy chuckled to himself, a laugh born both out of relief and of witnessing the predictable overreaction of Ben. He'd done it! And Mr Wiseman was right; it *was* possible to use the Pen to change the past. He'd managed to stop the accident. Now he couldn't wait to get back to the present to see the effect it would have on Ben.

Feeling pretty good about himself, Tommy backed away from the two boys and walked deeper into the woods. He was beginning to wonder at what point the Pen would return him to his bedroom and hoping that it would be less nauseating than the last time when he froze at the sight of something that his mind couldn't quite process. Standing in front of him, shaking his head in disapproval and tutting loudly, was Mr Wiseman. Tommy's instant thought was one of smug comprehension. So Mr Wiseman *had* been here first time round! He knew that he'd seen him in the woods two summers ago. But he had to think quickly. He couldn't stand here and chat, not with his younger self standing only a few yards away. That shouldn't be too much of a problem, he thought. This was the Mr Wiseman of two summers ago; they hadn't even met yet. The old man wouldn't know or even recognise him. Tommy could just walk past him without saying a word – maybe a polite little 'hello' but nothing more than that. As he made to pass him, his logic was proved incorrect almost immediately.

'I thought I told you not to use the Pen in this way, Master Parker?'

The words registered, but Tommy couldn't quite make sense of them. If this *was* the Mr Wiseman of two summers ago, then how did he even know him let alone know that he had the Pen? But more than that, if this was *his* Mr Wiseman, then how on Earth did he get in here? This was his memory! The old man turned and walked briskly into the woods. Tommy, struggling to keep up, called after him.

'Hey! How did you get here?'

'Not everyone needs a pen to travel through time, dear boy,' he replied, not breaking his stride. 'I trust that you were successful in your little quest?'

Again, Tommy couldn't help but wonder how the man knew so much.

'I think so. Ben managed to avoid the car. That should have sorted it all out now, right? When I go back, he won't have his limp will he?' he added hopefully.

'I would assume so, Master Parker,' Mr Wiseman replied in a rather off-handish manner. 'Although not even I can predict what other impact your actions could have had. How they will have changed not only Ben but also those around him.'

Tommy hadn't actually contemplated what other consequences there might be; he'd just concentrated on Ben's accident. What if Mr Wiseman was right? He'd been right about everything else so far. Perhaps Ben would be completely different? Perhaps Ben without a limp would have changed so much that they wouldn't even be friends anymore? He was beginning to regret using the Pen at all now. In fact, he regretted ever having the blasted thing.

'Hang on a minute!' he called. He had a question that had been bugging him for the last two years. 'That first time

Ben had his accident, I was positive I saw you in the woods. I was right, wasn't I? You were here all along.'

Mr Wiseman stopped suddenly and turned, looking him directly in the eye.

'Is that so?' he asked, 'Well ask yourself this: would I have been here at all had you yourself not returned?'

Tommy took a second to decipher the statement before responding in the only way he could.

'Huh?'

'Today is the first time I have set foot in these woods, Master Parker,' he said smiling. 'What you need to understand is that this *is* the first time that Ben had his accident. Or *not*, as the case may be. For now, thanks to you, there *was* no accident.'

He paused to let his words sink in before adding, 'Isn't time travel brilliant?'

Brilliant? Mind-boggling more like. The deeper he got into all of this, the more confusing it all became.

'But I must tell you again,' Mr Wiseman continued, this time in a more serious tone. 'It is not advisable to use the Pen to change history. I beg of you, do not use it in this way again. Not unless absolutely necessary. Not only is there the danger of you altering all sorts of events, but you also place yourself at risk to your surroundings. Unlike using it to simply *view* your memories, when used in this way you are as vulnerable in your memory as you are in reality. You cease being a mere observer and become a participant.' Mr Wiseman took a step closer to Tommy, so close that he could feel the old man's breath on his face.

'You are its Guardian now, Master Parker. And with that comes a great responsibility. Be careful, a completely different world exists within one's memories.'

Letting the words hang in the air between them, they looked at each other in silence until Mr Wiseman glanced quickly upwards over Tommy's shoulder before turning away and continuing at a brisk pace through the woodland.

Hearing a noise in the trees where Mr Wiseman's gaze had fallen, Tommy looked upwards. He could see a dark figure moving lithely across one of the uppermost branches, partially obscured by the leaves. He couldn't exactly make out what the figure was, but he could tell that it was like no creature he had ever seen before. It was dark in colour, almost black, its body similar to a human in shape, but the way that it crept deftly on all fours along the thin branch reminded him of a large cat like a panther. A shiver tingled down his spine. The creature looked like it was stalking something. In fact, it looked like it was stalking *him*.

The thing moved in front of the sun, creating a momentary eclipse and allowing Tommy a better look at it. It turned its head and looked straight at him, showing a pair of unnaturally bright, blood-red eyes. The creature then hissed loudly, exposing a pair of razor-sharp incisors. Tommy jumped a foot in the air and then ran off after Mr Wiseman.

'What the...!' he shouted, pointing over his shoulder and frantically looking around for the old man, but he was nowhere to be seen. He'd vanished into thin air. Glancing frantically behind him as he ran, Tommy could make out the dark shape of the creature as it moved quickly through the trees, following him from on high. He had the feeling he was being hunted. He ran as fast as he could through the woods, dodging trees and jumping over the small bushes and fallen branches. But the creature was quicker, gaining on him with every stride. In his panic Tommy failed to see a steep drop in front of him, causing him to tumble head over heels down the slope, crashing through nettles and scraping his knees as he fell. He felt light headed, his surroundings spinning faster and faster around him as he rolled downwards before he finally landing hard on the ground.

Dazed, he was surprised to find that the surface didn't feel like he thought it should. Expecting to feel the unforgiving stone and mud of the woodland floor, instead his hands found the soft welcome of carpet. Looking gratefully around him he saw that he was laying on his bedroom floor, the Pen at his side.

Tommy felt utter relief at having left his memory just before that strange creature had pounced. But he was positive that it had been chasing him. What *was* it? It was certainly like nothing he'd ever seen before, not even on any wildlife programme. As he made to get up he caught his reflection in the mirror on his bedroom wall. He noticed something on the Pen beside him. Picking it up he crawled eagerly to the mirror, thrusting it in front of the glass. He examined its inscription for a moment before letting out an excited gasp. It finally made sense! The reflection from the mirror had actually deciphered its meaning:

Author of Destiny! Of course! Thinking back to what Mr Wiseman had said to him, he realised now that he'd hinted at the answer all along. *Reflect on it some more, that should do the trick.* Why hadn't he thought of it before?

Standing excitedly, he rolled up his trouser legs, wincing at the pain from his grazed knees, blood trickling down both of his shins. Despite the pain he saw those injuries as a good sign. If his cut knees had transcended his memory, then hopefully Ben's limp would have been affected too. He eagerly checked the notepad on his bed, and his suspicions were confirmed. Unlike when he'd used the Pen before, this time the writing *hadn't* disappeared. That should mean that the changes he'd made would be permanent too.

He was very tempted to go and call for Ben right now to see if it had worked; he knew he wouldn't be able to wait until the morning, but his mum's booming voice made the decision for him.

'Tom!' she shouted from the foot of the stairs, 'dinner's ready. And don't forget you're helping Dad in the attic tonight!'

Morning it was then. And it couldn't come quick enough as far as he was concerned.

Stashing the Pen back into its hiding place, he slammed his bedroom door shut behind him and went downstairs for dinner. Had he heeded his mum's advice to keep his bedroom tidy, he would have noticed that the picture of him and Ben had fallen off the wall. Had he noticed the picture in his pile of dirty washing, then he may have picked it up. Had he picked it up, then he would have been surprised to find that the picture had now changed. For it now showed both he *and* Ben holding the football trophy.

Its inscription had changed too: *Tommy Parker & Ben Campbell – Joint Top Goalscorers 1994/5.*

— CHAPTER TWELVE —

Two Months, One Week and Four Days

'What's up?' Roy Parker asked with a smirk from behind his newspaper. 'You wet the bed?'

He wasn't used to seeing his son anywhere other than under his duvet at seven thirty in the morning. But today was no ordinary morning; this was the morning that Tommy found out whether the Pen had worked, and he couldn't wait to get to school to see whether it had altered Ben. He'd got up extra early, shoving the Pen deep into his trouser pocket, so he could leave early and find out.

'Very funny, Dad, I don't think that problem's hereditary though,' Tommy quipped, rather proud of himself for thinking of the comeback. He was in a particularly good mood today, and why shouldn't he be, what with all the excitement of entering his memory yesterday and now the anticipation of seeing Ben.

But there was something that was worrying him. That creature; animal in speed and appearance but with an undeniable intelligence about it. He was sure it had been stalking him yesterday, almost as if it had been watching him and had known exactly what he'd been trying to do. Could it be that the creature was some kind of custodian of memories, there to prevent him or anyone else from altering the past? It was possible he supposed. Heck, since finding out about the Pen *anything* seemed possible!

'Do you want a lift to school today?' his dad asked, putting down his newspaper and finishing off his cup of tea.

'No thanks,' Tommy replied, 'I'm gonna get in early, got an essay to finish off.'

Roy Parker almost choked on a mouthful of tea. 'Really?!' he managed to splutter, eyeing his son suspiciously.

'Yeah, why are you so surprised?'

'Oh, it's nothing. It's just you've not been yourself lately – getting up early, concentrating on your homework. And your mum tells me you've even been in the library most nights this week.'

'I'm just trying to make a good start to the year, that's all. I thought you'd be pleased?'

'I am, Tom, don't get me wrong,' he replied reassuringly, 'but... well, you'd tell us if there was something bothering you, wouldn't you? You know that you can talk to your mum and me.'

'Yeah, Dad, I know,' he replied genuinely, not adding what he was really thinking. *If only I could*. He could really do with his dad's advice at the moment, especially with this deadly Cult supposedly lurking about, but telling his parents would mean breaking the promise he'd made to Grandpa. Not only that, there was also what Mr Wiseman had said: the more people that knew of the Pen, the more dangerous the situation would become. The last thing Tommy wanted to do was put his parents in harm's way. He was the Guardian now. He and he alone had the responsibility of keeping it safe and keeping it secret. He'd just have to get used to it.

Eager to get to school, Tommy walked at quite a pace, lost in his own thoughts yet still brimming with excitement. He reached the front gates and made for his and Ben's form class, still wondering whether the whole thing had worked. It didn't take long for him to find out, as halfway across the playground he saw someone running towards him dressed in the school's blue and yellow PE kit.

'Hey, mate!' Ben shouted as he approached, 'what you doing here so early?'

It certainly looked like Ben, but there was something different. He was running… and fast! *Without* a limp too. It had actually worked!

'Ben! Look at you!'

'What?' He came to a halt just in front of Tommy. 'What is it?' he added, checking his clothes suspiciously. Tommy was astounded. Standing in front of him was his best mate, but he looked very different, slimmer than yesterday and so full of energy. Very much a healthier and more confident version of his old self. There was another thing too, Tommy thought whilst gawping at him. He didn't have a single bruise on him. Not one. Yet after yesterday's attack by Savage he'd had cuts and bruises all over the place. But now, nothing. Not a single mark.

'What are you staring at?' Ben asked uncomfortably, sticking a finger up one of his nostrils, 'have I got a bogey or something?'

'Hmm? Oh, no, no it's nothing,' Tommy rallied, still trying to make sense of it all. 'Seriously, there's nothing there,' he added, as Ben shoved his finger further and further up his nose.

Tommy wanted nothing more than to tell Ben about what he'd done for him, but he couldn't. He had to keep it secret. And he had to admit that it would be pretty hard to believe anyway. Composing himself, he managed to change the subject.

'What are *you* doing here so early anyway?'

'You know I've got athletics training in the mornings. Fender's pushing us all hard this year. Reckons I can get county trials if I keep at it.' Athletics training? *Ben?* Things certainly had changed. He'd known Ben was fast before the accident, but he hadn't expected this. Tommy's face flushed as he noticed a group of girls walking in their direction.

'Don't look now,' he said, causing Ben to inevitably turn and look. 'I said *don't* look now! Oh never mind. See?'

'What?'

'Jennifer. Jennifer *Fox*. She's walking this way. Ooh... hang on... she's coming over...' he added, smoothing his hair nervously.

Ben eyed him suspiciously. 'Yeah, but... of course she's coming over.'

To his surprise, Jennifer then drifted away from her friends and began to walk right towards them.

'Leave it to me, Ben,' Tommy said, bracing himself. 'I'll talk to her.'

This was it. Time to impress.

But it was Jennifer who spoke first.

'Morning, Benny, how'd training go?' she asked soppily, causing Tommy's jaw to hit the floor. She then did the unthinkable and landed a kiss on Ben's cheek. She might as well have plucked out Tommy's heart and stamped on it.

'Not too bad, Jen,' Ben replied nonchalantly. 'Broke my four hundred metre record again.'

What on Earth was going on? Tommy couldn't believe his eyes *or* his ears. Why was Jennifer even talking to Ben, let alone kissing him? And even more unbelievably, why was Ben being so cool about it?

Tommy could only watch on in horror as they then proceeded to cuddle and tickle each other in a manner that he considered totally inappropriate for the schoolyard. Especially this early and especially because it involved Jennifer Fox. *His* Jennifer Fox. He was about to tell them as much when they broke from their clinch voluntarily.

'You OK, Tom?' Jennifer asked him. 'You're acting a little weird. Well, a little weirder than usual anyway.'

He snapped out of his jealous trance.

'You two go out?'

'What?' Ben asked.

'Uh, I mean, you two go out,' he rallied. 'What I meant to say was: how long's it been now?'

They looked at each other, Ben trying his best to look indifferent, but Jennifer doing a pretty good impression of a lovesick puppy.

'Few months,' Ben replied.

'Two months, one week and four days,' Jennifer

announced, ruffling Ben's hair. 'Come on, Benny; don't pretend that you don't know. We were talking about it only yesterday.'

There it was again. *Benny*. Tommy had hoped he'd imagined it earlier.

'I'd better go,' Jennifer said, giving Ben a final peck on the cheek. 'See you at lunch.'

She then ran off after her friends, leaving Tommy and Ben alone. They exchanged glances for a moment, Tommy struggling to hide the devastation that his best friend would do a thing like this to him – stealing the one girl that he'd ever fancied. Ben, for his part, looked rather sheepish.

'*Benny?*' Tommy finally said.

'Oh don't! She reckons it makes us sound more of a couple. Y'know, *'Benny and Jenny'*. Gotta say I'm still not used to it. You won't tell Richie will you?'

Tommy wouldn't. He wouldn't tell anyone. He didn't even want to tell *himself* that they were going out. All the excitement of using the Pen had vanished. What *had* he done? He thought again of Mr Wiseman's words of warning. That if Ben had been altered then it would also have brought about other changes. It had clearly had an effect on other areas of Ben's life already. Tommy hadn't just fixed his leg; he'd also made it possible for him to pull the prettiest girl in school. *His* girl. Talk about a backfire.

'Right,' Ben said, interrupting Tommy's thoughts. 'I've gotta change before class. See you later.'

And with that he ran off again, leaving Tommy wondering just how many butterflies he'd upset yesterday.

CHAPTER THIRTEEN

Unwelcome Guests

G randpa walked leisurely into Harbour View, holding a bottle of milk in one hand and a handkerchief in the other, wiping away the perspiration which was glistening in the warmth of the morning sun. An early stroll to the local paper shop was the way Grandpa started most of his days, giving him an opportunity to fill his lungs with fresh air and get his legs into gear. Today's stroll, though, was a little bit too much like hard work. It wasn't that his bones were creaking any more than usual – it was simply too hot. Today felt like the hottest day of one of the hottest summers that he could remember. And he'd seen a few.

Pausing for a moment, he took off his tweed blazer (he wore it whatever the weather) and hooked it over his shoulder, letting it hang from his forefinger. Beginning to tire, he chose to take the short cut over the grass rather than follow the pavement. Halfway across he altered his course and headed towards a man of similar age who was washing his car. Or at least *trying* to wash his car – the man looked as though he'd gone twelve rounds with a giant octopus! A bucket of soapy water was next to him, and he had his sleeves rolled up to his elbows. He was soaked to the bone and more than a little preoccupied losing a fight with a runaway hose.

'Morning, George,' Grandpa said smiling. 'You alright there?'

George managed to wrestle the hose into temporary submission and look up to see where the voice had come from.

'Oh, morning, Len!' came the exasperated reply.

The momentary lapse in concentration proved fatal. George lost his grip on the nozzle of the hose, and it began to dodge about him like an angry cobra, spraying water all over him but missing his car completely.

'Need a hand?' Grandpa asked, his eyes following the hose as it danced about mockingly in front of him.

'No, no. I'm fine!' he replied, finally managing to get the hose back under control. 'I'm just washing the car with my new power-jet 3000, it's amazing! So powerful! It just doesn't know when to stop!'

'Well, as long as you're OK,' Grandpa chuckled, walking off towards his house. Grandpa could still hear the not-so-under-the-breath curses of George as he walked down his path. Closing his gate, he happened to glance over in the direction of Mr Wiseman's place, and as he did so he was sure that he saw the curtains in the upstairs window move. Curious, he looked more closely, hoping to see further signs of movement, but there was nothing. The curtains remained quite still. Grandpa moved on, laughing off the comparison he'd just noticed between himself and his grandson.

He opened the front door and welcomed the cool shade of his hallway. The noise the door made as he closed it meant that Grandpa didn't hear the low hum of the car engine that had pulled slowly into Harbour View – the large black car parking in the space next to George's. In his kitchen Grandpa whistled merrily as he poured himself a glass of ice cold milk. He had no idea that he'd never get to enjoy it. They'd finally found who they were looking for.

CHAPTER FOURTEEN

The Dead Arm

Tommy was relieved to discover throughout the day that interfering with history hadn't changed Ben *too* much (apart from the obvious of course). Although his body was now in full working order, he was still as clumsy and accident-prone as ever; a fact illustrated in Science when he almost set fire to Harriet Harper's hair with a Bunsen burner. And, although used to being teased about her bright ginger hair, the incident meant that she was then subjected to an endless stream of jokes about her being a 'fiery' redhead.

No, the only other real difference that Tommy could see was the way that Ben now behaved around girls. He was far more confident now, and why shouldn't he be? He'd managed to bag Jennifer Fox. He almost regretted ever helping him now; she was meant to be his not Ben's. He didn't show up for football at break either, which was very unlike him. If truth be told, Tommy was beginning to feel quite jealous. He was bound to have been with her, wasn't he? In fact, it had all got a bit too much for him in Maths when Ben borrowed his compass. Tommy had snapped at him for 'always taking his stuff' – a comment that probably had more to do with Jennifer than the compass.

Ben's newfound energy was further displayed at the end

of the lesson when Tommy was packing away his books. By his watch there were about twenty seconds left before the lunch bell went, and unlike yesterday, Tommy planned to be ready to go as soon as it sounded. Just as he was about to hand Ben his bag, he cut across him.

'I'll go, Tom, you know I always get the pick of the burgers.'

And with Tommy's protests drowned out by the dinner bell, before he knew it Ben had disappeared down the corridor, and he was left in the unfamiliar role of carrying the bags up to the Dutch Barn.

A few minutes later he dumped the bags down behind one of the pillars at just about the same time Ben tapped him on the shoulder and handed him a piping hot turkey burger. Now that *was* quick.

'How did you...?' But before Tommy could finish his sentence, Ben had already run over to the other end of the barn and started to sort out the two teams. *Did this Ben ever keep still?*

Within a few seconds the game was under way but with one noticeable difference – Ben was no longer in goal. Instead, he partnered Tommy in attack, and within minutes they had made their mark on the game, playing swift and intricate one-two passes and beating defenders with ease. Ben was the first to break the deadlock, latching on to a perfectly weighted pass before firing a powerful shot past the goalkeeper.

'Hotshot Campbell strikes again!' he yelled, wheeling away with his arm in the air.

'Bet you're glad you're not stuck in goal again?' Tommy called over to him, sharing in his revelry.

'Huh? I never go in goal,' Ben responded, slightly confused, before shaking his head and running off to close down a defender.

Of course. This was going to take some getting used to. Everything that had happened from Ben's accident to now had been changed. Ben had never been in goal because he never *had* to. He'd never had a bad ankle to begin with.

Despite his misgivings Tommy couldn't remember a lunchtime game he'd enjoyed more. He and Ben played so well together that between the two of them they scored a hat-full of goals. Even when Tommy had played a rare stray pass, Ben was so fast that he'd managed to get on the end of it – they were ripping the opposition apart. Having Ben at one hundred percent again was worth it. It was great seeing him totally happy again, even if it did mean that he'd have to get used to him and Jennifer being an item. He was his best friend; he'd just have to get used to it. He couldn't let a stupid little thing like a crush come between them. Girls were silly anyway – he had far bigger things to worry about.

All enjoyment soon drained out of him, however, when he glanced down the path and saw trouble approaching. Trouble in the form of Savage and Bogeys.

'Ben, quick! Over here!'

'What is it?' he asked, jogging over, rather annoyed at being distracted from the game.

'There, look,' Tommy said, pointing towards Savage, 'we should get outta here.'

'Why?'

'What do you mean "why?" After yesterday.'

'Nuh, I'm staying. I'm not scared, I showed him yesterday I'm not frightened of him, I'm not gonna start now.'

'Aren't you worried he'll beat you up again?'

'What do you mean *again*?' he asked, genuinely confused.

Tommy grunted in frustration.

'Like yesterday!'

And then, even before Ben could respond, realisation again dawned. Changing the memory had obviously affected yesterday's events too.

'What *are* you on about?!' Ben laughed, 'he couldn't even get close to me yesterday, let alone beat me up! Are you feeling OK, mate?'

He eyed Tommy closely, clearly bewildered by his behaviour. And why shouldn't he be confused? As far as he was concerned, yesterday's fight obviously hadn't even taken place. Their conversation was interrupted by Savage, who made a painful point of barging in between them.

'Where's your weird little friend today, Campbell? I owe him a hiding.'

Ben remained true to his word, refusing to be bullied.

'When are you gonna start picking on people who can stand up for themselves, Sav? Or do you only bother people half your size? Anyway, Art's not weird.'

Tommy stared, open-mouthed. Had he lost his mind? Nobody spoke to Savage like that and got away with it. Yet Savage didn't react. He merely grunted and stormed off across the Dutch Barn, his side-kick Bogeys snapping at his heels like an obedient dog.

'What are you playing at?!' Tommy asked incredulously when they were out of earshot.

'Ah, he's nothing but a bully; I've got no time for him at all. Besides, he knows better than to mess with me.'

'But he didn't think that yesterday...'

'And even if he'd caught me,' Ben interrupted, 'he wouldn't have done anything. Trust me mate, I know his type. Come on, look, he's joined the other team. Let's show him how it's done.'

As Ben took his position up front, Tommy was amazed at how the relationship between Ben and Savage had changed. Not only that, but from the way Ben had stuck up for Art again, it looked like the tension between them was a thing of the past. All in all, Tommy concluded that altering the accident had produced pretty good results. He felt foolish for worrying – Mr Wiseman had clearly exaggerated all of the dangers. So what if Ben had changed a little and got himself a girlfriend? It was hardly earth-shattering was it?

Tommy jogged towards Ben, making himself available for a pass. Ben played the ball to him before dodging a defender, sprinting away and finding space for the return. Tommy played it with perfect precision, leaving Ben to run onto it at full speed, ten yards out from goal. There were now only two things that stood between him and scoring: the last defender, Bogeys, and Savage who had gone in goal. Ben made quick work of skipping past Bogeys, which just left Savage to beat.

Tommy watched on as Ben stopped suddenly, trapping the ball under his foot. For a long second he and Savage just stood, glaring at each other like two gunfighters from the Wild West, both waiting for the other to make the first move. It was Savage who blinked first. Losing patience (if he ever had any to begin with), he came charging out of the goalmouth like a steam train, head bowed and arms pumping furiously. And yet Ben still didn't move. The Ben of yesterday would have turned and run the other way as soon as Savage had taken a step towards him, but today he was completely calm, standing there coolly, a confident grin on his face.

Savage was getting closer, a few more steps and he would be flattened. He moved with all the speed of a labouring steamroller, but unfortunately for Ben he would have the same kind of impact. Now only a couple of yards away, Savage raised his right leg and swung it with all his might towards the stationary Ben. It was clear from the manic expression on his face that he didn't particularly care whether he made contact with the ball or with Ben. Just then Ben quickly sprang to life, flicking the ball around Savage and stepping to the side and out of harm's way. The force of Savage's kick threw him off balance, causing him to spin like an overweight ballerina and land hard on his backside. The whole of the Dutch Barn erupted into raucous laughter at the sight of the school's meanest bully being left humiliated, rubbing his behind. Ben casually walked the ball into the goal before wheeling away in mock celebration, milking the emphatic cheers of the crowd. *What a turnaround!*

Only yesterday the roles had been completely reversed. It had been Ben laying on the floor in pain with Savage standing over him in triumph. Well, that's what had happened in Tommy's reality anyway. But today it was Ben who was the victor, and Tommy had no regrets, apart from the Jennifer situation of course.

'What a way to win the game!' an ecstatic Ben proclaimed whilst running around the Barn, arms spread wide, imitating an aeroplane. 'Here, Tom, grab this, I'll catch you up.'

'Where're you going?' Tommy asked, taking the bag from him.

'To give Bogeys a dead arm,' he replied mischievously, 'the idiot tried tripping me up yesterday.'

And with that, the new and improved Ben disappeared out of the Dutch Barn, once again leaving an astonished Tommy holding the school bags.

— CHAPTER FIFTEEN —

The Two Strangers

Tommy had to wait for almost an hour after school for Ben to finish rugby training. *Rugby?* What next?! Ben had always hated rugby. Just another of a hundred little surprises that Tommy supposed he was going to have to get used to.

Whilst Ben was training, Tommy had made good use of the time and settled in the school library again, hoping to find out even more about the Pen. But after many slammed books, frustrated grunts and cold stares from the librarian, he resigned himself to the fact that the only place he could get any proper answers was at Mr Wiseman's place. Another visit was required. He needed to find out just how far reaching the changes could be.

The walk home seemed to take half the time now that Ben's limp didn't slow them down.

'Did you see the look on Sav's face?' Ben chortled. 'It's all the boys were talking about in training. What a picture, I'd give anything to see that again!'

'Yeah, I know what you mean,' Tommy said smiling to himself, thinking that he may just use the Pen to do that later.

'Hey, Tom...' Ben ventured nervously, changing the

subject completely. 'Would you ever get an earring?'

'Huh?'

'Y'know, if it looked cool and everything? Would you get one?'

'You're kidding, right?'

Ben's cheeks turned red. Clearly he wasn't.

'So you're not kidding?'

'It's just that Jen thinks it might suit me, that's all.'

'Sure, I agree.'

Ben's hopes were raised.

'Yeah, and while you're at it, why don't you get a nice little bracelet too?' he added sarcastically. 'In fact, I think my mum's got an old brooch she doesn't wear anymore – you're welcome to have that.'

What *had* the Pen done to him? The old Ben wouldn't have even entertained the thought of getting his ears pierced. In fact, Tommy seemed to remember him once saying that it was only girls, hippies and pirates that had it done. Oh how he'd changed. That was the Ben of yesterday, and thanks to the magic of the Pen, yesterday now seemed a *very* long time ago.

'I was only asking your opinion,' he responded, having taken offence.

'Yeah, and can you imagine your mum's reaction? Not just hers but Richie's too? You wouldn't hear the end of it.'

'Well, I didn't say I was actually gonna get it done or anything.'

'Good! It's just not you mate. It's Jennifer talking. You shouldn't let her try to change you.'

Which, Tommy had to concede, was pretty rich coming from someone who'd just altered the path of his life completely.

'She ain't changing me!' he protested. 'I do whatever I want. I wouldn't wanna get a poxy earring anyway, so stop going on about it, will you?!'

Ben stewed for a while, much of their journey passing in silence before he finally spoke again.

'What's up with you lately anyway? You always seem a bit off when I mention Jenny. You're not still peeved at me 'cos of the whole Valentines card thing are you? I told you before, I didn't mean to take credit for it – it just kinda happened.'

The cheeky beggar! So that's how he and Jennifer had got together; he'd taken the credit for his anonymous Valentine's card! He knew he should have put his name on it! He'd spent all of his pocket money on that card, been late home for tea and all for nothing! Just for Ben to swoop in and take his girl.

'Besides,' Ben continued, 'I keep telling you; her mate has said she'd be up for a double date. All you've gotta do is say the word.'

This was news to Tommy. He considered for a moment the possibility that, for all he knew, Ben may well have discussed this topic with him a dozen times already, but he soon gave up. The whole parallel universe thing gave him a headache.

'Double date?' he replied, intrigued. 'Which friend?'

'I've told you before, I wish you'd listen. Helena. She

thinks you're cute.'

'Helena *Lundy* thinks I'm cute?'

'Yep.'

Well that *was* a turn up for the books! Tommy had never really looked beyond Jennifer before, had only had eyes for her, but Helena Lundy was pretty cute herself. In fact, he walked the rest of the way with a stupid grin on his face just at the very thought of her 'thinking he was cute'. It was amazing the difference that being fancied had on a person's morale.

Lost in a happy daydream, it wasn't long before they'd made it as far as the old Central School. Tommy looked up at the dark, towering structure – this place always gave him the creeps. Ben's focus, however, was elsewhere. He was staring at the large, red doors of the fire station.

'Tom...' he started, but was unable to finish.

'No we can't,' Tommy interrupted, noticing his friend's hopeful gaze.

'What? You don't even know what I was gonna say!'

'Can we have a go on the fireman's pole?' Tommy ventured in his best Ben impression.

Ben looked at him in disgust, as if that thought was the furthest thing from his mind, before saying, 'Well... can we?'

Some things really hadn't changed.

'Nah, not today, Dad's not working,' Tommy said, hoping that would put an end to it. He looked at the sky, which had become nothing but a mass of dark grey cloud. Where had the sun gone? The wind had got up too, blowing dust and grit in their direction. Shielding his eyes with his hand, he added. 'Besides, it looks like it's gonna pour down in a minute, we'd better get home.'

Tommy carried on along the street but stopped when he saw something that caused him concern. A few yards ahead of them a large, dark car had pulled up outside the Central School. He watched as the rear doors opened and two men got out, the car pulling off and driving up the road. He had a bad feeling about this. The two men were exactly how Mr Wiseman had described the Cult: dressed all in black and with black hats. And there was something about the way they moved and walked too – Tommy could just tell that they were dangerous. Apart from their clothes though, the men couldn't have looked more different. One of them was huge, as wide as a wardrobe and taller than anyone Tommy had ever seen. The other was short, probably about his own height, but, judging by the way he was gesturing to the bigger man, he appeared to be the one in charge. It was them, *Secuutus Pluma*, he was sure of it. And that meant that they could only be looking for one thing – the Pen.

Despite the blustery wind Tommy dared not exhale for fear that they'd hear him. He continued to watch as they stood outside the school grounds before walking through a gap in the wall where a gate had once been. *Why were they going in there?* Surely they didn't hope to find either him *or* the Pen in the abandoned school? Then Tommy's heart sank. Apparently, he hadn't been the only one wondering what they were doing.

'Oi, Mister!' Ben shouted. 'I wouldn't go in there if I were you, it's haunted!'

Quicker than a heartbeat, Tommy dived on him, wrestling him to the ground and behind a parked car. He clamped a hand over his mouth.

'Shut up!' he whispered through clenched teeth. 'You'll get us killed!'

Ben, his face largely covered apart from a pair of wide, confused eyes, managed to say through Tommy's palm, 'but those men... we gotta warn 'em... the Hintons...' Tommy placed his index finger to his lips.

'Believe me, Ben,' he said. 'Those guys aren't worried about the Hintons.'

Tommy peered over the bonnet of the car, hoping that they hadn't heard Ben's shout over the howling wind. Thankfully, there was no sign of them. He crossed the street, away from the school, his eyes not once leaving it in case they returned.

'What's up, Tom?' Ben demanded. 'Why are you so worried? It's just a couple of men. Come on. Let's see what they're up to...'

Before Ben could go anywhere, Tommy pounced on him for a second time.

'Whoa!' Ben yelped. 'Ever thought of joining the rugby te...?!'

'Please just trust me! Let's get outta here!'

Perhaps it was the look of fright on Tommy's face, or maybe it was the urgency in his voice, but for once, without question, Ben did as he was told. They walked along York Street at a quickened pace, a tense silence falling between them, Tommy drowning in a pool of panic. Everything that

Mr Wiseman had told him was going round and round in his head. *How had they found him so soon?* He'd only just got the Pen. And that was a close shave. Too close for comfort. His mind was now fixed on getting to Mr Wiseman's; he'd know what to do.

Over the noise of the wind and the even louder beating of his heart, Tommy heard a car approaching. Looking back towards the school, he saw that the dark car had returned; what's more, it was heading right for them. Its headlights shined on their backs, illuminating them both. They *must've* heard Ben shout; that's why they'd come back. And they were sitting ducks! Tommy always knew that Ben would be the death of him.

'Come on!' he yelled. 'Run!'

Again, without question and now looking equally as frightened as Tommy, Ben didn't need asking twice. He took off like a greyhound and was metres ahead of him in no time. They tried to outrun the car but it gained on them easily. There wasn't even a lane or a side-street for them to dart into to escape it. They were done for. The car overtook them and skidded to a halt. Both stopped running, Tommy breathing heavily and Ben looking like he could run another mile. *Some Guardian!* A few days on the job and he was about to lose the Pen and doom all of mankind! The car's rear door swung open and somebody stepped out. Tommy couldn't believe it – it was his mum getting out of the back of a taxi. It was a different car! Talk about paranoid. Any trace of relief was short-lived though. There was something about the look on his mum's face that he couldn't quite place, a look he hadn't seen since... and then it hit him. A look he hadn't seen since his nan had died.

'Tommy, get in. It's your Grandpa.'

CHAPTER SIXTEEN

The Old Guardian

The two men walked across a filthy wooden floor, both of them brushing the dirt from their black overcoats with black-gloved hands. The floor was barely visible through thick layers of dust, but what could be seen through the footprints revealed different coloured lines that created seemingly indistinct patterns on the hidden surface. The disturbed dust swirled around the shafts of light that had fought their way past the boarded windows, and hanging from the ceilings a number of thick ropes dropped to the floor. On the walls dozens of wooden climbing bars ran horizontally across the length of the room. Following old footprints, the men strode through a set of double doors and entered a long corridor. Behind the taller man a steady trail of red liquid spilled like the dripping of a leaking tap, marking each of his steps.

Halfway along the corridor the men turned left and down a stone staircase, descending into darkness. They were greeted by the Morse code-like flickering of a faulty ceiling light. They entered another small room, where Brother Lethely sat at a table playing with a cigarette lighter. Looking up at them expectantly, his optimism was quickly punctured as the short man shook his head in the negative and breathed the word 'no'.

They eyed the closed door on the opposite side of the room, both reluctant to enter. Finally, the short man walked towards it and knocked, waiting for permission before entering. The tall man shuffled in closely behind him. If he'd hoped to be hidden from view by his colleague, then he was sadly, and almost comically, mistaken.

Nidas, the Grand Master of *Secuutus Pluma*, was sat behind a desk, his scarred face illuminated by the lamp on the table. Not unusually, he didn't look happy. Again, it was the small man who bravely took the initiative.

'Boss, we got nuthin. Parker didn't have it.'

'I know,' Nidas said sternly, elevating himself to his full height, making even the bigger of the two men look average. 'But I gather that we are close. That it *was* with him.'

The two men exchanged bemused looks. *How did he know all this already?*

'Yes,' the smaller man answered. 'From what we found, he definitely had it. But he got rid of it – recently too. Brother Malus is going through some stuff we took from his place, piecing it all together. We'll find out who has it, and then it's ours. It won't be a problem boss.'

Nidas didn't seem reassured, 'And what of Parker? Did he talk?' he asked.

'No,' the small man said, almost in admiration. 'Tough as old boots, wouldn't say a thing.'

He looked at his taller colleague, who was wiping the blood from his gloves.

'Quicker than he looks too. Before we could restrain him

he managed to punch Brother Barbarus straight on the nose.'

Barbarus instinctively brought a bloodstained handkerchief to his now slightly squashed and misshapen nose. The beginnings of dark blue bruises were evident beneath each of his eyes. Musing aloud, Nidas ran a finger along the scar on his own cheek.

'Yes, the item certainly seems to unleash the fighter in people.'

He turned his back on the two men.

'Where's Parker now?'

The short man was quick to answer.

'He's no longer a problem. He won't be talking to anybody, we made sure of that.'

'Good,' Nidas said, removing a bottle of whiskey from the top drawer of the desk and pouring himself a glass. 'Go now and assist Brother Malus. We must retrieve the item before it eludes us once again. It will have its new Guardian already; we can't let them get too comfortable.'

Draining the whiskey in one swallow, he fixed the men with a cold stare.

'Be quick and be ruthless. Do not disappoint me.'

Barely a word was spoken during the taxi ride to the hospital. Brenda Parker sat silently in the passenger seat, whilst Tommy, after barraging her with an onslaught of questions, now sat quietly, desperately worrying about Grandpa. Ben sat next to him and fidgeted uncomfortably through the silence.

They were met outside the Intensive Care Unit by

Tommy's dad. Tommy could tell from the look on his face that it wasn't good news. He could see the worry and upset through his father's brave smile. He'd not once seen his dad cry; he wouldn't know how to react if he ever did. Roy Parker was always the rock upon which his family clung in times of crisis, and although the waters were choppy, he was holding firm.

'Hi, love,' he said, kissing his wife. 'Son, you OK?'

'Yeah, fine,' Tommy replied, not really meaning it. In truth, he was struggling to keep himself together. The hospital smell reminded him all too much of when he'd visited Nan here in her final days.

'Sorry you got dragged along for the ride, Ben. I'll try and get hold of your parents now.'

'That's OK, Mr Parker, they're out anyway.'

'How is he?' Tommy interrupted, unable to suppress his anxiety.

'Resting,' his dad replied, looking at him sympathetically. 'The doctor said we should let him sleep. He's had a rough day.'

Roy Parker looked like he'd had something of a rough day himself, slumping himself into a chair against the wall. 'I might have to go down to the canteen for some food in a minute if anyone's hungry?' he yawned.

Ben's ears pricked at that.

'What happened to him, Dad?' Tommy asked, cutting through the small talk.

'Heart attack. A pretty bad one. The police say...'

'Police?'

'Yeah, they're the one's that found him. They said he disturbed some burglars; the whole house has been ransacked. There was some kind of confrontation, and... that's what brought it on.' Roy Parker shook his head in disbelief before adding with an element of pride in his voice. 'Looks like he gave as good as he got though, he's got bruises on his knuckles. Bet they didn't expect that.'

It was then that Tommy knew for sure what this was all about. He'd suspected something on the way over, but what his dad said had just confirmed it. Grandpa's house being searched could mean only one thing as far as he was concerned – they'd found him. The Cult had figured out that Grandpa had the Pen, and then they went after him for it. He felt so guilty. It should have been him. He was the Guardian now.

'Can I see him?' Tommy asked hopefully.

'Maybe for just a few moments,' he agreed, realising that it would've been useless to refuse. 'But try not to wake him. Ben, we'll call your parents from the canteen.'

Left alone in the corridor, Tommy slowly turned the handle to Grandpa's room, preparing himself for what he'd find on the other side. Even then he wasn't ready. His eyes welled with tears and a lump formed at the back of his throat as he took in the scene. Lying in the darkened room was Grandpa, looking older than Tommy had ever seen him, attached by tubes and wires to all sorts of machines. His eyes were closed, and his chest moved up and down to the rhythm of one of the beeping monitors. He looked like he was in a deep and restful sleep. Standing by the bed, Tommy could only study his shoelaces, not wanting to look at how weak Grandpa had become. It pained him to see him in this condition.

'Hello, stranger,' Grandpa's voice said weakly, breaking Tommy from his trance. He looked up to find that his eyes were open and he was attempting a smile. Squeezing his hand, Tommy said softly, 'Don't talk Grandpa, the doctor says you should rest.'

'It'll take more than this to shut me up, son,' he said with a chuckle that turned into a wheeze and then a cough.

'What happened? Dad says you were burgled.'

Grandpa fixed Tommy with a serious look.

'That's what I told the police, Tom. That's what I *had* to say. But it was them. They finally found me. They wanted the Pen, Tommy, they so desperately wanted it.' His frail hand gripped Tommy's wrist tightly. 'Get rid of it son, please, for your own sake. They're dangerous people.'

Grandpa turned his head away in anger.

'I wish I'd never given you the blasted thing now! If I knew who they were... how serious they are... I'd have got rid of the thing years ago!'

Tommy could feel the Pen in his pocket digging into the side of his leg, almost as if it knew that they were talking about it.

'I know who they are, Grandpa,' he said. 'I know all about them. And I know more about the Pen too.'

Grandpa turned his head to face Tommy again, too weak to raise it from the pillow. His eyes had lost their sparkle.

'How?'

'Mr Wiseman.'

'Mr Wiseman?' he repeated in wonder.

The roles had finally been reversed. It was now Tommy who had all the information. Grandpa listened with captivated interest as Tommy told him every detail about his meetings with Mr Wiseman. About how he'd found a picture of him in a library book with Abraham Lincoln and then been brave enough to go to his house, where he'd been told all about *Secuutus Pluma* and his new role as Guardian of the Pen.

And, of course, he told him about the Pen's *other* use, the one that Grandpa had never known about. He nodded weakly when Tommy relayed the part about entering his memory to change Ben's accident and the effect it had had on him in real life, but then frowned with paternal concern when he told him about the creature that had chased him through the woods.

As Tommy neared the end of his tale, they heard the door creak behind them. Standing in the doorway, his jaw almost touching the floor in disbelief, stood Ben. How much he'd heard, Tommy didn't know, but judging from the look on his face he'd been there for some time.

'Ben!' Tommy shouted, 'this is priva–' But before he could even finish the sentence, Ben had closed the door and left the room.

'I can't believe him! Always gotta stick his nose into...'

'Don't be too hard on him, Tom,' Grandpa said, 'he's a nice lad. And what was it Mr Wiseman said "You're going to need your friends around you"?'

'Yeah, I suppose, but...'

'Come now, enough of that,' he said, returning to the subject at hand.

Grandpa shook his head, smiling slightly. 'Well, well... Mr Wiseman. I always knew there was something different about him.'

Tommy had to agree, but *different* somehow didn't quite cover it.

'Maybe you can meet him?' Tommy suggested. 'He knows so much about the Pen, he can answer all your questions.'

'Oh, I think it's a bit late for that now, Tommy. But you make sure you listen to what he has to say. Be careful. Those men that I met, the Cult, take it from me they're very dangerous men. You must find a way of getting rid of them, Tom, or of it. I don't want you having the Pen while they're around.'

Again, Tommy felt the Pen pressing against his leg, but he was forced to pay more attention now to the lump that had formed at the back of his throat.

'What do you mean it's too late?'

Grandpa didn't respond at first. It seemed a struggle for him to keep his eyes open, as if he were drifting in and out of consciousness. When he finally spoke, his voice was quieter, weaker than before.

'I'm an old man, Tom... and I'm tired.' He reached out for Tommy's hand and squeezed, his eyes glistening from the lights of the nearby monitor.

'You know, when your nan fell ill, towards the end when she wasn't quite herself, it was always when you came over that she was at her best. Her face would light up whenever she saw you marching up the path with your holiday bag over your shoulder. You kept her young, Tommy... you've kept us both young. And we're so very proud of you.'

Tommy felt a burning sensation in his throat. He couldn't contain it any longer; he began to cry, tears flowing freely down his cheeks. Grandpa smiled serenely, wiping Tommy's tears away with his thumb.

'Don't be sad, son, I'm happy. I no longer need the Pen to be with your nan. I'm ready to see her again now.'

Grandpa's breathing became laboured, the longer moments between breaths highlighted by the delayed beeping of the heart monitor.

'Enjoy life, son, don't live in the past as I did. Remember, life isn't measured by how many breaths we take, but by the moments that take our breath away.'

As Grandpa's final words trailed off, Tommy could feel the grip around his hand loosen. The rhythmic beep of the monitor was then replaced by a continuous monotone as a red light appeared on its display, flashing frantically.

Tommy knew that this was it. He squeezed Grandpa's hand and spoke his name, but he just lay there, unresponsive, a peaceful smile on his face. He was with Nan at last.

The door to Grandpa's room flew open, and half a dozen doctors and nurses spilled inside, hurriedly shepherding

Tommy out into the hall. He felt numb. He couldn't even muster the energy to protest or to ask them what was going on. The question would have been pointless anyway, he knew what had happened. Grandpa had gone.

'Tommy! What's happened?'

Brenda Parker was running down the corridor closely followed by his dad. Behind them, in the process of picking a fight with a vending machine at the end of the hall, was Ben. Turning at the commotion, he looked ashen faced, clearly concerned but at the same time reluctant to approach them, unsure whether he would be welcome at such a time.

'What is it, Tom?' his dad demanded.

'I dunno...,' he managed to say, 'the machine stopped beeping... and Grandpa...' Tommy could feel the tears well again, and his nose began to tingle. Placing a welcome arm around his shoulder, his mum sat him down on a chair, whilst his dad accosted a passing nurse. Tommy felt someone sit down beside him, and moments later a bar of chocolate fell into his lap.

'It's your favourite,' Ben said, trying to muster a comforting smile, which actually made him look like he had wind.

'Thanks,' Tommy said, fingering the wrapping of the chocolate bar, his eyes not leaving the door to Grandpa's room.

They sat there for what felt like an eternity, waiting for news until finally the door opened and a doctor stepped out, his stethoscope hung around his neck like a scarf. Roy Parker rose to meet him.

'How is he?'

The doctor paused, searching for the appropriate words.

'I'm afraid it's bad news,' he said mournfully, 'there was nothing we could do for him.'

With Tommy's fear confirmed he felt like someone had just kicked him in the stomach. All of the air had been knocked out of him; he felt suffocated, like the hospital walls were closing in around him. Somewhere a million miles away, he could hear the gentle sobs of his mum. He had to get out of there. He jumped up and barged his way past the doctor, running as fast as he could down the hall, taking the nearest stairwell to the exit so he could escape into the fresh air. He ran through the double doors and out into the car park, the air hitting him like a wave of sea water, barely making it to a nearby bin before being sick. Feeling a hand on his shoulder, he raised himself, and through watery eyes he saw Ben.

'It's OK, Tommy, get it all out. Don't worry about crying.'

But they weren't tears. It was odd. Since the doctor had come out and confirmed the news, he hadn't felt like crying. Of course he was sad – he loved Grandpa – but the foremost emotion in Tommy's heart at that moment wasn't sadness. It was anger. Anger and hate. Hate for the people who had done this to him. There'd be plenty of time to grieve later. For now, all Tommy could think about was revenge. Revenge on the Cult. Revenge on *Secuutus Pluma*.

CHAPTER SEVENTEEN

Ben 'Kung Fu' Campbell

'Your dad reckons you should come back in,' Ben said after a few minutes of silence. They were both soaked through. No sooner had they sat down on a bench there was a flash of lightning followed by a clap of thunder and seconds later the heavens had opened. Mother Nature herself grieving for Grandpa.

Tommy sat, numb, staring at a sodden cigarette butt on the floor, but he was fully focused on what had to be done. He'd immediately decided against contacting the police – they'd never believe him. His only option was to go and see Mr Wiseman and ask him what he should do. Could Mr Wiseman help him bring down *Secuutus Pluma*?

'I'm not going back in,' Tommy said firmly.

Ben was now so cold he could barely stop his teeth from chattering.

'Come on, Tom; let's go see your parents.'

'NO!' he shouted without intending to. He certainly wasn't angry with Ben. 'No. It can't happen like this!'

And then it occurred to him. A thought so obvious he was surprised that it hadn't come to him sooner. Could he do it? Would the Pen actually allow him to do this one important thing?

'Wait!' he exclaimed. 'I can change this... I can change *all* of this!!'

He stood up excitedly, feeling a new lease of hope. Why hadn't he thought of it before? Of course he could change it – he had the Pen! If he could do it for Ben, then surely he could go back and stop the Cult from attacking Grandpa?

'What are you on about?' Ben asked, clearly concerned for his friends sanity. 'You can change what?'

Tommy decided it was time to tell Ben everything.

'You heard me and Grandpa talking, right?'

Ben nodded.

'Well, how much did you hear?'

'A fair bit,' he replied, shrugging, 'but that was just some story you were telling him, right? I mean it wasn't real.'

Tommy shook his head eagerly.

'No, Ben. It's all true. Look!'

He pulled the Pen from his pocket and held it towards him.

'This is it. This is the Pen me and Grandpa were talking about. It's real, it's all real!'

For the second time in half an hour Tommy explained the full tale of the Pen. On more than one occasion he had to silence Ben, who had either snorted in disbelief or begun to ask a question, but now that he'd started, he had to tell him everything. He had to get it all off his chest. Ben looked at him in disgust as he told him about when he'd visited Mr Wiseman's place, but the biggest look of shock came when Tommy told him all about his own accident. About the fact that, for the last two years, Tommy had known him to have a limp.

'Come off it!' Ben protested. 'Now I know you're making it up. And you almost had me there too, I almost fell for it!'

'I swear it's true.'

'Nuh, you went too far. I mean look at me,' he said, dancing a little jig for good measure. 'My ankle's fine. It always has been.'

'Not until I used *this*,' Tommy interrupted, showing him the Pen again. 'Mr Barnes *hit* you with his car first time round. He did.'

Ben shook his head, refusing to accept what he was hearing. He walked back to the hospital entrance.

'It's true,' Tommy called after him, almost pleading.

Ben stopped and turned to Tommy, looking into his eyes. Tommy hoped that he'd see the truth in them.

'I'm not joking Ben. You heard my Grandpa too, he died for this thing.'

Ben didn't respond. He just stood there, raindrops bouncing off his head and dripping from the tip of his nose. Tommy cast his mind back to when Grandpa had first told him about the Pen – he hadn't believed it either, not until he'd used it. He couldn't blame Ben for his scepticism.

'Well, say that it *is* true,' Ben said, breaking the silence, 'then that means that these guys, those plumber blokes, have been looking for it?'

It's actually 'Pluma', Tommy almost said but decided against it.

'Yeah,' he replied, wondering where Ben was going with

this.

'Well,' Ben continued, approaching Tommy with some urgency, 'that means they're probably *still* looking for it!'

'Yeah, I know,' Tommy said, relieved that Ben was at least giving him the benefit of the doubt. 'That's why I stopped you shouting at those men outside the Central earlier. They were dressed in black – that's what the Cult wear.'

Tommy proceeded to tell Ben everything he'd been told about the Cult. The tattoo of the quill, their dress code and the fact that they were cold-blooded killers. Ben winced at the last part.

Finally, when Tommy had finished, a horror-struck Ben said quietly. 'You say they dress all in black?'

'Yeah, why?'

Ben pointed over Tommy's shoulder.

'Kinda like those guys?'

Tommy wheeled around. It was them, the two men from the Central. They'd found him!

They were stood about six feet away, staring menacingly at them, rainwater dripping from the brim of their hats. The shorter of the two boasted a sinister sneer, whilst the larger man simply stood impassively, pulling his leather gloves tighter onto his huge hands and puffing out his large chest. Tommy squinted through the rain, which was now coming down in sheets, trying to get a look at the men's faces. The big guy had two black eyes and a bloodied nose. *Could he be the one Grandpa had hit?*

Despite the fear of seeing them, of knowing what they

were capable of, Tommy felt anger burn up inside him again. These were the men that were responsible for Grandpa's death. They were the ones who had taken Grandpa away from him. Taking two brave steps forward and ignoring the gasps from Ben, Tommy shouted so he could be heard over the wind.

'YOU! You killed my Grandpa!'

The smaller man, Styx, just sniggered, not showing the slightest trace of remorse. In fact, his face seemed to light up at the mere mention of the pain and suffering that they'd caused.

'Listen, kid,' he said in a low, raspy voice. 'We can either do this the easy way or the hard way, it's up to you. Now, where is it?'

Tommy, who still held the Pen, managed to drop his arm to his side, shielding it from view. He allowed the sleeve of his school jumper to fall over his hand, concealing it completely.

'What are you on about?' he lied as convincingly as he could.

Styx smiled a satisfied smile.

'The hard way it is...'

Turning to his intimidating cohort, he barked, 'Barbarus. Go get it.'

The muscle-bound Barbarus strode towards Tommy, splashing through puddles and eclipsing the street light behind him as he approached. He was easily twice as tall as Tommy and at least four times as wide. Despite Tommy's own aggression he knew he'd be foolish to stand his ground against this man. He was just a kid. He had to make guarding the Pen his priority; he owed it to Mr Wiseman *and* to Grandpa. He had to run and hope that they were too slow to catch him. If he could just get away, he'd figure out the rest later. Unfortunately, in that split second's thought, Ben had appeared in front of him, placing himself as a barrier between him and the oncoming man.

'Tommy! Run!' he yelled.

'Ben, NO! What are you doing?!'

'Trust me, Tom, go! I can deal with this!'

Turning to face the two men, Ben bounced on his toes, his arms in the air, imitating a stance straight out of a martial arts movie.

'I bet these guys didn't know your best mate was a black belt in Karate, did they?!' he shouted, more at the two men than Tommy.

Barbarus raised a confused eyebrow. Evidently nobody of Ben's size had ever stood up to him before.

'Yeah, that's right, Barbara Bush,' Ben said, continuing his scare tactics and getting himself all worked up, 'they don't call me Ben 'Kung Fu' Campbell for nothing!' And with that Ben ran towards the huge man, leapt into the air and aimed a spinning kick at his head. He made the lightest of contacts somewhere near the killers' navel, before losing his balance and turning his ankle painfully, landing hard in a muddy puddle. Barbarus, who hadn't flinched during the attack, looked from the concerned face of Tommy to Ben, who was now rubbing his ankle. Having found Tommy's weakness, Barbarus set out to expose it, stepping forwards and hoisting Ben to his feet, placing a python-like grip around his neck and choking the air from him.

'Where is the Pen?' he demanded in a thick European accent.

Why did Ben have to be so brave? *And* stupid? If they'd both run when they'd had the chance then they could have got away. Seeing the genuine fear and pain etched on Ben's face, Tommy instinctively squeezed the Pen in his hand. He had a decision to make. But it wasn't really a decision. Ben or the Pen? It was no contest.

'OK, stop! Stop! I've got it here. It's here!'

He raised the Pen into the air, both men's greedy eyes following it as its design sparkled in the rain-specked light. Tommy saw the vice-like grip relax around Ben's throat, allowing him a chance to gasp at the air.

'Pass it over!' Styx said with a look of avarice.

Tommy took one last, regretful look at the Pen before tossing it in the direction of the cruel looking man, who caught it in his gloved hand. *Some Guardian*. He'd lost the Pen already. Who knew what consequences this would have on mankind? But he had no choice. Ben was more important – to him at least.

'Now let him go!' Tommy shouted at Barbarus.

The huge man tossed Ben like a rag doll, sending him half way across the car park and causing him to land in a crumpled heap on the floor.

'You really thought it would be that easy?' Styx said, his hungry eyes devouring the Pen. 'I told you we'd be doing this the hard way.'

He placed a hand into his overcoat and produced a handgun, pointing it directly at Ben who sat helpless on the wet tarmac.

'You're lucky, kid,' Styx said to Tommy. 'The boss says we can't hurt *you*, but he didn't say anything about your friend here.'

Tommy had never seen a gun before – not a real one anyway – and just the sight of it scared the life out of him. Despite his fear, though, he instinctively darted towards Ben and flung himself on him, blocking the line of fire.

'If you wanna hurt him, you've gotta get through me first!' he shouted, not ready to lose two people he loved today.

Styx weighed up the situation before slowly returning his gun to its holster.

'Come on,' he said to Barbarus, laughing. 'We ain't got time for this. We got what we came for.'

He then glared at Tommy.

'Your time will come, Parker. It won't be long now. Not long at all.'

With that threat the two men disappeared into the storm as quickly as they'd arrived. Tommy and Ben remained motionless, alone in the car park, in shock from their near-deadly confrontation.

'We should call the cops,' Ben finally said, rubbing his ankle.

But Tommy was in no mood to wait around *or* involve the police. He had to get the Pen back before the Cult did something terrible with it.

'Nuh, I'm getting the Pen!' he said. 'We need it for Grandpa. You coming?'

Ben looked from Tommy to the safety of the hospital doors. As tempting as it must have been, it took him all of two seconds to decide where his loyalty lay. He hauled himself up off the ground and jogged gingerly on his bad ankle, following Tommy across the car park and out of the hospital gates, his new limp reminiscent of the former self he'd never known. It appeared that their friendship knew no bounds.

— CHAPTER EIGHTEEN —

The Central School

By the time Tommy and Ben had reached the old Central School, the weather had grown even worse. The rain was now driving into their faces, and the wind was howling like a hungry werewolf, the strong gusts threatening to sweep them off their feet – but not even that could put Tommy off. He just *had* to get the Pen back. Every so often, flashes of lightning illuminated the town so brightly that it looked like it were daylight, and each flash was followed by a tremendous clap of thunder that would make Ben jump and clutch at his heart. This was not a storm that belonged in Little Millbrook; it seemed almost unnatural.

Tommy had decided that the obvious place to start looking was at the old school. They'd seen the men there earlier but the hardest part was convincing Ben about the idea. As soon as he'd even mentioned the plan, Ben loudly protested saying that they shouldn't go there for fear of antagonising the ghosts of the Hinton brothers. Tommy could only partially distract him by promising that he could have a go on the Pen when they got it back. Without the Pen there was no chance of changing what had happened to Grandpa, and if it meant that they'd have to face their fears in order to get it back, then that's what Tommy was prepared to do.

They approached the school cautiously, ducking down behind a parked car on the opposite side of the road. Surveying the area quickly, they saw no sign of the men from the hospital, which Ben took as irrefutable evidence that they'd come to the wrong place.

'Ah well, they're not here,' he said. 'Let's try...'

'Ben. We've gotta check *inside*.'

Tommy had never seen him look so frightened. The rain had flattened his hair to his head and had washed all colour from his face. The glimpse of the newer and more confident Ben had now all but vanished.

'Are you sure we've gotta go inside?' he asked for the tenth time since leaving the hospital. 'Can't we just wait 'til they come out? Or even call the police?'

'No, I told you before; the police would never believe us. Besides, we can't wait any longer; they might be in there using it right now.'

'But the *Hintons,* Tom...' he pleaded. 'I read somewhere that ghosts only hang around cos they've got no choice. That they don't leave 'til they get their revenge on whoever killed 'em. If we go in there, they might take it out on us!'

'You *read* somewhere?'

'Oh, OK, I saw it on TV! It doesn't mean it's wrong though. If we go in there we'll be asking for all sorts of trouble. Tom... we might not get out alive! And I'm not just talking about the Hintons. You saw those guys earlier, they had a gun! A *gun* Tommy! And that big guy's arm was really strong!' Ben massaged his neck for effect, the red marks still visible.

'I know, Ben, I know. You don't have to go inside if you don't want to. But I've got to; I'm the Guardian, aren't I? I've gotta get it back. Something bad's gonna happen if I don't. I've got to at least try.'

Tommy looked at the building's gloomy windows – which were now being battered by the storm – remembering the silhouette that he'd seen in the attic window. He wondered whether anyone was looking back at him right now. A flash of lightning startled him, bringing him out of his trance.

'Perhaps you could be look-out?' Tommy suggested, hoping that Ben would insist on accompanying him anyway. Ben's silence showed that he greatly preferred that option. It looked like Tommy would have to go it alone.

'Stay here then,' he said, trying to make it sound like he didn't mind. 'Yell if you see them. I'm gonna find a way in.'

Tommy hesitated by the gate as Ben took up a position that looked a little more like hiding than looking-out; he was crouching down behind a parked car. Just as Tommy was about to run into the school grounds, though, Ben whispered to him urgently.

'Hey, Tom! Someone's coming. Look!'

Tommy could see a slight figure walking along the street, towards him through the storm. He squinted through the rain, only making out who it was when they were just a few feet away.

'Jennifer?'

'Tommy?' she replied, just as surprised to see him.

'Hey, Ben, it's Jennifer.'

He sprang up from behind the car.

'Benny? What are you doing down there?' she asked.

'Huh? Oh I was just tying my shoelace,' he lied, pretty convincingly. 'What are you doing out in this?'

'I've just come from Eleni's house. We were practicing our dance moves for the new cheerleading team. It's going really well. Forgot my brolly, though, and the weather's absolutely horrid, isn't it? Anyway,' she said, looking at the imposing school, 'I could ask you two the same thing. You weren't about to go in there were you, Tommy?'

'Yep!' Ben replied for him. 'We were actually.'

Gone was the fear and trepidation, replaced now with an abundance of confidence and no small amount of swagger. The change in him was almost magical, and there were no prizes for guessing why. This was a good old-fashioned case of showing off.

'We both were, weren't we, Tom?' he added, winking at him. 'We've gotta get something of his Grandpa's.'

'But you can't go in there, Benny,' she said, looking concerned.

'Why? Cos of the ghosts? Like I keep telling Tommy, I ain't scared of them.'

Tommy rolled his eyes.

'No, not that,' she scoffed. 'I don't believe in all that. But still, it's dangerous in there; the whole place is falling apart. I don't want you going in there.'

She then threw her arms around his neck and cuddled

into him for what Tommy thought was way too long. It bordered on being awkward. They embraced and whispered to one another (no doubt he was telling her how brave he was and how Tommy wouldn't go inside without him) whilst Tommy waited impatiently by the entrance to the school, trying to spot the best way in.

'Have you two quite finished?' he asked after a while.

'Yeah,' Ben said, still holding on to Jennifer's hand. 'We're all yours.'

Tommy eyed them suspiciously as they both joined him at the gate.

'Well, Jennifer, guess we'll see you in school tomorrow?'

He couldn't have dropped a bigger hint.

'I'm not going anywhere,' she said firmly. 'If Benny is going in there to help you then I'm coming too.'

Tommy looked to Ben, who made a pretty good job of avoiding eye contact.

'I'm sorry, Jen, but you're not,' Tommy said, frustrated now at the delay. If they wanted to get all lovey-dovey, then they could do it on their own time. Not when he was trying to save Grandpa.

'Mate!' Ben jumped to her defence. 'I can hardly let her walk home alone, can I? Not in this storm.'

'Fine! Walk her home then! I'll do it alone.'

He dashed through the gateway and down the path, leaving the offended couple in stunned silence. He took cover behind a rusty old bike shed. From there he scanned the side of the building, looking for the best way in. Along the wall were a series of large, boarded up windows. Upon closer inspection, one of the boarding's had clearly been tampered with, the bottom corner pulled free from the frame. It banged rhythmically with each gust of wind, beckoning him inside. But it was a different, more welcome sound that startled him.

'There, look. That's our way in.'

It was Ben.

'I thought you weren't coming?' he asked, secretly relieved at having him there.

'What? And leave you without a bodyguard?'

'What about Jennifer?'

'I've had to send her off, haven't I?' he responded, annoyed with him.

'Thanks, Ben. Sorry if I was rude, I'm just really scared about Grandpa. I wanna get this over with.'

'That's OK, I understand. Let's do it then.'

'Right. I take it, as bodyguard, you'll want to go in first?' Tommy suggested.

'Well, I kinda thought I'd guard you from the back.'

Tommy smiled. At least he was here. The task ahead seemed more bearable now that Ben was with him.

'After me then,' Tommy said, jogging towards the window.

Ben pulled back the loose board, allowing Tommy to climb through the gap, and then followed him inside. They entered the school in the gymnasium. The floor was thick with dust, and ancient gym equipment was piled up along the walls. The wall bars, ropes and basketball hoops appeared almost untouched by the smoke and fire that had ravaged the school years ago. Except for some black scorch marks on the walls and ceiling, the gym looked pretty much like the one at their own school. Tommy turned to share this observation with Ben, only to find that he was now leaning out of the window again, this time holding the board back to help Jennifer as she clambered inside. They approached Tommy, who met them with a stony silence. Ben at least had the decency to look a little guilty.

'Sorry, Tom, but what could I do?' he said. 'Her hair will frizz if she walks home in this.'

Tommy looked to Jennifer, who was nodding furiously in agreement. *Her hair would frizz?* That wasn't his best mate talking.

'You've changed, Ben.'

He turned to Jennifer. 'OK, you can stay, but try to keep quiet. We don't know where these guys are.'

She seemed pleased, smiling at him sweetly.

'I'll be as quiet as a mouse, I promise.'

Tommy examined their surroundings, wondering where they should start.

'So, what are we looking for anyway?' Jennifer asked, immediately breaking her vow.

'Just something of my Grandpa's,' he replied dismissively, reluctant to tell her exactly why they were there. 'Some men stole it.'

'Not just anything, though,' Ben chipped in. 'It's this pen that can...'

'It's a pen that is very special to him,' Tommy interrupted, not wanting to tell Jennifer too much. He flashed Ben a look that told him to keep it to himself. 'It's a family heirloom.'

'Oh, OK. But why are we looking for it in here? Nobody's been in here for years.'

'You're just gonna have to trust us Jen. The men who burgled him – they've come here. I'm sure of it.'

'Burgled? Benny, you didn't say anything about them being *burglars*!'

She moved closer to Ben and held onto his arm. Clearly, that new information had frightened her, and now Tommy hoped to take advantage of the situation; he had enough to worry about without having to look out for Jennifer too.

'Actually, Jennifer, this could get quite dangerous. There's still time for you to leave if you want?'

She looked to her boyfriend for guidance.

'Hey, don't worry,' Ben said, much to the annoyance of Tommy. 'I'll look after you. Nothing's gonna happen to you while I'm here is it?'

She smiled and snuggled into his chest, leaving him free to look at Tommy and mouth the words: 'Let's go home'. Tommy ignored him. *So* brave.

'I think we should split up,' Tommy suggested after a few moments. 'This place is huge. It'll take ages to search otherwise. What do you think, Ben?'

He turned to find Jennifer standing all alone in the middle of the gym. Surely, he hadn't abandoned them already? He then noticed that one of the thick climbing ropes that hung from the ceiling was dancing about, apparently of its own accord. Looking up, he saw that Ben was now suspended fifteen feet in the air, halfway up its length.

'What *are* you doing?!' Tommy asked in an exasperated whisper.

Ben halted his ascent and responded, rather too loudly for Tommy's liking.

'Nuthin, I'm just trying to keep Jen distracted. See?' he said to Jennifer. 'Told you I could do it.'

'Will you get down! And keep quiet too; we don't know who else is in here! Anyway, did you hear what I said?' Tommy repeated as Ben slid down the rope. 'I think we should split up. We'll have more chance of finding it.'

He didn't like that suggestion one bit.

'No way! Whenever people split up in the movies it always turns out bad – especially for the side-kick! I don't want to fall into that trap. I think we should stay together; it'll be safer that way.'

'OK,' Tommy relented. 'You win. We'll do it your way. Let's just not waste any more time. Hey, hang on a minute! Look at this…'

Tommy had noticed two things on the floor; first were sets of footprints in the dust. But second, and more alarmingly, was what looked like a trail of blood that followed the footprints. They both headed towards a set of doors at the far end of the room.

'Look,' he said. 'They've definitely been here; this blood's not even dry.'

'Whoa! And look at the size of those footprints!' Ben contributed. 'Do you reckon they belong to that big guy? Barbarus?'

'Who's Barbarus?' Jennifer asked, beginning to lose her nerve again.

'They're bound to,' Tommy replied, ignoring her. 'They're twice the size of the other ones. And his nose had been bleeding, hadn't it? It's gotta be them. Guess we'd better see where they lead.'

'I knew you'd say that,' Ben replied, staring longingly at the window they'd just climbed through. Stepping back out into the storm seemed like a far more appealing option. 'OK, let's get on with it,' he added, leading the way along the trail of red. 'Don't worry, Jen, it's just one of the men we're on about, but you can leave them to me. Come on.'

Pushing the double doors open, they found themselves at the end of a long corridor, far darker than the gym, lit only by the faint electric orange hue of the street lights outside. It was the school's main corridor and a number of doors ran down it on both sides. To their right was a set of stairs leading up to the floor above, and every ten metres or so a new hallway ran off from the main corridor. The footprints and the line of blood continued straight ahead before veering off along a different corridor to the left. Tommy nodded after the footprints.

'I suppose we should...'

Ben anticipated how the sentence would end.

'Yeah. Since we're here.'

Jennifer tagged along, very much a reluctant passenger, latched firmly onto Ben's arm. But no sooner had they begun to follow the footprints than a loud bang, followed by a shrill, blood-curdling wail came echoing along the hall, causing the doors and windows to shake violently. Instinctively, Tommy shot through the nearest door while Ben, swivelling on his heels, pulled at Jennifer's arm and ran, desperate to find a place to hide. They headed for the furthest point away from the noise, running up the stairs that they'd passed, and up on to the next level. They hid in the first room they came to, waiting in complete silence, with only their fear and over-active imaginations to keep them company.

Tommy found himself very much alone in what was one of the school's old science labs. He'd hidden behind one of the long wooden counters and now had no idea where Ben and Jennifer had got to. His loneliness in this dark and creepy building made any bravery that he'd gathered seep out of him. He daren't move for fear that the shadows would be alerted and come to life. It was all he could do to muster the courage to peer over the counter to see if there was anything out there. If ever he wanted the invisibility that the Pen could give him, then it was now. That scream hadn't sounded human – no doubt Ben was convincing Jennifer that it must have been one of the Hinton brothers – and he may well have a point. There were certainly evil spirits lurking in Little Millbrook this night. Yet, to Tommy everything that they'd seen and heard since coming here had told him one thing: that they had come to the right place. The sets of footprints, the trail of blood, even that chilling scream. He was getting closer to the Cult and closer to the Pen; he could feel it. And all of that meant that he was getting closer to saving Grandpa. He *had* to go on.

Quietly, he searched the ruined lab for any clues, navigating his way around the smashed jars and beakers that covered the floor like a glistening carpet. He checked through cupboards, flicked through old textbooks and searched through drawers, looking for anything that seemed out of the ordinary. Whilst fiddling with an old gas tap he noticed a shadow moving across the long, Perspex window that overlooked the corridor. He froze again, terrified by the silhouette that was slowly stalking the deserted hallway. The silhouette belonged to a man – a man wearing a fedora hat. It was one of them – one of *Secuutus Pluma*.

Tommy daren't move; he just stood there, his hand quite still on the gas tap, watching as the shadow walked the length of the window. He willed it to pass the door and move on to a different, faraway part of the school, but as it approached the door the shadow slowed to a halt. Then the man turned and faced the room, looking through the opaque window. It was all Tommy could do not to scream. His eyes bore into the door handle, praying that it wouldn't turn. But turn it did. He dropped to the floor behind the counter just as the door opened. The man stepped into the lab, eyeing it suspiciously. Something had caught his attention, and he began to walk the aisles methodically, in between the long wooden desks, sweeping the classroom row by row. Tommy could only rely upon the sound of the man's footfall, each step announced by the crunching of broken glass underfoot as he remained on all-fours, crawling away from the man's search. As the man walked the length of the first row and turned into the second, Tommy crept deftly, rounding into the third row just a split-second before he'd have come into his view, grimacing at the pain from the cuts being inflicted on his hands and knees. But still the man came. *Crunch, crunch, crunch.* Nearing the end of the second row Tommy once again timed it perfectly, turning the corner into the next, narrowly avoiding the mercenary's line of sight. Tommy was running out of desks; he'd crawled almost to the far corner of the room now, and soon the man would only have one more row left to search and Tommy would have nowhere left to run. Now in the final row, he slid along on his hands and knees, trying desperately not to succumb to panic. If the man continued, then he'd have no choice but to show himself and run.

Tommy listened as the footsteps closed in on the end of the previous row. Any second now the man would be exposed to a scared little boy cowering in the corner of the room. Tommy closed his eyes and hoped for a miracle as the footsteps seemed to grow louder and louder.

Crunch. Crunch. Crunch...

With Tommy lost to them a long moment passed with neither Ben nor Jennifer saying a word. They just crouched side by side beneath a desk in a disused classroom on the first floor. Looks like splitting up was no longer a choice.

'What *was* that?' Ben finally asked, his voice shaking slightly. 'It sounded like somebody screaming.'

'I know,' Jennifer replied, the unforgettable noise still ringing in her ears. 'It sounded like someone being hurt.

Benny, what's going on? What are we really doing here?'

'Look, Jen, I can't tell you too much OK? I promised Tommy. But it's like he said, we've got to get something of his Grandpa's. Then we can get out of here.'

Jennifer wasn't satisfied with the explanation at all, but Ben didn't give her any time to interrogate him further.

'That scream,' he said, 'it sounded like a kid. And it came from the basement. That's where the fire started. It's *them*, Jen, I know it is. It's the Hintons! It's cos we're here, on *their* territory, they're trying to scare us off. I told you they were real!'

'C'mon, Ben, it's not them, it can't be. We shouldn't worry about things that don't exist.'

He held her by the shoulders, fixing her with a serious stare.

'Look me in the eye, Jen, and tell me that you don't think it's the Hintons.'

'I don't think it's them,' she replied slowly.

Ben continued to glower at her for a few seconds, his eyes as wide as saucers, as if trying to hypnotise her.

'Ah, you blinked!'

'Oh stop it, Ben! You're trying to frighten me! Whatever it was, I'm pretty sure that it wasn't ghosts!' She crawled out from under the desk and made her way to the door. 'We'd better find Tommy; he must be really scared on his own. We really shouldn't separate like this.' She opened the door carefully and peered into the corridor.

'OK, Ben, it's clear. Ben? Ben?'

There was no response. Ben was too busy, bent double,

picking up what looked like miniature totem poles made out of papier-mâché – the remnants of a school project long forgotten. He collected them in handfuls, using his jumper as a makeshift basket, precariously balancing as many of them as he could.

'What are you doing?' she asked.

'What does it look like? I'm setting a booby trap. Here, gimme a hand with these.' He struggled to the door with the little models and then laid them out in the corridor like ten-pins. 'C'mon, pass me some more.'

'We're wasting time.'

'Best hurry then,' he said, continuing his work until one section of the corridor was completely cut off by the arrangement of foot-high models.

'There!' he said, proudly assessing his work. 'This'll tell us if there's anyone else here. Anyone *human* anyway. I saw it on a survival show once. Now they won't have the element of surprise. If they come for us, we'll know about it, and I'll be able to take them out.'

He said it like he really believed it.

'Where next d'ya reckon?' he then asked, looking to her for guidance.

There were half a dozen classrooms on this level and loads more corridors leading off to other parts of the school. It could end up being a pretty long night.

'Well, I think we should go back downstairs and find Tommy.'

'Nah, he'll be OK for a bit; he wanted to split up anyway, didn't he? We may as well have a look around now that we're up here. Let's try down there,' he suggested, eyeing a door near the far end of the hallway. 'We can start up that end and work our way back.'

Leading the way, Ben focused on the room in front of him. He had no idea what to expect on the other side, and he had to be ready for anything. For all he knew, this door could lead them directly into the Cult's lair. Or, even worse, the room could be the hang-out area for the Hinton ghosts. He twisted the door handle and flung it open, prepared to fight whatever was inside. It was a store cupboard.

'They're lucky they're not in there,' he postured. 'They would have had it then.'

The cupboard housed a load of dust-covered shelving units filled with pots of water paint and hundreds of used paintbrushes. Various brooms and buckets were strewn across the floor.

'Must've been for art class,' Ben deduced expertly as Jennifer had a look around inside. He followed her in and closed the door behind them.

'What did you close that for?' she demanded, uncomfortable with the sudden blackout.

'I thought we could regroup in here and come up with a plan.'

'Regroup? We've only gone ten yards.'

'Yeah, but we don't wanna be too gung-ho do we? We don't really know what's out there yet.'

Their eyes took a couple of seconds to adjust to the darkness before they realised that, in fact, they weren't in complete darkness at all. There was a fraction of light coming in from somewhere that dimly lit the room. Jennifer fumbled her way over to the source of the light, near the tallest unit against the far wall. She shifted a few items to one side, causing even more light to be thrown into the storeroom. Behind the shelves, hidden from view by some of the old boxes, was a hole in the wall about the size of a fist. The hole was at Jennifer's eye level, and when she looked through it she found herself staring down into the school gym. The bird's eye view enabled her to see the wall bars, gym equipment and basketball hoops, the nearest of which was directly beneath them. She could even see the trail of footprints on the floor and, through the dust, could make out the coloured tape that marked the lines of the basketball court. At the far end of the gym was the boarded up window through which they'd climbed.

'What is it, Jen? What can you see?'

'It's the gym.'

Ever the gentleman, Ben unceremoniously barged her to one side. 'Oh, lemme see. Cool! Who d'you reckon put this hole in then?'

'That's what I was thinking. It could have been some of the school children, back when it was open? You know, to spy on PE lessons?'

'Nah, look how smooth it is,' he replied, running his fingers along its edges. 'Whoever did this had proper tools and everything. It's gotta be adults.'

He made a very good point.

'But why would an adult have done it? Surely a caretaker or teacher wouldn't have done it?' she commented.

'Unless somebody else did it,' Ben replied dramatically. 'Perhaps someone who'd made it as a look-out post. Y'know, to see who was coming into the school.'

Jennifer spent the next few minutes moving about more boxes and utensils, searching for anything that seemed to be out of the ordinary. The only problem was that she hadn't the faintest idea what she was looking for.

'What is it we're after again?'

'An old pen. I doubt they'd have stashed it in here though,' he replied.

She continued to have a look around anyway; it seemed better than doing nothing.

'Where next?' she asked after she'd finally exhausted her search of the small room. Ben himself had spent the whole time sitting on an upturned box in the corner, pointing at the places that she'd missed.

'We just keep looking around, I suppose, room by room, until we find something. Those men have got to be in here somewhere. I just hope Tommy's having more luck.'

...Crunch. Crunch. Crunch.

The man rounded the final counter. He was positive he'd seen movement in the classroom, and if there *was* anyone here then they'd be in this final row; he'd covered every other part of it. He turned into the last aisle but found nothing but an empty floor. He was alone. Maybe he'd been mistaken. Perhaps his eyes had played tricks on him. It *had* been a long few months; the Grand Master had barely let them rest as their search for the Pen had intensified. But now that they had it there would be no stopping them. The tide had finally turned. Soon they could put this sleepy little town behind them and then really get to work.

Determined not to leave an inch of the room unsearched, he walked to the end of the row. If he had to, he'd search inside every cupboard. Any intruders would pay for sticking their noses into the Cult's business. Especially if it was this new Guardian. He made his way methodically along the cupboards under the nearest counter, opening the first one. Nothing. He moved on to the second one; a rat scurried out of it and disappeared into a dark corner of the lab. He then moved on to the third cupboard and placed his hand on the handle. He was just about to open it when he heard a noise, something moving about on the floor above. He had them now! He straightened himself and pulled his leather gloves tight, striding across the broken glass and out into the corridor. He slammed the door behind him, intent on flushing them out.

Ben opened the store cupboard and stepped back out into the corridor.

'There was a big classroom down here,' he declared. 'Let's go and have a look there... hey! Jen, look!' he whispered urgently.

The models Ben had so carefully placed across the hallway now lay on their sides, haphazardly strewn across the length of the corridor.

'How did they...?'

'Sshh!' she whispered. 'I think someone's here – I just

heard something in that classroom!'

They stood rooted to the spot, neither daring to speak, Jennifer strained her ears for any sign of movement, but the only thing that she could hear was Ben's erratic breathing.

'It can't be human, Jen,' he said, struggling to control the tremor in his voice, 'we'd have heard them. It's gotta be the Hintons! I told you they were real!'

'No, wait. Listen,' she said. 'I can hear footsteps.' She dragged Ben to one side. 'Quick, get in here!'

They clambered into a low cupboard that was against the wall, barely managing to squeeze themselves in. It was a tight and very uncomfortable fit. They lay in wait for the footsteps to draw near. Jennifer had purposely left the cupboard door ajar in the hope of catching a glimpse of whomever was walking the corridors, not sure whether she wanted Ben proved wrong or not. Perhaps a harmless ghost or two would be far more preferable than meeting one of those men that had stolen from Tommy's Grandpa. She was distracted by an unfortunate and most definitely unwelcome noise.

'Oh, Ben! Have you just broken wind?' she whispered, prodding him angrily and bringing her perfumed sleeve to her nose.

'Sorry,' he replied, 'I can't help it when I'm nervous.'

Jennifer held her breath. It was probably safer out there facing whatever threat it may be than being stuck in a cupboard with Ben and his troublesome flatulence. They soon heard one of Ben's models being kicked across the floor. Seconds after that, somebody walked past them –

somebody wearing a pair of large black shoes, black trousers and a dark trench coat that hung just below the knee. A person who was very much human. It wasn't ghosts.

The man came close to the cupboard, impossibly close. Jennifer was sure that he must have seen her looking out at him. But then he walked from view.

'What's going on, Jen?' came a whisper, 'I can't see a thing back here.'

'It's one of the men you're looking for – I think he's going back downstairs. He looks dangerous, Ben! Can we please just go now?'

Ben chuckled quietly to himself.

'What's funny?'

Jennifer failed to see the funny side of being stuck in the Central School with these people.

'My booby trap worked,' he declared proudly. 'We'd have walked straight into him if it weren't for that!'

Ben was right. His trap had certainly given them enough warning. Jennifer eased herself out of the cupboard, checking carefully that the coast was clear.

'C'mon,' Ben said, 'let's follow him. He could lead us right to the Pen. We can't leave until we've got it.'

Tommy watched through a crack as the man checked the two cupboards next to his. His heart almost stopped as a gloved hand moved towards him. He held his breath, praying for a miracle. Just then a noise in a different part of the school caught the man's attention. He waited for a while in case the slamming of the lab door had all been a ruse orchestrated to flush him out of hiding. Then, carefully, he opened the door to the cupboard and, like a battered old accordion, unfolded himself onto the floor. That had been *too* close.

He peered out into the corridor. Not a soul in sight. He heard noises from the top of the stairs, which sounded like things being kicked over, and then the low curses of a man. Seconds later, what appeared to be a cardboard version of a decapitated American Indian bounced down the steps and rolled along the corridor, landing at his feet. Not something you see every day. As if it were a sign, the model's eyes looked straight along the trail of blood, serving as a reminder of the path he'd been on. He took up the course again, following it along the corridor and to a turning off to the left which led him to another set of steps. These steps looked even less inviting than the ones behind him. These steps went *down*. Down into the basement; into the belly of the haunted school. And it was a path he knew he had no choice but to follow if he wanted to keep alive any hope of seeing Grandpa again. So down he went, one terrified step after another, descending further into darkness and into a battle against an unknown foe.

Ben and Jennifer peered over the banister in time to see the top of the black fedora disappear around the corner and into the hall below. Ben led the way down the stairs, carefully peeking around the corner into the corridor. The man had already made it halfway along it, and, as they watched him he turned left, down a smaller corridor and out of sight.

They waited a few seconds before scurrying along after him. Ben noticed that they were also following the trail of blood.

'Jen,' he said turning to her. 'If you want to go, then now's the time. I can see you out as far as the window.'

She squeezed his hand.

'I'm going where you're going,' she replied warmly.

He blushed. She really did like him.

They turned into the smaller corridor and found themselves approaching another set of steps. This time leading down to what Ben assumed was the basement. A distant glimmer of light ahead disappeared with the sound of a closing door. They followed the steps down, Ben's shoes feeling as though they were filled with lead. It took all of his willpower to continue. If he didn't feel the need to act brave in front of Jennifer, then he probably would have bolted for the window himself.

'It's down to us now, Jen,' he said quietly, trying to convince himself more than anyone else. 'Even if we have to take on the Hintons as well, we have to go on.'

'Oh, Ben, don't you get it?' Jennifer whispered. 'There *are* no Hintons here. There's no such thing as ghosts. This place isn't haunted, it never was. It must be this group of men that you and Tommy are on about. All the screaming, all the banging over the years, it's probably been them all along. If this is their hide-out, then they might have been using it for years.'

Ben stared at her blankly. She made a very good point. Why hadn't he thought of that?

'How did you get so smart, eh?' he asked her.

'Because I listen in class. Plus I grew out of ghost stories way back in junior school.' She winked at him, making him blush again.

At the bottom of the steps, they found themselves in a narrow hallway so dark that they had to feel their way through it. A few metres on, it opened up into a wider area which actually turned out to be a room that contained a desk and a chair. There was a closed door at the far end and, on the adjoining wall, a battered looking locker about the size of a wardrobe. A recently discarded cigarette still glowed in an ashtray on the desk, and the brickwork displayed the worst example yet of the damage from the fire all those years ago.

'This must be near where the fire started,' Ben whispered, 'look at the state of the walls.'

'Ssh...' Jennifer urged. 'Did you hear that? Voices. In there...'

She pointed to the closed door and moved as lightly as she could. A number of voices could be heard, one of which Ben recognised instantly – the unmistakable, raspy tones of Styx, the rodent-like man who'd pointed the gun at him and Tommy earlier. They leaned against the door, straining to hear the conversation within.

'Psst! Over here!'

Ben jumped.

A noise was coming from the locker.

'Psst! Ben, quick, it's me!'

The door of the locker groaned open and Tommy stepped out, trying desperately to muffle the sound of the rusty hinges.

'Thank heavens you two are OK! I thought that guy was going to find you.'

'Don't thank heaven, thank me!' Ben replied. 'I set a booby trap didn't I, Jen?'

She smiled and nodded. Tommy had the distinct impression that she was humouring him.

'We followed him down here.'

'Yeah, well he's back in there now,' Tommy said, pointing to the closed door. 'There's a few in there, I think. I saw at least two more when they opened the door. That's gotta be where they're keeping the Pen.'

'Come here, you can hear them.' Ben made room for him by the door. 'Listen.'

The men were mid-conversation.

'...it was easy boss,' Styx said. 'He was just where you said he'd be, visiting his *poor* grandfather – like taking candy from a baby.'

The sarcasm in the man's words angered Tommy. For a second he felt like barging straight into the room and throttling him. Then a deeper, more commanding voice spoke.

'Disappointing. I expected more from this new Guardian, more of a challenge. But we must be wary nonetheless. I have warned you of the danger he poses to our cause. This is the Guardian that *He* told us about. The youngster is more important than he knows.'

There was a pause.

'No matter. Now that we have the Pen,' the

commanding voice continued. 'We can end his threat before he is even born. Brother Malus, did you discover what I asked of you from the grandfather's house?'

'Yes, sir,' said another voice. 'Piecing together what we've found at the Parker place, the exchange took place on the fourth night after the landings. At the church of the forgetful town.'

On the other side of the door, a confused Tommy looked from Ben to Jennifer, both of whom could only shrug their shoulders.

'Very good,' said the leader. 'Very good. Then we finally know when to do it. The place where we were betrayed so long ago. Now we can avenge those acts and eliminate Parker too. In one swift motion, killing off the line of Guardians for good. Soon their futile resistance will be at an end.'

'And with this,' he continued, 'we can finally release *The Creperum*. Too long has it been gone. Too long has mankind kept it at bay. What an honour it is that I, Nidas, will be the one to unleash it. The world will never be the same again. *He* will be pleased. *He* will be *very* pleased.'

Raucous laughter broke out, the vibrations of which could be felt through the door they leaned on. So *this* was Nidas. The terrifying Grand Master that Mr Wiseman had told him about. Tommy's head almost exploded trying to figure out what he'd just heard. *What were they talking about? An exchange?* Were they on about the time Grandpa was given the Pen? It had to be. And they mentioned a church. He was pretty sure Grandpa had said that it was in a church in France that the man had given it to him. Did the Cult really intend to use the Pen to go back and stop all of it from happening? To tip off the Cult during the war and get to it before Grandpa even knew he had it? But that wasn't all; by the sound of it they actually intended to *kill* Grandpa back then too. The knock-on effects would be disastrous! This *Creperum* thing didn't sound too good either – whatever that was. His mouth finally caught up with his thoughts.

'We gotta stop them,' he said, turning to Ben. 'They mean business. They're gonna use it to kill Grandpa.'

Ben looked at him for a second, his expression a mixture of fear and pity.

'But, Tom, he's already dead,' he replied, clearly not understanding what Tommy had meant.

'What?!' Jennifer exclaimed. This was news to her. 'Oh, Tommy! I didn't know your Grandfather had died. What happened?'

'It was these lot,' he replied, angered by the very thought of it. 'But we're gonna change all that.'

Jennifer backed away from the door, terrified by the new information.

'Benny, you didn't say anything about them being *killers*.'

'Uh, didn't I?' he replied awkwardly, suddenly preoccupied with a bit of dirt on his trousers. 'Didn't I mention it earlier? Sorry.'

'Well, if they really did do all of that, then we have to leave right now and call the police,' she pleaded, trying to pull Ben back into the corridor. He placed an arm on her shoulder to calm her.

'You can if you want to, Jen,' he said calmly. 'But Tommy thinks that we can fix this, and if he's right, then I'm staying.' He turned to Tommy. 'Now run that by me again. How can they hurt your Grandpa if he's already dead?'

'I don't mean they can hurt him now. I mean they can do it back then, during the war. They're gonna use the Pen to go back and kill him when he was young. If they do that, then my whole family's gonna be wiped out. We'll never exist! That Guardian they're talking about eliminating Ben – it's me. Don't you see? If they go back and kill Grandpa, my dad will never get born. *I'll* never be born!'

It seemed to take an age for comprehension to finally dawn, the look of fear on Ben's face intensifying. Despite this he clenched his jaw tightly and, when he spoke, his words held a steely determination.

'We can't let them kill your Grandpa, Tom... not again. What do we do?'

Tommy backed away from the door, looking around for something that he could use as a weapon, but all that was there was a chair, which looked far too heavy and, on the table, the rather filthy ashtray. Neither was a match for a handgun.

'Hang on,' Ben said, 'I've got an idea.'

'It doesn't involve going for help, does it? Cos I've told you–'

'Gimme a break, Tom, I know that.'

He pointed to the locker against the wall. 'Get in there again. Me and Jen will distract them. With any luck, they'll leave the Pen behind, and you can grab it. At the very least it'll cause them to split up. Then we'll meet out by the bike shed, OK?'

Ben made grabbing the Pen sound easy, but Tommy was willing to bet his bike that it would be much harder trying to do it for real.

'OK,' he agreed. 'What you gonna do to distract them?'

Ben escorted Jennifer out of the room and back towards the stairs.

'Dunno yet. We'll think of something, though, won't we?' he said to Jennifer, who, since hearing that the men weren't just thieves but also murderers, had gone into a state of shock. She just stared at him blankly. 'That's my girl.'

'Tom, we'll give you a minute, and then we'll do it. Good luck,' he said, and then he and Jennifer disappeared into the dark corridor.

'Yeah, you too,' Tommy whispered to the empty room, feeling awfully lonely all of a sudden.

CHAPTER NINETEEN

Ben 'Tarzan' Campbell

Tommy climbed back inside the locker and winced as its hinges let out a dull creak. He pushed aside some junk, squeezed himself in and closed the door behind him. No sooner had he begun to wonder how Ben would distract the men, than a loud slamming of doors came from the floor above, echoing loudly through the basement and down into the room where he hid. The banging was accompanied by Ben yelling at the top of his voice (and in his best impersonation of a ghost) 'Woooo! I'm the Hinton boys! I'm the Hintons! I'm coming to get you!' He looked through a gap in the locker door and braced himself. Almost immediately, the door to the room was thrown open, and Styx rushed out, standing just a few feet from where he hid.

'What is it?' the voice of Nidas asked from the other room.

'I don't know. It's coming from upstairs!'

Following Styx out of the room was Barbarus, and then a third man emerged, one who Tommy had never seen before, and, if he had his way, would never set eyes on again. This man, who strode angrily into the room, was even larger than the gargantuan Barbarus. He was the oldest of the Cult members by far and, having removed his jacket and hat, was now stood in a white shirt and a pair of black braces pulled tightly over his muscular shoulders. He looked menacingly around the room, and Tommy was forced to throw a hand over his mouth to suppress a gasp of horror when his gaze fell upon the locker. An ugly scar ran down the length of his cheek, which gave him the look of a battle-worn, albeit well-dressed, pirate. Tommy held his breath as the man continued to stare suspiciously at the locker, only exhaling when his eyes finally passed over it and onto a different part of the room.

Then the man spoke, 'Brother Malus,' he said, in the same commanding voice that Tommy had heard earlier. 'Guard it. We won't be long.'

The men moved with surprising speed out of the room and to the floor above. Tommy hoped Ben knew what he was doing; he wouldn't fancy having any of those chasing him. But at least Ben had managed to draw three of them away, and now there was only one person left to guard the Pen. The odds were much better – still stacked against him, but better nonetheless. It was time to execute phase two of the plan.

Tommy stepped out of the locker and tiptoed towards the open door. He poked his head inside and saw that the remaining Cult member was just a few metres away, sat on the side of a desk with his back to him. He scanned the rest of the room. It was much larger than the other one. In fact, Tommy couldn't see where the walls ended as both sides disappeared into darkness. A large boiler stood against one of the stone walls, and next to it a faint flicker of light emanated from a large hole that had numerous bricks, rubble and loose soil lying at its entrance. It looked like some sort of passageway or tunnel. Tommy supposed it was probably what the Cult had been using to enter and leave the school undetected. The damage from the fire was also at its most evident here, leaving Tommy to wonder whether it was in this very room that the blaze had claimed the lives of the Hinton brothers.

The man took a long drag on his cigarette and glanced nervously towards the tunnel. Whether it was the thought of intruders or the fact that he himself believed in ghosts, Tommy didn't care; whatever it was, he hoped that he was suitably preoccupied to take his mind off guarding the Pen. Tommy surveyed the items on the desk. It didn't take him long to find what he was looking for. Directly under the lamp, its brilliant design winking at him invitingly, was the Pen. With the watchman still looking in the other direction and not wanting to lose the element of surprise, Tommy ran over to the desk and grabbed it, darting out of the room before the man knew what was going on. He bounded up the stairs two at a time, squeezing the Pen for dear life and vowing to never let it out of his grasp again. He emerged into the main corridor, relieved to find that it was empty. Mixing urgency with caution, he then walked at a fast pace along the hallway and back through the doors of the gym, following the trail of blood like it were breadcrumbs, all the time hoping that Ben and Jennifer had managed to get out of the school unharmed. The adrenalin was coursing through his body, and his pace quickened as he began to sense the freedom that lay only a few metres ahead. In his mind, he began to plan what must be done next. *Meet Ben, get to Mr Wisemans, use the Pen to save Grandpa...*

His thoughts were interrupted by a sight that made his heart sink. In the gym and standing directly in front of the boarded window was Barbarus. He glared at Tommy through his blackened eyes and began to smile. Tommy turned his head. Just a few feet to his right was Styx, a sadistic sneer etched on his leathery face. Tommy instinctively thought about running back the way he'd come, but then, as if hit by a bolt of lightning made of pure ice, he was frozen to the spot by a deep and measured tone that came from behind him.

'Ah, our young Guardian. We meet at last.'

With Jennifer securely hidden back in the cupboard on the first floor, Ben shouted the first thing that came into his head (some ridiculous comment about him being a Hinton ghost) and then proceeded to slam a number of classroom doors, making as much noise as he could. He then dodged the remains of his own booby trap and hid himself in the stockroom at the end of the hall, crouching between two shelving units and listening hard for any sign of movement. There was nothing. Surely they had heard him? He'd made enough of a racket!

Just as he'd decided to go back and cause more chaos, he heard them – footsteps rushing about in the main corridor below. He skulked back into the shadows and pressed his back firmly against the wall, praying that Jennifer would stay quiet and avoid detection. He chewed on his fingernails compulsively, a habit his mum continually nagged him to break. Minutes passed as he continued to stare at the door handle, willing it not to turn. A noise from above broke his trance; it had come from the spy hole that they'd found earlier. After a few seconds of trying to convince his legs that it was safe for him to stand, he raised himself to the level of the hole and looked through it. His eyes widened in terror at what he saw. The man, that giant man who'd strangled him earlier, was searching the gym, sweeping it like a well-trained soldier would sweep an enemy camp. Barbarus moved with stealth, every light step he took contradicting his true bulk. He continued his search of the gym, peering behind the dusty gym equipment and crash mats that were piled six-feet high. With every potential hiding place being examined without success, Ben grew more and more relieved, thankful that neither himself nor Jennifer had chosen to seek refuge behind them.

Barbarus was now at the window. He examined the loose board and then looked to the floor. Kneeling, he removed a glove from one of his shovel-like hands and then touched the fresh footprints in the dust. He raised his head, looking to the double doors directly beneath Ben.

'We've got company. Kids. Three of them,' he said, loudly enough for Ben to hear.

'Any sign of them?' a gravelly voice replied. Ben recognised it instantly.

'They're not in here.'

The owner of the other voice, Styx, entered the gym.

Unlike the military Barbarus, Styx moved more like a fox stalking his prey, his shoulders hunched, leaning forward slightly as if ready to pounce. He scanned the room suspiciously. These two men now stood between them and their exit, and Ben couldn't think of another way out, not at ground level anyway. He cursed as a third person entered the gym. This one moved with far more urgency than the other two and had made it halfway across the room before he halted suddenly, having seen Barbarus by the window.

It was Tommy.

And he was in such a rush to get out that he hadn't even noticed them until it was too late. Then another – and Ben could hardly believe his eyes – even bigger man entered the gym behind Tommy. He was trapped now. Ben watched helplessly as the new entrant, who had a greyish white buzz-cut, spoke to Tommy in tones too quiet for him to hear. Whatever was said couldn't have been good, as Styx suddenly pounced towards Tommy and seized something from his grip. Styx handed the item proudly to the older man. The Pen! Tommy had managed to get it back! But now Ben didn't fancy their chances of getting it off them for a second time. He racked his brain, trying to think of a way to save Tommy, but he struggled to look beyond the obvious facts: he was just one boy. One boy against at least three dangerous men, two of which could easily win a tag-team match with a pair of grizzly bears. Plus he had Jennifer to think about too. He had to get her out safely.

Ben continued to listen as the men surrounded Tommy, backing him into a corner near the crash mats. Tommy looked so much smaller than them, completely at their mercy, only alive because they hadn't decided to kill him – yet. The grey haired man continued to talk, as if delivering some sort of a lecture, and Ben was amazed at his friend's bravery. Despite being surrounded Tommy didn't cry, beg or struggle with them – in fact quite the contrary. On more than one occasion, Ben heard him shouting at them, loudly vowing revenge for what they had done to his Grandpa.

As they continued to talk, a fourth Cult member joined them, taking up a watchful position at the rear. Ben knew that he had to do something soon, before even more of them arrived. Or worse still, before they decided to hurt Tommy. Standing there, in the loneliness of the dark storeroom, he decided that it was time for him to show as much bravery as his friend had. He was their only hope now. He took one last look at the men before he left the safety of the small room, stepping anxiously out into the corridor and psyching himself up for the battle that lay ahead.

Before Tommy had time to think, Styx had pounced on him and wrestled the Pen from his grip, passing it to his boss. Styx laughed a wheezy laugh, staring triumphantly at Tommy, whose eyes were full of nothing but hatred for the man. It was the second time today he'd taken the Pen from him, and Tommy vowed that, should he manage to get it back, there wouldn't be a third.

Barbarus approached and gripped Tommy firmly, turning him roughly to face Nidas. It's fair to say that Tommy wasn't prepared for what he saw. Having seen him through the gap in the locker, he'd seen that he was big, bigger even than Barbarus. But now, close up, he was without a doubt the scariest man Tommy had ever laid eyes on. He looked about Grandpa's age but was clearly so much fitter and more powerful. And if the sheer size of him wasn't enough to give you nightmares, then the disgusting scar on his face would certainly keep you up at night.

Nidas caressed the Pen fondly, tracing its grooves with his fingers, his gaze not once leaving Tommy, all the time examining him with those cold, grey eyes. Clinging onto the hope that Ben and Jennifer had managed to escape, Tommy did his best to keep his fear at bay, convincing himself that they were now sure to return with the police. He realised that he'd been foolish to think they could take on the Cult alone; these people were professionals. He just had to keep them busy until Ben arrived with the cavalry.

'Who *are* you?' Tommy asked, looking at Nidas and speaking as boldly as he could in the circumstances.

The huge man remained silent, continuing to stare at him, evaluating his every breath.

'I am the person you least wish to meet,' he said finally. 'The old man may have spoken of me. I am Nidas. Grand Master of *Secuutus Pluma* and possessor of the Pen of Destiny. I am also the man who is going to end the reign of the Guardian once and for all.'

There was an awkward silence as his words hung between them.

'Umm, no,' Tommy said defiantly, still doing his best to stall. 'He didn't mention you at all actually. Couldn't have thought you were that important.'

Nidas' eyes flashed angrily at his insolence, but the loss of composure was only momentary. Tommy was surrounded. Styx to his left, Barbarus to his right and Nidas directly in front of him. Then all heads turned as a fourth member of the Cult, the one who had meant to be guarding the Pen, rushed into the gym, looking panic-stricken. Realising that it had been retrieved, a look of relief broke on his face. Nidas fixed him with a glare as he placed the Pen into the breast pocket of his shirt. Tommy's heart sank. The Pen was now in a place where nobody in their right mind would even attempt to remove it. And with every second that passed by, any hope of saving Grandpa slipped further and further away.

'Of course,' Nidas said with an air of arrogance, 'the old man *would* have told you about us, the true keepers of the Pen of Destiny.'

'You're nothing but MURDERERS!' Tommy shot back before Nidas could continue. The thought of Grandpa in that hospital bed had caused anger to rise within him, his words spewed out of him like an erupting volcano.

'You killed my grandpa!'

Nidas considered him for a moment.

'Your grandfather was just one of the many sacrifices to our cause. He was forced to learn the hard way what it is to cross us, as did the Guardian before him. As you will too. You should have known better than to involve yourself in our business. All Guardians meet with an unfortunate end. Especially you, the so-called *Chosen One*.'

Chosen One? He'd only had the Pen five minutes. Why did they think he was so special?

'Since time began,' Nidas continued, 'we have sought out the Pen in order to return it to its creator. And, of course, to use it to release *The Creperum*.'

At the mention of that last word, Tommy saw a hint of madness in the man's eyes. A word that he'd never heard before today, but if Nidas enjoyed the thought of it, then he knew that it couldn't be good. Nidas tapped his breast pocket and took a step forward. Tommy backed away until he could go no further, his back pressing against the gym equipment. The Grand Master then unbuttoned the cuff of his right arm and rolled up the sleeve of his shirt, showing his exposed arm to Tommy. On his thick forearm was a tattoo of a quill. Tommy studied it. Mr Wiseman had told him about this. That all members of *Secuutus Pluma* were branded with the mark of a quill – the symbol of the Pen of Destiny.

'You may have been told of this,' he said, showing him the tattoo. '*This* mark however,' he continued, fingering the ugly scar on his cheek, 'was given to me by a friend of your grandfather. One of our own who let his conscience get the better of him. Needless to say, it was the last mark he made in this lifetime.'

Nidas continued to stroke the shiny scar tissue, his eyes drifting into a distant memory. A memory that Tommy didn't ever want to enter.

'The old man always chose worthy Guardians. It surprises me that he has chosen so poorly this time. You are young – the youngest of all. A very weak choice. He is wrong about you, I think. It is time to bring an end to the era of the Guardian for good. Now is the time of *Secuutus Pluma*.'

'You'd really kill a kid?' Tommy asked him.

Nidas laughed loudly, his booming tones shaking the very floor of the gym.

'You think that we wouldn't hurt children? Let me assure you, we do what is necessary. It certainly won't be the first time we've had to eliminate troublesome children. Only a few short decades ago, we had to take care of some juveniles in this very building. Two foolish brothers who'd involved themselves in things that didn't concern them – much as you are now. It is a happy coincidence that since their passing rumours of their ghosts have kept other curious children away from this place.'

So there it was. An actual admission from Nidas that the Cult had killed the Hinton brothers. Tommy felt sorry for those boys. In his current predicament he could well imagine how frightened they were before they were killed. And with no sign of help coming, it looked as though he was going to share their fate.

His eyes flitted around the gym, desperately searching for a way out, but every exit was blocked. Then he caught sight of something near the doors, a new figure entering the gym. But it wasn't another of the Cult – it was Ben! Tommy had conflicting emotions. He was happy that Ben had evaded capture, and was now here to help him, but also frustrated that he hadn't escaped and raised the alarm.

Maybe Jennifer had managed to get away. Perhaps if he kept them distracted for long enough, then Ben would be able to make a run for the window anyway. Clearing his throat and putting as much steel into his voice as possible, he stepped towards Nidas.

'So that's how you get your kicks is it, you over-sized bully? Hurting children and defenceless old men? You wouldn't be so tough if all my mates were here!'

He could see Ben in the background, creeping his way quietly towards the window. A few more yards and he'd be home free. *Yes, Ben! Go. Go and get help!* And do you know, that's probably what any sensible person would have done. Ben, however, had other ideas. Instead of crossing all the way over to the window, he approached one of the lengths of rope which hung from the ceiling, took it in his grasp and started to climb the nearest set of wall bars, holding the end of the rope in his mouth like a seaman ascending the rigging of a ship. Couldn't he ever do things the easy way?

'I'm glad that you mentioned your friends,' Nidas said, drawing Tommy's gaze back to him. 'There are three sets of children's footprints here today. Where are the others?'

'I don't know what you're on about,' Tommy lied, fearing that Ben would show himself soon enough anyway. 'I came here alone. My mates went to get the cops, and they'll be here any minute.'

From the corner of his eye, Tommy could see Nidas' mouth move. He knew that he was talking to him, but he could no longer hear him; his attention now belonged to Ben, who had reached the top of the wall bars and was now standing at his full height, holding the rope in both hands like a pirate atop his mast. Tommy willed him not to give away his position; there was still time to run and get help, but that just wouldn't have been Ben.

'OI! YOU LOT!' Ben shouted, the top of his head almost touching the ceiling. Each of the Cult spun around in shock – not at the fact there was another intruder in their midst but that he'd been stupid enough to show himself so easily.

'LET HIM GO! AND GIVE US BACK THE PEN!'

Silence followed the demand. For a second or two everyone, including Tommy, stood wordlessly staring up at him, scarcely able to believe what he was doing. Nidas himself even faltered for a moment, thrown by Ben's bare-faced audacity. He quickly collected himself, however, and responded in an equally booming and amused voice.

'And should we refuse?'

'Well, then you'll see that they don't call me Ben 'Tarzan' Campbell for nothing!' came the equally confident reply.

Barbarus, his mouth agape, stood side by side with Tommy, his normally brutish features fixed into a look of confused astonishment. Tommy could only shrug his shoulders and add matter-of-factly. 'His middle name's Ian.'

Having made the announcement, Ben, still gripping the rope, leapt off the wall bars and yelled as he swung through the air in a large arc towards them. He travelled right in between the group of men and then released his grip on the rope, landing like a cat at Tommy's side.

'Alright?' Ben said, looking at him excitedly, the

adrenalin evident in his every movement.

'Yeah.'

'Good.'

Tommy waited for Ben to do something. The Cult too, having been caught off guard, also stood in disbelief.

'Well?' Tommy asked after a long pause.

'Well what?'

'Well what's the plan?' he whispered urgently through gritted teeth, looking from Ben to Nidas, who now looked on with amused interest.

'Uh... I thought you might have one...' Ben replied sheepishly, his excitement quickly fading. Styx chuckled huskily. Barbarus, who had temporarily allowed himself to be distracted, was now fully alert and ready to pounce when given the order. The unreadable eyes of Nidas remained fixed on Tommy, the outline of the Pen visible in his shirt pocket. There was no way they'd be able to get it back now, not from him.

Luckily for them, someone did have a plan. Jennifer emerged from the shadows and shouted, 'RUN!'

For a second the Cult sentries were caught off guard, moving far too slowly to stop them from making a run for the doors of the gym. The men grasped at air as the boys dodged between them and ran for the double doors, and back out into the main hallway, straight past Jennifer who quickly turned and followed them. Although terrified at the situation, she kept her head, and shouted, 'Quick! This way!' She grabbed Ben by the arm and dragged him onwards, driven on by the heavy footfall of the men as they bounded across the wooden floor of the gym after them. With the only sure route of escape behind them, they ran as fast as they could along the corridor, frantically searching for another way out. As their pursuers emerged from the gym, Tommy followed Jennifer and Ben down the steps into the basement. He tried to tell them that Jennifer was leading them into a dead end, but he couldn't find the breath. As they entered the room with the locker, they could hear the sound of their pursuer's footsteps on the stone staircase behind them – they'd be on them in seconds. Then an image flashed into Tommy's head. That hole in the boiler room wall – the passageway! It must lead somewhere! He barged past Ben and Jennifer, pulling them into the boiler room and pushing them towards the hole in the wall.

'Quick! Through there!'

He slammed the door shut and dragged a chair in front of it, jamming it under the handle. The second or so that it took him to do that proved costly. As soon as he'd turned to follow them, both the door and the chair followed him across the room; the large, black boot of Barbarus appearing where the door had just been. Jennifer screamed and ran into the tunnel, but Tommy and Ben both froze, in awe at the brute strength of the man. Barbarus filled the entire frame with his bulk, his massive chest rising and falling calmly, his lungs heaving to replace the oxygen lost in the chase.

Moving to one side, he allowed Styx to enter. His far scrawnier chest wheezed rapidly, sounding like the pea in a referee's whistle. His face was blushed and ruddy, the picture of a man who had let his vices, and some school kids, get the better of him.

Tommy glanced anxiously at the passageway, weighing up whether they could get there before being grabbed. Then a few things happened at once, all very quick and shocking. Styx leapt forward to grab Ben. Tommy reached out for Ben's arm, pulling him away and towards the light of the tunnel. But the most astonishing thing of all, causing both him and Ben to do a double-take as they ran, was the sight of the heavy lamp-lit desk sliding miraculously across the room and in front of the oncoming Styx, blocking his path and causing him to crash into it. Tommy and Ben wasted no time in pressing their advantage, darting into the tunnel after Jennifer.

Neither could resist glancing back to see what had assisted them in their escape, but they weren't prepared for what they saw. Suspended in mid-air, near where the desk had been, were two small figures, both giggling hysterically at the sight of Styx struggling to collect himself. The figures had a dull, grey complexion, almost transparent in appearance. But it wasn't only their appearance that was shocking. They were actually *floating* in the air! As Tommy stared from the tunnel's mouth, the smaller of the two figures looked directly at him, flashed him a broad, goofy smile and let out a shrill laugh as he returned his attention to the dumbfounded men of the Cult, joining his brother in hurling various objects at them. Ben watched on in amazement, and it required a firm yank on his arm before finally joining Tommy in running down the dark tunnel. It was immediately obvious to them both that they had just met the Hinton Brothers.

Nidas arrived just in time to see a heavy book bounce painfully off the top of Styx's head. What Nidas didn't see was who had thrown it – whoever it was had disappeared. Styx let out an angry growl and swiped at the air, hitting nothing. Barbarus and Malus also seemed to be doing battle with an invisible enemy.

'You've allowed them to escape?' Nidas asked calmly, his disapproval evident.

'But boss, look!' Styx shouted, pointing at the ceiling, his anger soon replaced by confusion.

Nidas surveyed the room with his cold eyes. There was nothing to see. The Hintons had vanished as quickly as they'd appeared. He looked into the dimly lit passage.

'No matter. Even if the tunnel doesn't finish them off, we can end this young Guardian before he even begins.'

— CHAPTER TWENTY —

The Tunnel

They caught up with Jennifer fifty metres along the tunnel. She was cowering and slumped against the wall, cursing Ben for involving her in all of this. As he approached, she jumped up at him and unleashed a flurry of well-placed slaps before she finally relented, burying her face into his chest and sobbing uncontrollably. Tommy watched with a great deal of relief, glad that he didn't have a girlfriend; they looked like hard work.

He was surprised at how deep the tunnel ran. It would have been awful if it had only been a few metres deep, leaving them trapped for the Cult, but happily they found themselves running along what turned out to be a very long, dank tunnel, with the sound of water continuously dripping from its stone ceiling. It narrowed as they progressed and became so tight that they could only move in single file. Ben had taken the lead and was setting a rather quick pace. Tommy, bringing up the rear, concluded that the passage had been excavated long after the school had been built. They ran in near darkness; only thrown into light periodically by wall-mounted torches, the flames of which licked greedily at them as they passed.

They ran for an age and, with every metre that they

covered, Tommy noticed a slight decline taking them deeper and deeper underground. Such was the subtlety of the gradient that he doubted he'd have noticed it had it not been for the water dripping from the ceiling which formed into a small stream that ran steadily at his feet. He encouraged Ben to force the pace despite the fact that he and Jennifer were already struggling to keep up with him.

'What did I tell you?!' Ben shouted excitedly over his shoulder. 'I *told* you they were real! I *told* you they were hanging around for revenge! But did you two believe me? Nope. I'm telling you, if there's one thing I know about, it's ghosts!'

'Keep moving!' Tommy urged as he slowed slightly. 'They might be following!'

Jennifer hadn't said a word since her attack on Ben earlier.

'You OK, Jen?' Tommy asked.

She didn't respond.

He'd never seen anyone in shock before, but the way that she was behaving made him think that this was his first. Poor thing, she'd only popped out to practice her dance moves.

They continued further along the tunnel, Tommy repeating to himself everything that he'd overheard back in the school. It was bound to be important somehow. He had to remember it so that he could tell Mr Wiseman later. *The Church in the forgetful town on the fourth night of the landings. Church. Forgetful town. Fourth night. Landings. Creperum. Creperum. Creperum.* But what did it all mean? And that part about him being more important than he knew, that couldn't be true – he'd lost the Pen twice already.

As he wrestled with yet another cobweb, Ben turned to face them, jogging backwards. Just as he was about to say something, he tripped and fell on a thin, almost invisible wire that had been stretched across their path at ankle level. It was a fall that may well have saved his life. No sooner had he landed on his backside, than a heavy block of wood whooshed out of the darkness above, missing his head by inches. Protruding out of the wood were dozens of sharp nails, and had Ben not fallen so quickly, then the deadly item would have embedded itself into his face. Thank heaven he was so clumsy! Jennifer emitted a scream that echoed all the way back to the school.

'Woah!' Tommy yelled, skidding to a halt. 'What was that?!'

Ben stared up at the offensive piece of wood, realising just how close he'd come to certain death.

'Where did that come from?' he asked, shaking and pulling himself up off the floor.

'Up there,' Tommy said, pointing into the darkness. 'And look here,' he said, kneeling to examine the wire on the floor. He followed it with his fingers as it ran up the wall and towards the ceiling. 'It was a trip cord!' Ben examined the wire himself before approaching the wood and touching one of the razor-sharp nails.

'Ouch!' he said, sucking a trickle of blood from his forefinger. 'Now *that's* a booby trap! These blokes mean business, don't they?'

The tunnel was getting more dangerous with every step, and still they didn't know where it would lead them. Tommy checked behind them, sure that he'd heard something in the shadows. An eerie feeling crept over him, making his skin crawl, almost as if the very darkness that surrounded him was coming to life.

'C'mon, let's go,' he said urgently, squeezing past them to take the lead.

He led them for a while longer, carefully tempering urgency with caution, wary of any other traps that the Cult may have set for them.

'I bet it wasn't a patch on yours mate,' he said to Ben after a while.

'What?'

'The booby trap. I bet it wasn't as good as yours.'

'I know,' Ben replied seriously. 'Mine was good wasn't it, Jen?'

Still nothing.

Tommy upped the pace a little. They must have gone on for at least another half mile, continuing their gradual descent, before their surroundings began to change. The narrow tunnel began to widen, and a brighter glimmer of light appeared before them, more potent than the torches that had previously led their way. Tommy couldn't imagine where the light could be coming from – it was dark outside now. And that wasn't the only thing that bothered him. Between the scuffed sounds of their footfall, Tommy was positive that he could hear the thunder of heavy rain up ahead. But he knew that couldn't be true; how could it be raining underground?

The mystery of the subterranean rainstorm was solved a few metres further, when the tunnel gave way to something that none of them expected to see under Little Millbrook: a magnificent forty-foot high waterfall inside a huge cave with stalactites hanging from its roof like overgrown icicles. The chamber was illuminated by hundreds of torches, and a labyrinth of other tunnels disappeared off it in various directions. Water cascaded over the topmost rocks and came crashing down into the pool below, creating a billowing cloud of mist that sprayed the surrounding area. Tommy could feel the speckles of water cool his face, clear proof that the scene before him was not a mirage. It was amazing that this thing actually existed beneath the town where they'd all grown up.

'Wow...'

'What the...?!' Ben proclaimed, equally as astounded. 'Where *are* we?'

'I haven't a clue. We've gotta be somewhere under the town, though, we can't have gone more than a mile or so.'

Tommy marvelled at its beauty, wondering how many people were aware of its existence. Clearly, the Cult had found it whilst digging their tunnel, but Tommy doubted whether many other people knew of it; that sort of thing would be hard to keep secret. 'We've gotta find a way out,' he said, scanning the cave for an exit. There must have been a dozen dark archways scattered about the cave, presumably leading off to further tunnels, and for all they knew, each one could lead to a dead end. But then Tommy saw something high up in the cave, just to the side of the waterfall. An archway, larger than most of the others, with a bright torch flickering in its mouth. Of all possible avenues, this one seemed the most likely to lead them to the surface.

'Look, up there!' Tommy pointed. 'That's gotta be the way out.'

Ben followed Tommy's finger to the well-lit archway, and even Jennifer, who was near-catatonic, seemed to return to them briefly, no doubt buoyed by the mention of an exit.

'How we gonna get up there?' Ben asked.

Tommy had to admit that it looked an impossible feat. It would be suicide for them to climb up the rocks against the force of the waterfall, they'd be sure to slip and fall into the churning water below. As they moved through the spray and closer to the waterfall they found that good fortune smiled on them yet again. Alongside the waterfall, ascending towards the ceiling and leading directly to the exit, was what looked like a stone staircase. Whether natural or man-made, Tommy couldn't tell; he was just relieved that it was there at all.

'C'mon, quickly,' he said, leading them across the cave and towards the steps. 'I think they're coming. I heard something in the tunnel. Let's move!'

They raced together through the watery mist and towards the stone steps. They climbed slowly, careful not to lose their footing on the moss which had made the steps treacherously slick. Leaning on each other for support, they finally reached the top, exhausted, their legs numb from the climb. At the entrance to the new passageway, Tommy paused to catch his breath and looked back over the cave one last time. Through the billowing spray he could just make out the shape of a figure entering the cave from the tunnel to the school. It was Barbarus. Their eyes met for a brief moment before Tommy rushed after Ben and Jennifer. He promised himself that the next time he saw Barbarus, he wouldn't run.

'They managed to avoid the trip wires, boss,' Styx said, breathing heavily. 'One nearly got 'em though.'

Nidas had taken up his seat behind the desk in the boiler room. He refused to look at Styx, choosing instead to study the Pen as he rolled it playfully between his large fingers.

'Boss? I said the lucky b–'

'I heard you,' Nidas interrupted, finally looking at him. 'Call Barbarus back. There's no need for us to chase them now. They are no longer a threat.'

Styx looked confused.

'But we can catch them.'

'Call him back. Now we have this,' he said, indicating to the Pen in his pocket, 'it is only a matter of time before I dispose of the Guardians for good.'

Nidas continued to stare at the Pen, a twisted smile on his face.

'I need you all here whilst I run a little... errand.'

The new passage had led them to yet another set of steps, and as they climbed Tommy had an overwhelming feeling of familiarity. The higher they went, the more he began to recognise his surroundings. They went through an archway and entered a far larger room. It was ancient, but this time there was no doubt that it was man-made. Only then did it dawn on him where they were.

'Ben, we're in the fort!'

'Huh?'

'The fort! Look!'

Ben took a moment to take it all in, studying its high ceilings and ancient stonework.

'Remember, Ben? Over there,' Tommy said, pointing to a raised stone platform. 'That's where you fell and hurt your knee!'

Or had he? Tommy wasn't so sure any more. Ever since he'd used the Pen to change Ben's accident, he'd begun to doubt whether *any* of his memories had actually happened at all.

'You're right, that really hurt!' Ben said finally, to Tommy's relief. 'We're only in the bloody fort!' he added, happy that they'd ended up in a place that they both knew. 'See, Jen? We're almost home!'

Jennifer barely acknowledged him. She was as white as a sheet and looked about herself furtively, apparently expecting an ambush at any moment. Tommy could scarcely believe it. They were now in the fort, which meant that they'd travelled through the underground tunnel all the way from the Central School and over to the coast. It was crazy: a tunnel actually existed between the two most haunted places in Little Millbrook.

'Come on,' he said. 'This means we're only a few

minutes from Grandp... I mean from Mr Wiseman's. We gotta hurry.'

Tommy had to push Grandpa to the back of his mind. The thought of him not being around anymore was too much to bear, and right now he had to focus. He needed Mr Wiseman. Only he could give him all of the answers that he needed. He'd explain everything. Then he could concentrate on saving Grandpa.

Eager to push on, Tommy rushed through the fort's entrance and into the woods. The violent storm was still battering the town and Harbour View was about ten minutes away. Tommy intended to do it in five.

He soon had cause to stop dead in his tracks. In front of them, standing in the rain and wearing a funny looking overcoat, was none other than Grandpa's curious neighbour.

'Mr Wiseman! What are you doing here?!'

They really had to stop meeting like this. Yet just his presence was somehow reassuring. After the peril of the tunnel and their brush with the Cult, the mere sight of this magical little man reinvigorated him, instilling him with a sense of renewed hope that all was not lost. That there was still a chance to save Grandpa.

Tommy rushed to him, his words tripping over themselves as they hurriedly competed to leave his mouth.

'We're coming to find you... Cult... they... and now... well... it's Grandpa!'

Mr Wiseman raised his palm, smiling softly. His large owl-like eyes seemed to exude warmth despite the ferocious weather.

'Slowly, Master Parker. Take your time. What is the matter?'

'It's Grandpa! He's dead!' Tommy blurted out. There. He'd said it. Hearing it aloud seemed to highlight the reality of what had happened. He had the same sickening feeling he'd had when he'd first heard the news, and for the first time today he was grateful for the rain; it hid his tears.

'It was them,' he continued, 'the Cult. They attacked him and now they've got the Pen. We've gotta get it back. We've gotta change it all!'

Mr Wiseman's expression didn't change a bit. In fact, Tommy had the unsettling feeling that, somehow, he already knew.

'Be calm now, Master Parker,' he said simply, before turning his attention to the other two. 'Master Campbell, I presume? How do you do? And who is this?' he enquired, looking at the mute Jennifer. 'I see that you've collected someone new along the way.'

'I'm... uh...' she couldn't finish her sentence.

Ben couldn't do much better. After doing nothing but stare stupidly at the old man since he'd appeared, he could do no more than nod vacantly. This was the first time Ben had officially met Mr Wiseman, and evidently it had the rather unusual effect of rendering him speechless.

'Well, nice to meet you both,' he continued. 'I see that you two have already proved yourself invaluable to our young Guardian here, and for that I am grateful. Come, walk with me.'

'Walk? We haven't got any time!' Tommy shouted,

angered at how trivial Mr Wiseman seemed to find his news. Grandpa was dead! Hadn't he heard him?

'All in good time, young man.'

The calm reply only served to infuriate Tommy further.

'*Time?!* We haven't got time!' Tommy shouted. 'They've got the Pen! And they could be destroying my family right now for all we know!'

'And where do you propose we start, Master Parker?'

Tommy stared at him, breathing heavily. His mind had gone blank. He didn't have a clue. His only aim was to get to Mr Wiseman and hope he'd be able to tell him exactly what to do. Now that he'd found him, he had no idea what to do next.

'I always find,' Mr Wiseman continued after a polite pause, 'that in times of crisis it is best to calm oneself and think logically. Only then can a problem be overcome.'

With that advice Mr Wiseman whipped around and walked briskly along the pavement towards Harbour View, his coat flicking rainwater at Tommy. At least they were going in the right direction. Maybe he'd take them to his house, where he'd have a plan ready and waiting, perhaps even some other people there to help them or an arsenal of weapons they could use against the Cult.

'Now, tell me *all* that has happened since we last met,' Mr Wiseman commanded.

Tommy told him everything: the Cult's attack on Grandpa, the confrontation with Barbarus and Styx outside the hospital, and their unpleasant meeting with Nidas in the Central School. Ben bounced around at Tommy's side as he spoke, nodding furiously and grunting at all of the scary parts. Tommy relayed every little detail he could think of, right up to their journey through the secret tunnels before they'd met him.

'And Nidas,' Tommy said, nearing the end of his story. 'He said that now they have the Pen they'd be able to destroy the Guardians once and for all! Especially me. He reckons *I'm* the important one! He's really got it in for me for some reason.'

Throughout the narrative Mr Wiseman had walked along briskly, but upon hearing this last part his stride faltered. It was barely noticeable, but Tommy definitely saw it.

'And they said something about the *'Creepers'* or something like that? Some word I didn't know anyway.'

'Yeah, it was Creepers,' Ben confirmed.

'*The Creperum?*' Mr Wiseman asked, definite concern in his voice now.

'Yeah, that's it,' Tommy said.

'Yeah, *Creperum*, that's what I meant,' Ben added.

'What does it mean?' Tommy asked.

Mr Wiseman flashed Tommy a look that worried him. There was fear in the old man's eyes. The moment passed quickly, though, Mr Wiseman collecting himself and ignoring Tommy's question completely.

'Was there anything else?' he asked. 'About how your grandfather came into possession of the Pen perhaps?'

Of course! How had he forgotten that part? About the church and how the Cult had discovered the exact time when Grandpa had first received it.

'Yes! Yes, they did say something about that!' Tommy almost yelled. 'Remember, Ben? In the basement, when we were listening to them talking. What was it he said? Something about the exchange taking place in a church? They *must* have been talking about when Grandpa was given it.'

Turning to Ben, he was met with nothing but a blank expression.

'Can you remember what they said?'

'Umm... I wasn't really listening, mate. Sorry,' he replied sheepishly.

'Oh, what *was* it?' Tommy said, thinking out loud, angry with himself that he'd forgotten. 'One of the men said something about an exchange; that *had* to mean the Pen. And he said that it happened after the landings, whatever that means.'

'It was the *fourth* night after,' a fragile voice said.

They all turned to look at Jennifer.

'He said it was the fourth night after the landings,' she repeated.

'Yes! Yes, that's it! Well done, Jen!' Tommy declared, delighted that she'd been clever enough to remember.

Ben placed a proud arm around her, which she very quickly shrugged away.

'It was the fourth night after the landings!' Tommy continued. 'That's what he said. And something about a forgetful town, too. He said that the exchange took place on the fourth night after the landings, at the church of the forgetful town. That's definitely it! And Grandpa told me that a German man had given it to him in a church during the War, so it all kinda ties in,' he concluded, pleased that they'd been able to remember it all.

Mr Wiseman nodded thoughtfully, smoothing his chin with his hand, but still he didn't respond. It was too much for Tommy to take. Every second that slipped by was taking him further and further away from Grandpa.

'So what are we gonna do?' he demanded. 'Can we stop the Cult or what? We just need to get the Pen back and change what happened to Grandpa, right?'

Mr Wiseman considered his question for a moment, looking a little uncomfortable.

'Master Parker, your young lady friend here...'

'Uh, she's *my* lady friend actually,' Ben interjected.

'Yes, quite. Well this young lady has been through quite enough for one day. Why don't we let her get on her way? There's no need for us to trouble her again tonight.'

Tommy got the hint immediately. Mr Wiseman clearly didn't want to discuss matters concerning the Pen in front of her. Too many people knew about it already.

'Yeah, Jen, you've been great, but you'd better get home. Your parents will be going nuts.'

'What do you think, Jen?' Ben asked her, desperately wanting to be part of the discussion. 'Do you want to go home? I can walk you if you like?'

She gave him a frosty stare, which thawed when she turned to Tommy and Mr Wiseman.

'Well, my parents will be worried.' she said. 'It's getting

pretty late.'

She turned to Ben again and said sharply, 'but I'm quite capable of walking home on my own, thank you very much. You've done quite enough for one day.'

Tommy hadn't failed to notice that she'd stopped calling him 'Benny'. There was definitely trouble in paradise.

'What do you want to do about those men, Tommy?' she asked. 'Shall I get my parents to phone the police? If they've harmed your grandad, then we really should get some help.'

Tommy looked to Mr Wiseman.

'You just leave that to us,' the old man answered. 'Enough innocents have suffered at their hands already. There's no need to add to that number.'

Unsure but too tired to argue, Jennifer walked off into the night. Ben followed her in an attempt to smooth things over, but after a few moments of hushed argument that ended in him being slapped in the face, he returned rather sheepishly to where Tommy and Mr Wiseman stood.

'Everything OK, mate?' Tommy asked.

'Yeah,' he replied, rubbing his cheek. 'She just wanted some time to herself. She'll be fine though. I'll call her in the morning.'

They then followed as Mr Wiseman set off down the street.

'So what do we do now?' Tommy asked him. 'If we can get the Pen off them, can we use it to save Grandpa or not?'

'I fear that it's not quite that simple. The fact that *Secuutus Pluma* has acquired the Pen of Destiny means only one thing: that they intend to use it to visit the exact point in time where the previous Guardian passed it to your grandfather. There, they will look to eliminate them both. Should they succeed, then I fear that they will have won – the chain will be broken, and the Guardians will be no more.'

'But there is more than that,' he continued. 'There is something else that you have told me tonight that is very worrying. Very worrying indeed. But I need to check on something first.'

'So how do we do it then?' Tommy asked eagerly. 'How do we get the Pen back?'

'I suspect they'll want to put their plan into action as quickly as possible,' Mr Wiseman answered. 'And there is only one sure place that they will be.'

'Where?'

'This 'forgetful town' they spoke of. You must go there and stop them. Only there will you find success.'

'OK, so where is this place? Let's go!'

Mr Wiseman stopped again and looked at Tommy seriously.

'I'm not sure that you fully understand. The question isn't just *where* it is, Master Parker, but also *when* it is.'

Of course, Tommy thought, the exchange would have taken place during the War, when Grandpa was in the army. He felt stupid that he hadn't thought about that before.

'Well, that's it then,' he said in defeat. 'How can we possibly stop them if we can't even get there? We'd need to have the Pen before we could even think about going back.'

'You leave that part to me,' Mr Wiseman interrupted,

quickening his pace. 'You just concentrate on finding out the exact details of the location.'

Leave that part to him?

'What do you mean I've gotta find out where the location is? I haven't got a clue. I thought you'd know!'

'With that I cannot help you. But remember this – you are not alone. You may not have the Pen, but you still have your friends.'

'Great! So you're telling me I've gotta rely on Ben to figure it out? We've had it! No offence, Ben.'

'None taken.'

With the distraction of the conversation, Tommy hadn't even noticed that they were almost at Harbour View.

'I cannot assist you with the specifics,' Mr Wiseman said. 'It is the Guardian's responsibility to protect the Pen. I *am*, however, able to tell you that all of the answers that you seek you will find here.'

He waved his arm out in front of him as they rounded the corner into the street where Tommy had enjoyed some of his favourite moments. Just the sight of the place made him feel a little safer, and even the storm seemed to have abated slightly. But there was one thing missing – Grandpa. It didn't feel the same without him.

'So the answers *are* at your place?' Tommy asked.

'No.'

'At Grandpa's then?'

Perhaps he'd kept the location of that church written down somewhere? he thought.

But once again the old man merely shook his head and

250

smiled.

'No. The answer is there,' he said, indicating to a house in between Grandpa's and his own. 'There is another friend who can help you now – Arthur.'

'*Who?*' Ben asked.

'Art,' Tommy answered impatiently.

'Indeed,' Mr Wiseman continued. 'Master Campbell has already proved most valuable to your cause. It is now time for another of your friends to prove himself.'

They stood in silence under a street light and looked over to Art's house, the silence finally being broken by the noise of a faraway car and then a badly suppressed giggle.

'What is it now?' Tommy asked.

'His name's Arthur!' Ben chortled as they both took a step towards the house of their friend. A friend whose world they were about to turn upside down forever.

CHAPTER TWENTY-ONE

Convincing Arthur

Art closed his bedroom curtains in an attempt to shut himself off from the rain driving against his window. He'd never seen such a storm and would be happy if he never got to see one like it again. He hadn't always been afraid of them, but ever since he'd seen a documentary about thunderstorms they scared him half to death. Especially the thunder. Yep, he was a brontophobe for sure. He'd looked that word up as soon as he realised that he was afraid of storms, finding it somewhat ironic that his phobia sounded just like one of his favourite dinosaurs.

Another reason for him disliking this particular rainstorm was that it had had the effect of distracting him from his homework all night. He'd struggled to take his eyes off it, spending half the evening at his window looking out into the dark skies, trying to guess where the next bolt of lightning would come from. He counted the gaps between each flash of light and the rumble that followed, positive that the storm was getting closer to its final destination – his house. The aggressive storm wasn't the only strange phenomenon that night either. Earlier, Art had witnessed none other than Mr Wiseman going out into it. What a strange man. Hardly ever going out at all and then choosing to venture out in weather like this!

Finally, though, there seemed to be a break in the storm. The lightning had stopped, and even the rain had eased a little, the heavy beating of it against his window being replaced by the continuous dripping of water from the overflowing roof guttering. Distracted, Art found that he was no longer in the mood for homework, so instead he wasted a bit more time changing into his favourite pair of pyjamas and pulling on his dressing gown before finally sitting back down at his desk. The history essay he'd started hours ago lay unfinished before him, a textbook open beside it. He reviewed what he'd written before glancing at his alarm clock – almost 9:30pm. His mum would be up soon with a hot chocolate; maybe that would help him concentrate. He hoped that she'd put an extra couple of marshmallows in because of the storm. He'd like that.

Art whiled away a few more minutes, studying the star chart on his wall, but then felt a pang of guilt as he looked at the poster next to it. It was a poster of Albert Einstein, one of his heroes, whose large and knowledgeable eyes now stared right back at him and his unfinished essay.

'C'mon,' Art said defensively, 'even *you* needed a break sometime.'

Defiantly pulling open the top drawer of his desk, he rifled around in it for a moment before producing a comic book. He sat back in his chair and was just about to turn his back on the world of scholars and enter the marvellous world of fictional superheroes when he was disturbed by a loud knock at the front door.

They had waited until Mr Wiseman had walked down his path, disappearing from view, before knocking on Art's door.

'So what exactly did you think Art was short for?' Tommy asked as they waited for a response.

'Dunno really, just thought it was the only cool thing about him. I didn't know it was short for Arthur.'

They were interrupted by the slow opening of the front door and the face of a concerned looking woman peering out from around its side.

'Hi, Mrs Ford,' Tommy said brightly, hoping he'd be able to charm his way in. 'Sorry to call so late. Is Art there?'

'Hello, Tommy,' she replied sternly, opening the door fully. 'It's awfully late, boys. He's doing his homework. I'd rather you didn't disturb him tonight.'

So much for the charm offensive.

'You must be Benjamin?' she added, looking over Tommy's shoulder at Ben, who up until now had been busy studying his shoelaces. Tommy said a silent prayer. *Please be polite, Ben.* He'd been hoping to do all of the talking himself. The last thing they needed now was for Ben to come out with some smart remark and annoy her even more.

'Uh, Ben, yeah,' he said, looking up from his shoes. 'Pleased to meet you, Mrs Ford. Art's told me so much about you,' he added smoothly, stepping in front of Tommy and thrusting his arm out to shake her hand. *Thank God for that.* Tommy's prayers had been answered.

Now just leave it there, Ben, and I'll take over, he thought.

'Mrs...' Tommy began.

'I hope you don't mind me saying,' Ben continued,

talking over him, 'but you don't look anywhere near old enough to have a son our age.'

Uh oh, he's gone too far. Way too far. But he hadn't. To Tommy's surprise, any sign of Mrs Ford's frustration instantly disappeared, her mouth broadening into a wide smile.

'Oh, Ben, what *are* you like?' she said, clearly flattered, fluffing her hair up at the back with her hand.

Tommy couldn't believe what he was witnessing. *Was Ben really flirting with Art's mum?* Eeewwww!

'We really won't be long, Mrs Ford, I promise,' Ben continued, pressing home the advantage. 'We just need to ask him something about our history project.'

'Well,' she said, pretending to think about it, 'I suppose it won't do any harm. Just so long as you're quick.'

She stepped to one side and beckoned them in, smiling like a school girl when Ben threw her a cheeky wink. Tommy led them to the staircase.

'By the way, Tommy, how's your grandfather?' she asked. 'Miss Tunley said that she saw an ambulance over there earlier. I hope everything's alright?'

Tommy's stomach lurched at the mention of Grandpa. Fighting to keep his emotions at bay, he called back from halfway up the stairs.

'Everything's fine, Mrs Ford. He just had a bit of a fall, that's all. He'll be back to normal in no time.'

And if everything went according to plan, he would be.

'Well, you be sure to give him my best wishes. Tell him that I'll pop over with some scones when he's feeling a little better.'

'Sure thing, Mrs Ford, thanks.'

But Tommy was hoping that the Ford family could offer him far more assistance than just a few scones. With Art's help he hoped to acquire the information key to getting the Pen back *and* saving Grandpa.

No sooner had he and Ben stopped at Art's bedroom door than it swung open and they were met by their friend who looked even more surprised and confused than his mum had.

'What are you two doing here?' he asked, 'and where have you been? You're soaked.'

In contrast, Art looked extremely warm and dry, modelling a very fine pair of dinosaur pyjamas that were hidden behind his fluffy, blue dressing gown.

'What's up with him?' Art said, pointing at Ben who was trying desperately not to laugh.

'What is it?' Art demanded.

'Your name's Arthur!' Ben exploded, unable to control himself any longer.

'Oh grow up, will you!' Tommy scolded, eager to quiz Art for the information they needed. 'Come on, Art, ignore him. Are you gonna let us in, or does he have to flirt with you too?'

'Huh?'

'Oh, never mind,' Tommy said, deciding that disclosing that particular piece of information would only make matters worse. He pushed Ben into the bedroom and closed the door behind them. Ben couldn't resist a further comment as he entered, 'Nice Pjs, mate.'

Once inside, dripping rainwater all over the carpet, Tommy spent a few seconds looking around the room, trying to find the right words. The room was the complete opposite of his own – being as it was, extremely tidy. He decided that the direct approach was best.

'Art, we need your help.'

'Can't it wait? Have you seen the time?'

'No, it can't, it's urgent. It's about my grandpa.'

'Is he alright? Mum said...'

'I'll explain everything later,' Tommy interrupted, 'but right now we really need your help.'

'OK, but you'll never guess who I saw out in the rain earlier.'

'Mr Wiseman? Yeah, we know. We've just been with him.'

That certainly got Art's attention.

'What?!'

'Like I said, I'll tell you later. Grandpa's in trouble, serious trouble, and Mr Wiseman thinks you can help.'

Tommy stared at Art for a long moment, hoping that his friend would see in his eyes just how serious their predicament was.

'OK,' he said finally. 'What do you need me to do?'

Tommy had already decided against telling Art *everything* – the less he knew the better. For one, there was no way he'd believe them. He was too sensible to believe in the Pen and its magical powers without proof; he'd just think that they were winding him up. But more importantly, he wanted Art to stay out of harm's way. The less he knew about the Pen, about Nidas and about *Secuutus Pluma* the better.

'We just need you to solve a riddle,' Tommy said. 'We think it's about the war, but we're not sure.'

'Go on,' Art said, intrigued, surprised that they were bringing up such a topic themselves. The breadth of their conversation was normally limited to football and comic books.

Tommy composed himself before he spoke again, rehearsing the line in his head to make sure he got it right.

'OK, it's this: *On the fourth night of the landings, at the church of the forgetful town.*'

There was a pause.

'What?' Art asked. 'That's it?'

'Yeah,' Tommy replied, disappointed. He'd half expected Art to have an instant revelation as to its meaning. 'Does it mean anything to you? Anything at all?'

'OK, OK,' Art said, picking up the challenge and gesturing for silence. 'Lemme think for a minute.'

He walked over to his bookshelf, selected a hardback book from one of the shelves and sat down at his desk. 'Right. You think it's got something to do with the war, do you? Well that would make sense. The only landings I know of are the...' Art mumbled as his concentration became dominated by his research. He thumbed his way through the pages of the book. Tommy moved closer to the desk, a butterfly of excitement beginning to flutter in his belly. He knew Art wouldn't let him down.

'Right, here we are,' Art continued, before adding casually, 'and, Ben, put it back.'

Tommy watched as Ben sheepishly rummaged inside his jumper, returning a comic that he'd taken from Art's desk. Tommy shot him daggers.

'What? I was only gonna borrow it.'

'Go on, Art,' Tommy said, buoyed by the new hope.

Art continued. 'Right, here it is. Normandy Landings, June 6th 1944. That *has* to be what the first part means.'

Tommy and Ben looked at one another blankly.

'The *what* landings?' Ben asked. It would have taken them a decade in the library to have even got this far.

'The Normandy Landings,' Art replied. He looked at Tommy for support but was met by an expression as equally as blank as Ben's. 'Oh, don't you two *ever* listen in History? The D-Day Landings? World War Two? Allied forces invading Nazi-occupied France? Is *any* of this ringing a bell? Come on, we did this last year! And get off the bed, you nincompoop,' he directed at Ben, 'you're soaked!'

'Hey, don't call me that!' Ben retorted. 'What *did* you call me anyway?'

Art looked to the heavens.

'Must I really educate you *all* the time? Nincompoop. From the latin: *non compus mentis*. Someone without all their mental faculties. In other words – YOU!'

Art carried on about his business, huffing and puffing, wiping the rainwater off his duvet and criticising them for not listening in class, but Tommy didn't hear him. He was attempting to process this new information about World

War Two. If Art was right, and, let's face it, he was always right, then it all made sense. It would tie in exactly with what Grandpa had told him about how he'd come to have the Pen. And he always used to talk about D-Day too. He hadn't realised that could be what the 'landings' part meant, though. Tommy wished he'd concentrated a bit more on Grandpa's old stories now; he'd give anything to have that chance over again. Anyway, at least they were getting somewhere. Now all they needed were the specifics.

'What about the rest?' Tommy pressed. 'The bits about the *fourth night* and the *forgetful town*?'

Art mused for a moment. He pulled another book from the shelf, this time an atlas, and began to study a detailed map of France. He began talking to himself and marking particular points on the map.

'Well, the fourth night would be the 9th June, and if they started here, or here... then by the fourth night they'd have moved inland a bit... of course, it would depend upon which beach they'd landed on... so all we gotta do is look for a forgetful town near the coast...'

Again, Tommy and Ben exchanged looks. They were impressed, *very* impressed. They'd never have got this far. Art scrutinized the map for a moment longer before raising it proudly, his finger pointing to a town near the north-west coast of France.

'Here you go! There's your forgetful town!'

'What?' Tommy said excitedly. 'You've found it? Are you sure?'

'Well,' Art explained, 'like I said, quite simple really.

Once you figure out that it was the Normandy Landings then you know which area to look at. All you have to do then is find a forgetful town and you've got it. There, look.' He handed Tommy the atlas. 'La Ville Distraite. *The forgetful town.*'

'But are you sure that's what it means?'

'Positive. I've been doing extra French classes, haven't I?'

'Yes, you have! Brilliant, mate! Just brilliant! You're a blinkin' genius!' Tommy exclaimed, virtually jumping with excitement.

Art returned to the first book and after a minute or so looking in the index flipped it to the relevant page. All three leaned over the desk to look. It showed a black and white picture of a town ruined by war. An old church stood at the centre of the picture, half of one of its walls blown apart by a bomb blast. A number of soldiers stood posing in front of it, the tired lines on their faces illuminated by the light from the camera's flash. In the background, a group of children ran across the town's square, one of them holding what looked like a large stick, although Ben was adamant that it was a rifle. Beneath the photograph was its description: *Allied soldiers celebrate the liberation of La Ville Distraite – June 9th 1944.*

'Art, that's it!' Tommy said. 'It *has* to be! And look at the date – June 9th. That's the fourth night after they landed. I wonder if Grandpa's there?' Tommy scanned the faces in the picture. 'I can't see him.'

'So what *is* all this about?' Art asked.

'You'll find out soon enough,' Tommy replied. 'Get dressed. We need you to explain this to someone.'

'Huh? Why?'

'Cos we won't remember the dates or the French or anything.'

Art pulled his dressing gown closed, gripping it to his chest, clearly reluctant to go anywhere at such an hour. 'Well, who do I need to explain it to?'

'Mr Wiseman, of course!'

The look of horror on Art's face told them that he would take a lot of convincing.

— CHAPTER TWENTY-TWO —

The Mysterious Memories of Mr Wiseman

To say that Art was reluctant to go to Mr Wiseman's house was an understatement – Tommy and Ben almost had to drag him there. While Art was getting dressed, Tommy picked up his history book, the one with the picture of La Ville Distraite in it, before shepherding him out of his bedroom, down the stairs and straight out the front door. Ben even had the where-with-all to shout, *'Goodbye, Art!'* as they all left, in an attempt to fool his mum.

'Why do we have to go *there*? Are you mad?!' Art asked as soon as they were clear of his house. 'And why do *I* have to come?'

He struggled to keep up with them as they crossed Harbour View towards the old man's house. A light was on in the front room, and the distinct shadowy figure of Mr Wiseman could be seen moving about in the window.

'Like I said,' Tommy replied, 'you need to explain it all to him. Trust me, Art, we've gotta do this. It's Grandpa. He was hurt earlier, and Mr Wiseman is the only one who can help.'

Art came to a sudden halt.

'How bad is your Grandpa, then?' he asked, a look of concern etched on his face.

'Tom? How bad is he?' Art repeated. 'Is he gonna be alright?'

Tommy refused to dwell on it.

'He's fine, I'll explain later. We just need to hurry and then everything will be OK.'

Art still didn't move. He just stared fearfully at Mr Wiseman's silhouette.

'Look, Art,' Ben intervened, 'you like pens, don't you?'

The question clearly confused him.

'What? Pens? Well, I suppose.'

'Then you're just gonna *love* this!'

With Art in tow they continued towards the house, Tommy reaching the gate first, with the other two lagging behind slightly – understandably hesitant considering the years of horror stories that they'd heard (and invented) about the man who lived there. Remembering the last time he'd stood at this gate, Tommy sympathised with his friends, who were surely remembering the horror stories themselves. Or so he thought. Ben, it appeared, was cut from a different cloth entirely. Buoyed by the fact that he'd already met Mr Wiseman that night, he was filled with a new confidence, jostling past Tommy excitedly and barging through the gate, causing it to creak loudly.

'I've always wanted to go in here!' he exclaimed, contrary to any previous opinion he'd had on the matter. 'I wonder what it's like inside.'

He was halfway down the path before Tommy could even coax Art to the gate, having to push him through in front of him in order to guard against any last minute escape.

'Hey, Tom!' Ben called back. 'There's that ball you lost last summer and... *Wow*! Look at this weird knocker!' referring to a brass cauldron on Mr Wiseman's front door. 'Can I bang it?' he asked hopefully.

'NO!' Art shouted instinctively. 'I mean, don't. Let's think about this.'

If he reacted this badly to meeting a friendly old man, Tommy wondered just how he'd react should he be faced with meeting Nidas or Barbarus. Hopefully he'd never have to find out.

'Go on, Ben,' Tommy encouraged. 'There's nothing to worry about. You'll see Art, he's OK – *really* he is. Just a little different, that's all.'

'Different' being the biggest understatement of the century.

Ben rapped the door knocker loudly, its tattoo echoing down the hall inside. The door opened shortly after, and Mr Wiseman stood in the doorway, smiling at them broadly.

'Can we come in?' Ben asked, straining his neck to look past the old man and into the house behind him. Mr Wiseman smiled warmly again and stepped to one side. Ben, not wasting a second, darted into the hallway leaving Tommy having to bundle a reluctant Art over the threshold on his own.

'He's done it!' Tommy blurted as soon as they were inside. 'Art's figured it out! We know when it happened!'

Art blushed silently, his head bowed low so not to make eye contact with their host.

'Then we've no time to lose,' Mr Wiseman replied,

turning from them instantly and making for the living room. His speed of movement surprised them all. 'Nice to finally meet you, Arthur,' he added without looking back.

They followed him and watched as he stood calmly in front of a roaring fire, waiting to hear Art's announcement. Ben and Art, strangers to these new surroundings, gaped open-mouthed at the clutter that was before them, their eyes trying to take in the treasure trove of weird and wonderful items.

'Well?' Mr Wiseman asked.

'Tell him, Art,' Tommy said.

There was a long pause. He looked at Art, whose attention was fixed upon an item on the mantelpiece just over Mr Wiseman's shoulder. It was the chalice that Tommy himself had noticed during his first visit.

'Art?' Tommy said again.

'Holy...' Art mouthed.

'Sh–' Ben interrupted, apparently thinking of something else entirely.

'Grail!' Tommy exclaimed. 'Yes, I'm as shocked as you are Ben, but there's no need to swear! C'mon, Art, tell him what you told us,' he continued. That chalice was a whole other topic, and one that would have to wait. There were more pressing things at hand right now. 'Tell him about the French town.'

Art finally found the courage required to direct his attention to Mr Wiseman.

'Go on, Arthur,' the old man encouraged, 'what was it you discovered?'

Art swallowed hard.

'Well, it's like I told these two, that riddle they had, it's all about D Day – probably on the 9th June – and a town called La Ville Distraite in France, *the forgetful town*.' He managed to cram everything into one hurried sentence. 'At least that's what *I* think anyway.'

'And look!' Tommy said, opening the book and thrusting it in front of Mr Wiseman. 'There's the church.'

Tommy was more than a little surprised by the old man's reaction.

'That's it!' Mr Wiseman said, clapping his hands together excitedly. 'Well done, dear boy! I knew that you'd do it. I knew you'd get there in the end!'

'What?' Tommy exclaimed. 'You already knew?'

'There's not much I don't know, Master Parker,' came the dismissive response, the old man now busying himself amongst some of the clutter.

'Then why didn't you just tell us in the first place? Look at all the time we've wasted!'

'Yes,' the old man replied, his back to him as he rummaged around in a chest of drawers. 'But look at what you've gained.'

He turned to face him.

'Learn to value your friends, young Guardian. You've overcome this obstacle together. The chance to share the company of those closest to you should never be underestimated *or* taken for granted. The times spent with the ones we care about are ones to treasure. Your grandfather would agree with me there, I think. Besides,

I've been researching something else. Something altogether more worrying.'

'Will somebody PLEASE tell me what's going on?' Art demanded.

'You've told him nothing?' Mr Wiseman asked Tommy.

'Well, no,' Tommy replied before looking at Art. 'I didn't wanna worry you. Besides, there's no way you'd believe it all, not without proof, you're too intelligent for that.'

'But I believed you, Tom,' Ben interjected innocently, looking up from behind a suit of armour that he'd been examining in the corner.

'My point exactly.'

Before Ben could take offence Mr Wiseman steered the conversation back to the point at hand.

'There are forces at work here that are more dangerous than Nidas and more important even than your grandfather,' the old man said. 'Every few centuries a war occurs. A war where all of the memories of mankind's evil deeds attempt to break the confines of memory and escape into reality. Now that Nidas has the Pen, he has the power to unleash that evil. He can bring on the darkness. He can unleash *The Creperum*.'

There was that word again.

'But I still don't get it!' Tommy declared, flustered now. 'Why me? Why does he think *I* can stop him? I'm just a kid!'

Mr Wiseman looked at him sternly.

'Young Guardian, you don't have a choice: You *have* to stop him. You ask yourself "why you"? The Pen has always belonged to those that are noble and true: Mr Churchill. Da Vinci. President Lincoln. The list is endless. And all of these former Guardians had to, at one time or another, keep *The Creperum* from our doors. Whenever it attempted to seep into our world, they ensured that it was stopped – at any cost.'

'The Pen came to your grandfather not because *he* was the chosen Guardian. No, it came to him as a mere vessel, a stepping-stone, to *you*. You are the Guardian, Master Parker. You are *The Chosen One*. You always have been.'

The size of the task weighed even more heavily on Tommy's shoulders. All he wanted to do was go back and save Grandpa. He wasn't ready for a war. He was too young. Too frightened.

'*Chosen One?* But I'd be no good at all this – I'm useless. I've shown you that already!'

'It's not what you've done, Master Parker, it's what you're *going* to do.'

He let his words hang for a moment as each of the boys attempted to find the depth of their meaning.

'What *are* you going on about?' Art pleaded again.

'You will know everything soon enough, Arthur,' Mr Wiseman replied, 'and I think it best that we actually *show* you what's going on. Bear with me a moment, won't you?'

The old man returned to the chest of drawers he'd been searching and seconds later produced a large brass key.

'Ah, here it is!' he said, holding it aloft. 'Come on, follow me all of you.' He looked to Tommy.

'You'll be pleased to know, young Guardian, that it is

now time for you to take the next step in saving your grandfather.'

Mr Wiseman beckoned for them to follow him into the hallway.

'Come now, we've not a moment to lose, the race is on. Oh yes, the race is most definitely on!'

They followed him until he stopped abruptly at a door just before the kitchen. He turned and looked at them individually, holding the brass key in front of him.

'This key,' he said, pointing it towards the door, 'will allow you access to the very place where you can save your grandfather.'

'What? Your basement?' Ben asked, confused.

Mr Wiseman chuckled.

'In a way, young man, in a way. This door will lead you to where you need to go.'

As he looked at Tommy, all warmth and humour left his face. He spoke very seriously, his tone one of warning.

'It is very important that you get to your grandfather before Nidas does. He knows where to find him now and has probably made the journey already. The consequences should you fail to stop him will be catastrophic. Should he succeed, then *Secuutus Pluma* will be in a position to alter everything that has happened from that point to this – the birth of you, Tommy, even the outcome of the war. But not only that. It was hearing mention of *The Creperum* that had me very concerned. Should Nidas succeed in unleashing it, then it will be the end of the world as we know it.'

All three boys looked at each other, the fear and

confusion evident on their faces.

'But what is it?' Tommy asked. 'What exactly is *The Creperum*?'

Mr Wiseman exhaled for the longest time before speaking again.

'It is as I have said: *The Darkness*. A supernatural entity made up of mankind's worst memories. It is fuelled by every bad thought or nightmare ever had, all of which can be conjured into physical form. If released, then every man, woman and child will be forced to face their own worst fears – it will be an unwinnable battle. You may have heard it referred to as the apocalypse or Armageddon. Whenever a volcano erupts or an earthquake or hurricane hits, then that is *The Creperum* attempting to break through into our world. It must be stopped, Master Parker. Nidas must not succeed.'

Tommy looked at his friends, both of whom were staring wide-eyed at Mr Wiseman.

'Only with the Pen can Nidas release his army. Without it *The Creperum* will remain trapped where it belongs – in a world of nothing but bad memories.'

'I cannot tell you what you will find when you enter this memory,' the old man continued. 'I cannot tell you of the exact dangers. All I can tell you is this: you will each have to face your own fears, your own worst memories. Be ready for anything. The only way to stop Nidas and his invasion is to exit the memory with the Pen and therefore close the link he would have forged between it and the real world. Do not fail, young Guardian. The world cannot afford for you to do so.'

'But I don't get it,' Tommy said in frustration. 'How can we get there without the Pen?'

Mr Wiseman smiled calmly. There was a mischievous sparkle in his eyes that reminded him of Grandpa.

'You just leave the finer details to me,' he replied with a wink. 'I may be old, but I still have a few tricks up my sleeve. I've been around a while, and I've seen a lot of things. I'll allow you to borrow one of *my* memories. Only a loan mind; at my age I can't afford to be giving them away. But remember this: no matter what happens, you cannot interfere with the original course of events. You *must* allow the previous Guardian to pass the Pen to your grandfather. Allow that to happen and only *then* concern yourself with stopping Nidas. Should you stop the original exchange from happening, then an unpredictable chain of events would be set in motion.'

'What are you all on about?!' Art exclaimed. '*Memories?* Have you all gone mad?'

His protests fell on deaf ears.

Mr Wiseman placed the key into the lock of the basement door and turned it.

'Are you coming too?' Tommy asked hopefully, realising how lost he would feel without his advice.

'No. I will be there in memory only. This is a task that you and your young friends must complete alone. But be warned: you won't be able to leave the memory without the Pen. Fail, and you may remain trapped in there forever.'

He opened the door, stopping Tommy for a moment as he eagerly rushed forward.

'Be brave, my young warriors. Remember, *Secuutus Pluma* fear the Guardians above all else. They fear the brave and the loyal. Believe it or not, they are more afraid of you than you are of them.'

'I doubt that!' Ben huffed. 'Have you seen the size of them?'

'The size of a person isn't measured by their body, Master Campbell. It is measured by their heart. There is no doubt that the members of the Cult have made the wrong decisions; they have chosen the side of suffering. But you three, you are all pure of heart – you won't need to go searching for the path you are to follow. Your destiny will find *you*. And you are all destined for great things, of that I am certain. You won't let me down. Come quickly then,' he continued, ushering them through the door to the top of the stairs. 'Down here.'

It was pitch black, so dark in fact that Tommy could only just make out the first couple of steps.

'Hey, how come your house has got a basement?' Art asked. 'Mine hasn't got a basement.'

'Let's just say that I've extended the property somewhat. Quickly now, down the stairs.'

Tommy fumbled about, trying to feel for a banister, but instead all he found was solid wall. He tentatively stepped down, closely followed by Ben and then Art. They had only descended a few steps when Tommy felt Ben stumble behind him.

'Where's the light switch?' Ben asked, grabbing onto Tommy's shoulders for support.

They were surprised to hear that the response came not from directly behind them, but from the top of the staircase. Mr Wiseman hadn't followed them down.

'Lights?' he replied, a childlike mischief to his tone. 'I think you'd rather not see what was to come next.'

And with that Tommy felt the staircase suddenly disappear beneath his feet, transforming itself into a smooth, slippery slide. He lost his balance instantly, flailing his arms about in an attempt to grip onto something, but there was nothing there to grab. He could hear the shouts behind him and could feel that Ben and Art had also fallen. Together they slid down into the darkness, picking up speed as they went, sliding much further than any normal staircase would have taken them. Tommy then felt the dizzying sensation he'd experienced when entering his own memories, the dark walls that surrounded them suddenly came to life in swirling colour. He felt his stomach lurch forwards as if he'd gone over the brow of a hill too quickly, and he could just about hear the faint calls of 'good luck!' from behind them as they continued to slide uncontrollably into the unknown; into a battle of good versus evil; into the mysterious memories of Mr Wiseman.

Nidas sat at the desk in the boiler room of the Central School. He'd sent his henchmen away – this was a task he had to complete alone. His long and dangerous journey had brought him here, to Little Millbrook, but soon it would return him to his younger days. For now that he knew the exact date, he could extinguish the threat of the Guardians forever. Not in centuries had such an opportunity presented itself and it was he, Nidas, who would be the man to achieve it. Achieve his destiny.

In the dim lamplight he closed his eyes and searched calmly for the distant memory that he required. The memory of a time when he had just entered adulthood, a young man of eighteen, with he and his brethren hot on the heels of the traitor Lothar. He thought back to the smells and colours of war-torn France, of how comfortable he had been surrounded by all of that fear, death and violence. He remembered that small town and the church where they had cornered him.

He opened his eyes, smiling sadistically. The scar tissue on his cheek twisted and glistened in the lamplight. It was he who would go down in history as the one who had unleashed *The Creperum*. It was he who would bring about the end of days. Taking the Pen of Destiny, he scribbled a date and location into a small notebook and willingly surrendered himself to the sensation that followed. A sensation he himself had never experienced but one that he had studied for decades – the sensation of entering into his own memory. And when he returned he'd be bringing *The Creperum* with him.

— CHAPTER TWENTY-THREE —

Saving Private Parker

Tommy landed with a thump onto a hard surface, and Ben and Art landed close beside him. They found themselves on the floor of what appeared to be a large, dark cellar. But it wasn't the basement to Mr Wiseman's house, that was for sure – it was far too big. From the look of it they were in the cellar of some kind of restaurant, with numerous crates of rotten vegetables and innumerable empty bottles stacked up against the walls. Tommy picked himself up and brushed the dust off his clothes, eager to establish their whereabouts so that they could figure out where they needed to go next. All he knew was that they had to get to Grandpa – well, to the *young* Grandpa anyway.

He ran to the nearest light switch and flicked it up and down a few times. Nothing. No electricity.

'Where are we?' Art asked, trembling, rubbing one of his knees, injured from the fall. 'What just happened?'

'That – was – COOL!' Ben commented helpfully, jumping excitedly to his feet.

Tommy shushed away Art's questions and made for a small window near the ceiling, wiping the grime from it and standing on one of the crates, so he could see through.

'We've gotta get upstairs,' he said, 'I can't see anything

from here – no church, nothing.'

Ben, meanwhile, had busied himself trying to force open a small storage unit at the other end of the room.

'Hey, Art, what does this mean?' he asked, pointing to a sign on its front. Art studied the sign.

'*Crème glacée*? It's French for ice cream.'

As the words came out of his mouth, he suddenly seemed to realise the possibility that the unbelievable may have just actually happened to him.

'Tom,' he added, swivelling round to face him, '*why* is that sign in French?'

'There's no time, Art,' Tommy dismissed, running to a nearby door. Ben followed, but Art, like a toddler lost in a supermarket, remained rooted to the spot.

'Tell me,' he pleaded, tears beginning to well in his eyes. 'Where *are* we?'

'Later.'

'No, NOW!' he finally bellowed.

His force brought Tommy to a halt.

'I may not know much about what's going on here,' Art continued, 'but from what I can gather you wouldn't have got very far without me. You at least owe me an explanation!'

And he was right, Tommy thought. This whole adventure was frightening enough as it was, but at least he and Ben knew *why* they were here and what they were doing it all for. They were here through choice. But not Art. They'd done nothing less than force him to come with them. The truth was the least he deserved.

'OK,' Tommy said, turning from the door. 'You're right,

you do need to know. Please don't get upset, Art, I'm sorry.'

Tommy looked at Ben and then nodded to the door.

'Check where that leads will you?'

When they were alone, Tommy told Art everything. It took him less than a minute to get him up to speed, in the briefest way possible, everything that he and Ben had gone through. About the Pen, its powers and the mission they were on to save Grandpa. He kept the bit about the monstrous Nidas until last. As expected, his story was met with no small amount of scepticism.

'Rubbish!' Art said raising his hand, preventing Tommy from interrupting him. 'You're asking me to believe that we're now in Nazi-occupied France? No, wait a minute, not just that, but you're saying that we're in Nazi-occupied France *inside* someone's memory – inside *Mr Wiseman's* memory. And all of this because of some magic pen that your grandad found? Rubbish. Sorry, Tom, nothing against your grandpa, but that's ridiculous.' By now Art was stomping around the cellar and waving his arms about excitedly.

Tommy took his time, careful to find the appropriate response. They desperately needed Art on side, but they also had little time for delay.

'It's all true, I swear it. How else do you explain how we got here? And we really need your help. We can't do it alone.'

Art seemed to take an age weighing-up his options before finally realising that he didn't really have any. He was here, wherever *here* may be, and the only way out was to complete their task.

'OK,' he said, 'let's just do what we need to do and get outta here.'

'Thanks,' Tommy replied gratefully, leading him to the door. He then remembered a small detail that he'd left out earlier.

'Oh,' he said clicking his fingers, 'there is one other thing. You know the Hinton ghosts?'

'Yeah?'

'Well they're real too.'

'Of course they are,' Art replied, shaking his head. 'You're mad. And if Ben believes in all this then he's mad too. It's just not possible. Time travel, falling into memories, magic pens – none of it is real.'

'And yet here we are,' Tommy reminded him. 'We've gotta hurry too – Grandpa's life is depending on us. We've gotta find him before Nidas does.'

They were interrupted by the sound of quick footsteps approaching the cellar door. A moment later, Ben came hurtling through, bouncing about excitedly and pointing to where he'd just been.

'Tom, you won't believe it. It's amazing! We're actually there... I mean *here*... I mean we're not in Little Millbrook anymore!' he said, barely pausing for breath. 'There's a café upstairs and outside there's loads of crumbling buildings and loads of smoke and stuff. Everything's in French, Tom! He did it! The old man only went and bloody did it! I think we're actually in France! Oh, and that church we're looking for – I think I can see it at the other end of the square.'

Tommy looked hopefully to Art who, although frightened, nodded his approval.

'It doesn't look like I've got much choice does it?' he said. 'I'm in.'

'That's the spirit!' Ben said cheerily, leading the way back up the stairs. 'Now keep it down, there's a group of men just outside the window. I think they're foreign though. I couldn't understand a word they were saying.'

The café was full of wooden tables and chairs. One side of the room had a long glass counter that, in more peaceful times, would have undoubtedly displayed all sorts of cakes and tasty pastries.

'Show me where those men are,' Tommy whispered, fearing that they could be some of Nidas' cronies.

Ben led them to a window that was partially covered by a pair of torn curtains. The silhouettes of a group of men could be seen moving about outside, and a conversation was taking place. They crouched beneath the window and listened as the voices chatted loudly.

'See,' Ben commented after a few seconds, 'they're foreign. Art, you're good at languages, where are they from?'

'England.'

'What?'

'He's right,' Tommy said, shaking his head at Ben. 'That's English they're speaking, you idiot. They've just got accents. I think one's from Newcastle.'

'Why would Mr Wiseman send us to Newcastle?' Ben asked.

'We're in France,' Tommy replied. 'Just look around

you. Everything in here is French. We're definitely in the right place. They must be British army.'

Tommy peered through the window in an attempt to get a better look at the soldiers. It was night-time now and pretty dark, but he could make out about half a dozen or so men gathered outside, smoking cigarettes and taking the opportunity to relieve themselves of their equipment. They were definitely British army – he could tell by their uniforms. One of them leaned against a wall, picking the dirt from his boots with his fighting knife, whilst the others rested on their rifles, their faces dirty with a mixture of mud and blood. Their mood and expressions conveyed a sense of both exhaustion and accomplishment. They'd worked hard for this break. Art's head joined Tommy's at the window as he too examined them.

'They've probably come up from the beaches,' he said, 'marched inland for miles and miles, trying to reclaim the towns. I bet they're knackered.'

'Grandpa's not there,' Tommy said, scanning the men's faces.

'Are you sure? He'd look much younger.'

'Positive. I've seen loads of old photos of him when he was in the army, none of these guys look anything like him. Look there, though, at the other end of the square. You're right, Ben, it's the church. It's gotta be the one we're looking for. Grandpa could be in there already.'

Ben joined them at the window. 'Do you think Jen will be OK with me?' he asked.

'What?' Tommy replied, still focusing on the task at

hand. 'Oh, Ben, I've kinda got bigger things to worry about right now.'

'Yeah, yeah, 'course. I'm sure she'll be fine anyway. I mean, I *was* pretty brave wasn't I? Hey, look at that one there,' he added, easily distracted. 'He's got a hand grenade on his belt. Cool!'

He looked to Tommy. 'D'ya reckon there's any spare ones laying about?'

Ben with a hand grenade. Now that *would* be a recipe for disaster. Tommy looked at Ben in disapproval.

'What?' Ben said, 'I'd just use it to scare Richie, that's all. So, we going to this church or what?'

'You bet we are,' Tommy replied, approaching the main door of the café. He opened it carefully, praying that they wouldn't find another group of soldiers on the other side. Thankfully, all he found was a desolate courtyard, the door hidden from the soldier's view. Art, out of fear rather than enthusiasm, never left Tommy's side as he followed him into the yard. Though the whole town was a picture of a crumbling, smouldering war-zone, the church stood firm, its clock tower climbing sixty-feet into the night sky, dozens of bats flitting in and out of the belfry. The stone-arched double doors of the entrance faced them invitingly. A full moon shone brightly like a giant spotlight in the clear night sky, illuminating the square and allowing them to see each of the buildings that stood between them and the church. Together, they quietly conspired, planning a route that would provide them with the most sheltered path across. Directly opposite was a building with abandoned vehicles in front of it. If they could get to that point, the cars and vans would provide them with perfect cover from the soldiers. The last thing they needed was to be found out and questioned by them – even if they were the good guys. A few metres further on, in the centre of the square, was a large stone fountain; that would be checkpoint number two. Then from there, a final dash to the church where they could shelter beneath the tall obelisk monument, and plan their final assault.

'Where'd Ben get to?' Art asked.

Tommy looked back into the café. Ben was stood at the opposite end of the room, holding something that looked rather long and offensive.

'Wish I had my cricket bat,' he said, walking over to them and slapping the object against the palm of his hand. 'But this'll have to do.'

As he neared, Tommy saw that he was holding a wooden chair leg.

'What've you got that for?'

'I found it over there. If you think I'm taking on that big lump without a weapon, then you've got another thing coming.'

There was no time to argue.

'Fair enough,' Tommy whispered, turning his back. 'Follow me and keep low.'

The laughter from the group of soldiers disguised the sound of their footsteps on the gravel as they ran towards the building opposite. Tommy led the way, crouching low, with Art close behind him and Ben bringing up the rear, his chair leg at the ready to fend off any attack. All of the buildings in the square bore the marks of heavy artillery fire, and one particular building still burned steadily into the night, crackling loudly every couple of seconds. The smell reminded Tommy of bonfire night.

They managed to make it to the first checkpoint without drawing attention to themselves, finding refuge behind an abandoned vehicle. It was only a brief stop. Tommy then shepherded them to their next target; the fountain in the centre of town. Taking advantage of a further chorus of laughter from the soldiers, they dashed out and made a run for checkpoint two. As they moved, Tommy allowed himself a glance over at the group. The soldiers had changed position slightly and were now stood shoulder to shoulder with their backs to him. In front of the group was another man holding an old fashioned box-camera. A blinding flash lit up the square and all of the men cheered loudly. A memento of their triumph.

As they dived to the ground behind the fountain, Tommy looked at Ben, wooden chair leg in hand, and felt a strange, unsettling feeling. There was something very familiar about all of this, kinda like déjà vu. He peered over the fountain to look at the soldiers and then back to a confused Ben, still holding his wooden stick. He brought it to his chest protectively, worried that Tommy was going to confiscate it. Tommy racked his brain. *Where had he seen this before?* And then it suddenly dawned on him. Everything fell into place. As mind-warping as the truth was, there could be no other explanation.

'No way!' he exclaimed.

'What is it?' Ben asked.

'Art, that picture in your book. The photograph of the town, of *this* town!'

'What about it?'

'Well, y'know those kids in the background? I think it was us!'

'Huh?'

'Remember one of the kids had a stick?'

'Rifle,' Ben corrected.

'No,' Tommy said, pointing at Ben's weapon. 'Stick. It was you! That rifle was *your* chair leg!'

'What are you on about?' he replied defensively. 'I've never been here before in my life. How could I be in that book? It was taken fifty years ago!'

'We *are* fifty years ago!' Art said. 'Fifty-two to be exact.'

Art seemed to catch on much quicker with the whole space/time continuum thing.

'Think about it,' Art continued. 'The reason we're in the photo that was just taken is because it wasn't *just* taken at all. It was taken fifty-two years ago! We *are* fifty-two years ago!'

Tommy felt sorry for Ben. Attempting to understand all of this looked like it was frying his brain. Ben's eyes then widened as he looked at the piece of wood.

'This is freaky!' he exclaimed a little too loudly, 'we've been in that book for ages then.'

Then, having realised something else, he smiled.

'Hey,' he said proudly, 'I'm in a book!'

'Keep it down,' Tommy whispered, looking over to the church. 'There's someone over there.'

They crouched behind the fountain, peeking over the stone basin. The figure of a man emerged from the shadows, running towards the arched doors of the church. He appeared frantic, out of breath, and he was continually looking over his shoulder. Reaching the entrance, he pushed the heavy doors open. A loud *clang* was followed by a droning echo from within as he closed them behind him, disappearing inside.

'Who was that?' Ben asked.

'I dunno,' Tommy replied honestly. Even though they couldn't see his face, it didn't look like Grandpa, and he was way too small to have been Nidas.

'Well let's find out,' Ben said, standing.

Tommy yanked him back down. 'Wait! Look!'

Coming from the same shadows, half a dozen other men now walked with a purpose towards the church. Tommy recognised their attire instantly, and, from the gasp to his right, it appeared as though Ben had also realised who they were. *Secuutus Pluma.* They walked menacingly, stalking the lone man, pausing only as they reached the closed doors. One of them barked orders at the group, and two of their number immediately disappeared around the far side of the church, two others going in the opposite direction. The two that remained were by far the largest of their number, and one of them in particular was huge. So large, in fact, that he looked just like a younger version of Nidas.

'Of course!' Tommy said, slapping his forehead. It had

suddenly dawned on him. 'That's how he's managed to come back here – he was here first time round!'

He looked to his friends, who weren't quite on his wavelength yet.

'Nidas,' he explained, 'that huge guy over there, that's him when he was young.'

Ben and Art shuffled closer to get a better look.

'Jeez, he's massive!' Art said. It was the first time he'd set eyes on him.

'Well, if that's the young Nidas,' Ben said. 'Then where's the other one? Y'know, the old one?'

'That's what we've gotta find out,' Tommy replied. 'And soon. Before he gets to Grandpa.'

He was worried now, more so than before. There were too many Cult members in this memory for his liking. They'd seen six so far, which meant there'd be seven in total, including *two* versions of Nidas. Things couldn't get much worse. *What was he thinking?* Of course it could. Nidas could succeed in releasing *The Creperum!* They *really* had to get that Pen back!

The church doors opened again, and this time the young Nidas and his friend disappeared inside.

'They've gone in,' Tommy said, confirming the obvious, the fear of having to act growing more intense with each passing second.

Ben turned to Art. 'Look, I've met these guys before,' he said, almost showing off. 'They're very dangerous, OK, so we've gotta be careful.'

'I don't see Nidas anywhere, though,' Tommy added,

his eyes flitting around the square. '*Our* Nidas I mean.'

'Look again,' Ben whispered. 'Over there.'

And sure enough, moving out from behind a wall not fifty yards from their own position, was Nidas. Looking exactly as he had the last time they'd seen him in the Central School, he moved towards the church, paying no heed to his war-torn surroundings, focusing only on his goal – eliminating Grandpa.

'*That's* him?' Art asked, his voice shaking. Clearly, the mere appearance of Nidas had the same effect on him as it had on Tommy and Ben.

'Afraid so,' Tommy replied.

'That's why I needed this,' Ben said, tapping his piece of wood. 'Bet he won't take me so lightly this time.'

As much as he wished he was right, Tommy doubted that very much. He kept his eyes trained on Nidas, unwilling to let him out of his sight, even for a second. *But what will Nidas do?* Dare he break Mr Wiseman's rules and interact with the Cult of this time? Or would he just play the waiting game and not make his move until Grandpa had been given the Pen? All they could do was wait and find out. They had to stick to him like glue and then try and sabotage any move that he made. After all, they did have quite a valuable weapon for once (and it wasn't Ben's chair leg): they had the element of surprise. Nidas had no way of knowing that they'd found a way to follow him into his own memory. Their presence here would be totally unexpected.

But then, when he thought that things couldn't really get any worse, Tommy saw something new that knocked the wind right out of his sails.

'Hey, Tom,' Ben ventured having followed his gaze. 'Bet there are snipers up there in that bell tower. Tom?' he continued, 'I said I bet there's snipers up there.'

Confused by his silence, Ben watched as the colour drained from Tommy's face until it matched the same milky-white shade of the moon.

'What's the matter?' he asked.

'U-u-p-p th-th-ere...' Tommy managed to stammer. 'T-top of the bell tower.'

At the highest point of the church, sat atop the tower, was a small figure crouched low and balancing impossibly on the edge of the slanted roof, its silhouette boldly outlined by the moonlight. The figure looked right at them, its red eyes glowing in the darkness. Tommy recognised the shape instantly. Ben and Art, of course, did not, for they hadn't yet had the misfortune of seeing one. Until now that is. It was one of those horrid creatures that had chased him in his memory.

'It's one of those things,' Tommy explained. 'One of those creatures I told you about. We've really gotta hurry now.'

'What are they?' Art dared to ask.

'You don't wanna know. In fact *I* don't wanna know, but they're vicious and like nothing I've ever seen before. And they're even worse close up, believe me.'

Tommy returned his focus to Nidas, who was almost at the main doors of the church. Rather than opening them, he chose to walk to the far side of the building, rounding the corner and disappearing from view.

'Let's follow him,' Tommy commanded, standing up. 'Just make sure you watch out for that thing up there,' he added. As it happened, Ben and Art hadn't taken their eyes off it anyway. It remained sat, predator-like on top of the tower.

'Come on!' Tommy urged, 'Nidas has gone. We can't worry about that thing now. If you see it getting close, just yell, but we need to save Grandpa.'

They crossed the square undetected, reaching the huge double doors of the church. Eager to find Nidas again, Tommy hugged the cold stone of the church and peered around its corner.

'These doors ain't half heavy!' Ben grunted.

Tommy spun round to find Ben pushing against one of the doors with all of his might, his deadly weapon discarded on the floor beside him.

'It won't open.'

'Ssh!' Tommy whispered, pulling him away from the door. 'We can't just walk in there; they'll all see us, *including* Grandpa! Besides, you gotta turn the handle, you idiot. C'mon, let's try round the side.'

They were forced to stop in their tracks and dive behind a nearby bush, as Nidas was directly in front of them, a mere twenty metres away. He was talking to somebody – or to some*thing*. Tommy looked hard, scarcely believing his eyes. It was one of those creatures! Nidas actually seemed to be having some sort of conversation with it. They watched and waited for a moment until Nidas gestured and then pointed to a faraway corner of the town square. The creature ran off on all fours, quicker than any man, dog or horse and vanished out of sight. Nidas then disappeared through a gaping hole in the side of the church. It had clearly been damaged by some sort of blast. A pile of rubble littered the ground around it, leaving an unconventional threshold. They crept along the wall and huddled around the hole to look inside. It was situated about half way along the nave, and dozens of candles lit the church interior, throwing flickering shadows onto the walls. It was utter chaos inside. Pews were overturned, copies of the Bible and loose hymn sheets littered the floor and rats scurried from place to place.

'C'or, looks like a bomb's gone off in there,' Ben commented seriously.

'You don't say?' Art tutted sarcastically. 'I can't believe that we're actually in World War Two; this is one of my favourite periods in history! Shame about the rats though. I hate rats.'

'Well, we're not hanging around,' Tommy said. 'As soon as we do what we need to, we're outta here.'

'Hey, look over there,' Ben interrupted.

Inside the church, sweeping the length and breadth of the nave, were the Cult men they'd seen outside a minute ago. All six of them were here now, searching under pews and behind curtains, clearly looking for the man who'd run from them. There was no sign of the old Nidas though. *Their* Nidas. Where had he got to? He'd only just come in here.

They watched on silently as the men, with military precision, covered every inch of the church in search of their prey, finally congregating at the front near the pulpit. There they plotted their next move. Their discussions were interrupted by a sudden movement near the chancel. The man that they sought suddenly appeared from behind a curtain and jumped down the steps towards them, shouting as he went. He barged past them and ran towards a door at the rear. The Cult were on their toes instantly, chasing him through the exit, drawing their weapons and yelling insults at him as they went.

'Who's that they're chasing?' Art asked as the last of them disappeared through the door.

'That must be the man who gave Grandpa the Pen,' Tommy guessed. 'But did you hear how much noise he made? He could've stayed hidden or sneaked past them. It was almost like he *wanted* them to follow him.'

Tommy pondered for a moment.

'That must be it!' he decided. 'He's leading them away from Grandpa. Away from the Pen!'

Tommy looked at the now eerily silent church. *If that were true, then where was Grandpa?* More worryingly, for that matter, where was Nidas? Another figure then slowly emerged from behind the curtain. He'd crawled out from beneath a choir stall, hidden from view in the chancery. It was a young British soldier. *Grandpa!* He was wearing an army uniform, and Tommy could see some sort of handgun in a holster on his waist. The young Grandpa pulled himself to his feet and looked cautiously around the church , dusting himself down as his eyes scanned the interior. His face told a story of confusion and fear, but despite the fact that he was half a century younger, Tommy knew instantly that it was Grandpa. His features were unmistakable.

Grandpa stood near the altar, scratching his head and looking at a small item in his hand – the Pen. Tommy desperately wanted to run over and introduce himself. To explain everything to him and take him clear of the danger, but he knew that he couldn't. He mustn't interact or interfere, not yet. That's what Mr Wiseman had told him, and he had to trust in him. So instead he and his friends just waited. Waited in silence. Waited for Nidas to make his move.

They didn't have to wait long. Ben noticed it first. He nudged Tommy with the chair leg and indicated to the far end of the church, where there was something moving. Somebody stepping out of the shadows. They knew right away that it was Nidas. He walked slowly down the aisle, drawing his weapon from his coat as he approached the young Grandpa, who was totally unaware of the threat. Tommy had to do something; he couldn't lose Grandpa again. And what was more, losing *this* Grandpa, as a young man, would also mean losing his entire family. A thought that he couldn't bear. Tommy made to get up but was stopped by a hand gripping his forearm. It belonged to Art.

'No, Tommy, wait, it's suicide,' he whispered urgently.

'I know, Art, but I've got to. He's gonna kill Grandpa.'

But Tommy had underestimated him. It wasn't cowardice that made Art intervene.

'I *know* we've got to,' Art said, 'but not like this. I've got

293

a plan.'

He grabbed a handful of dirt from the ground and rubbed it into his face. He then pulled at his jumper, ripping it at the neck, and smeared it in mud.

'What are you doing?' Tommy asked.

'He doesn't know me, does he? I'll distract him while you try and find a way of getting your grandpa out.'

'No, Art, wait...'

But it was too late. Art had already skipped over the fallen debris and entered the church. This wasn't what Tommy had wanted. It should be him going in there now, not Art.

'He's crazy!' Ben said, awestruck at his bravery. 'I didn't think he'd have the guts to do that! Who'd have thought it, eh? Art – the man with the plan!'

They watched as he clambered over a toppled pew and made his way towards the aisle and into Nidas' eye-line. Art approached him, speaking in a loud, clear voice that echoed through the church.

'Monsieur, monsieur, je recherche ma famille, ils suis absent! Veuillez m'aider!'

They didn't have the foggiest idea what he'd said, but Tommy knew full well that it didn't matter. What mattered was that he'd said it loud enough for Grandpa to hear. *Well done, Art!* He'd given him the heads up.

The young soldier turned, looking for the source of the noise. Nidas glared at this scruffy French boy who'd come between him and his prey. He lowered his gun in an attempt to hide it from Grandpa, but he hadn't been quick enough.

Grandpa had seen it and was now clearly worried by the threat that this huge man presented. Art continued to approach Nidas as he raised his gun again, taking aim at Grandpa. Art jumped forward, managing to knock Nidas' arm upwards just as he fired his shot, sending the bullet high above its intended target and knocking the gun out of his hand and under one of the nearby pews. Tommy marvelled at the bravery, but fortune didn't favour them completely. The bullet Nidas had fired had hit some stonework, breaking it loose and causing a heavy load of bricks to avalanche down upon Grandpa as he tried to make good his escape. The bricks hit him near the shoulder, sending him sprawling onto the cold floor of the church, where he lay, unconscious.

'C'mon, Ben,' Tommy yelled. 'He's lost his gun!'

They charged over the obstacles screaming Art's name, Ben swinging the chair leg over his head like a medieval warrior. Nidas, for his part, appeared genuinely shocked by their presence.

'You?!' he shouted in anger. 'How can *you* be here? This is *my* memory!'

'Yeah? Well, we Guardians know a few tricks ourselves!' Tommy retorted confidently, glad for once that he had the upper hand. 'And there's plenty more where that came from too, so you better give me back my Pen or else you're gonna get it!'

Art retreated to a safer distance, sensibly placing a fallen pew between himself and Nidas. Ben stayed near the hole in the wall, tapping the chair leg repeatedly against his hand in an attempt to look menacing whilst Tommy, although making sure he kept his distance, positioned himself in the centre of the aisle, facing Nidas. The Grand Master towered over Tommy, staring him down. He looked from Tommy to Ben and then to Art, before smiling that familiar evil grimace that served only to accentuate the ugly scar on his face.

'Ha, I see that you've recruited another friend into this pathetic little rebellion? You Guardians always insist upon putting those dear to you in danger.'

A sudden 'Yelp' caused all eyes to fall on Ben, who was now wincing, attempting to pull a splinter out of the palm of his hand. Nidas laughed loudly.

'Do you really think that you three weaklings have a chance of stopping me? I am Nidas. I don't need weapons to complete my task.'

He glared at Tommy.

'I can finish you with my bare hands!'

Any false confidence that Tommy had immediately drained from him when he witnessed the pure evil in the eyes of his enemy. He instinctively retreated with each step that Nidas took forward, bringing him closer to the altar and to his fallen grandfather. He glanced around in desperation, but Art was frozen to the spot with fright, trembling more and more the closer Nidas came to Tommy. And... Ben, well Ben, wasn't anywhere to be seen. He'd either fainted and fallen from view, or he'd left. Tommy scanned the church quickly. *Could he really have deserted him? Right when he needed him most?*

Tommy's expression betrayed his thoughts and Nidas

picked up on his disappointment. He laughed again, louder than before, the noise echoing violently around the building, making the pipes of the church organ drone deeply.

'Ha!' he sneered. 'Your friends don't dare to help you now, Parker, not even the stupid one. What a shame, the only one of you impudent enough to bring a weapon has decided to run off with it!'

And it was true. Ben had run away and left him to die at the hands of this mad man. Tommy was scared. Still backtracking, he felt his heel hit something solid. Looking down, he saw that he'd reached the steps of the chancel. Just a few feet away lay Grandpa, still unconscious and very much as helpless as he was. But seeing him there served to strengthen Tommy's resolve. He had to make one final push; if it was to end now then he'd rather go out fighting.

Then something on the floor flashed at him. A twinkling of candlelight reflecting off a piece of metal on Grandpa's belt. His gun! *Of course! Grandpa was armed.* If he could just get to it before Nidas...

Tommy found his voice again.

'I'm warning you,' he said. 'Give me back the Pen!'

'Or what?' Nidas replied, mocking him.

With Nidas now just ten feet away, Tommy had to make his move. He knelt down at Grandpa's side, unfastened the button on his holster and took out the gun. He stood again and, though shaking violently, pointed it directly at Nidas' chest.

'Or this!' Tommy shouted, more scared now than ever.

The sight of it had the temporary effect of halting Nidas,

but his calm expression gave Tommy the unnerving feeling that this wasn't the first time he'd stared down the barrel of a gun. He hesitated for only a moment before taking a long stride forward, testing Tommy's resolve to the limit.

'Don't! I'm not afraid to use this,' Tommy shouted, waving the gun at him for the avoidance of any confusion. 'Give me the Pen, and I'll let you walk outta here unharmed.'

Nidas made a show of considering the offer for a few seconds. He then raised his right hand and slowly, delicately, placed two fingers inside the breast pocket of his shirt. He removed the Pen, holding it out in front of him for Tommy to see.

'You really want this?' he asked.

Tommy nodded, wondering what sort of game he was playing.

'Well, let me ask you this important question: do you really think that you deserve to possess it? More so than I? This is the Pen of Destiny. You know nothing of its true potential.'

'Give it to me,' Tommy replied. 'It belongs to me, you'll only use it to do bad things.'

Nidas laughed again, revelling in Tommy's fear.

'It's too late,' Nidas boasted 'I've already used it to do *bad things*. I've already summoned *The Creperum!* You've lost. You just don't know it yet. Soon mankind will be no more. If you want the Pen back then you'll have to kill me for it, and I don't believe that you're ready to do that. You are not brave enough to take the shot. It is why you Guardians will never succeed.'

Tommy lowered the gun a few inches. Seeing his resistance waver, Nidas walked towards him, but Tommy, fuelled by self-preservation, instinctively raised the gun again and pulled the trigger, firing a warning shot high above Nidas' head. The force of the shot stung Tommy's hand, pain shooting up his forearm. It also stopped the killer in his tracks, clearly surprised by the young Guardian's bravado.

'I said stay there!' Tommy yelled, the sound of the gunshot still ringing around the church.

And then, from high above them, came a voice.

'OI, WATCH IT! You nearly had my head off!'

Tommy, Nidas and Art immediately looked upward. Twenty feet above them, perched on the narrowest of window ledges, was Ben. In one hand he had hold of a scrunched up floor-to-ceiling curtain and in the other his chair leg.

Tommy felt ashamed that he'd doubted Ben. Of course he wouldn't have deserted him – he was too stupid for that!

'What are you doing?' Tommy called up, not taking his eyes off Nidas but also recalling Ben's farcical rescue attempt in the school gym.

'Stupid boy!' Nidas himself chided. 'Do you learn nothing from your mistakes?'

Ben was most offended. 'Just shut it, you big lump! Didn't anyone teach you that practice makes perfect? You're not all there! You're mental! Nothing but a big, old... nincompoop!'

Tommy managed to shoot a glance over to Art, who

was smiling. It seemed Ben did listen to him after all.

'I'm the guardian *of* the Guardian,' Ben continued, 'and you *will* leave my friend alone!'

'What did you call me?' Nidas asked, his turn now to be offended.

'I called you a big, ugly nincompoop!' Ben shouted in response. He then confidently jumped off the ledge, tightly holding onto the curtain with one hand. He swung in an arc towards his target, his free arm held out in front of him – the chair leg pointed at Nidas, like a medieval knight charging with his lance. *Here we go again*, Tommy couldn't help but think, realising that Nidas was right and Ben hadn't learned from his previous mistake. This time, though, rather than swinging lazily towards them as he had in the school gym, Ben's orbit seemed far more purposeful and aggressive, his weapon aimed directly at Nidas' head. Such was the pace at which he travelled even Nidas appeared wary and was sensible enough to try to get out of the way. As Ben neared the huge target, he drew the chair leg back and took an almighty swing at the killer, missing his head but making contact with the arm he'd raised to protect himself. Tommy winced at the sickening sound of wood on flesh, and in that split second he realised what Ben had done. The arm that he'd hit was Nidas' right arm. And it was his right hand that held the Pen of Destiny! Ben had known what he was aiming for all along! Such was the force of the blow, that the Pen flew out of Nidas' grasp and sailed through the air on the same trajectory as Ben, the two of them landing almost simultaneously at Tommy's feet.

'Alright, mate?' Ben said, smiling excitedly. They both looked at the Pen for a moment, Tommy still pointing the gun in Nidas' general direction.

'Well, pick it up!' Tommy urged, as Nidas rubbed his right arm and searched the floor around him for his lost treasure. Ben did as he was told, quickly grabbing the Pen before running behind Tommy, realising that the gun was a bit more of a deterrent than his piece of wood. He looked at the unconscious form of the soldier at their feet, who was now beginning to stir.

'So that's your grandpa huh? Weird...'

'Hold it right there!' Tommy shouted.

Ben froze.

'Not you!' Tommy added, his eyes flicking to Nidas. 'Him!'

Nidas, his face crimson with rage, had steadied himself and was now marching down the aisle towards them.

'I said STOP!'

But this time there was no stopping him. Nidas didn't heed Tommy's warning, nor did he wish to stop to discuss the situation. The tables had been turned. The Pen was no longer in his possession, and Nidas wouldn't stop until he'd retrieved it. He continued to stalk angrily towards them, and now they had nowhere to go. They couldn't just run; Grandpa was still helpless beside them. They had to make a stand. Tommy *had* to use the gun; there was nothing else that would stop him. *Was Nidas right about him? Was he really ready to kill for it?*

With Nidas now only a few feet away, Tommy steeled

himself. He closed one eye and pointed the gun at Nidas' chest. He squeezed down on the trigger and waited for the loud bang that would inevitably follow and change his life forever. A bang that would turn him into a killer, just like Nidas. But it wasn't a bang he heard. Instead, there was a loud *clanging* from the main doors of the church, a clang that caused Nidas to spin around and Tommy to take his finger off the trigger.

Entering the church, apparently drawn by the noise, was Grandpa's platoon. And what a welcome sight it was. A dozen or so alert, battle-hardened soldiers, ready to take on any enemy threat. At last! The cavalry!

Satisfied now that Grandpa would be protected, Tommy lowered the gun and pulled Ben towards the hole in the side of the church.

'Art, run!' Tommy shouted. He was already half way there.

The soldiers swarmed into the church, guns raised and clearly surprised to find that three children and a gigantic old man were the source of all the commotion. They were even more concerned when they saw that one of their own was lying injured on the floor.

'Hey! What's going on in here?' the lead soldier demanded.

Nobody was prepared to stay to offer an explanation. Tommy, Ben and Art all fled towards the exit, and Nidas, realising that without a weapon he was no match for an entire platoon, made to follow the boys out of the church. He paused only to stoop at Grandpa's side and try to grab *his* version of the Pen of Destiny – the Pen that Grandpa would go on to hide in his attic and one day give to Tommy, thereby triggering this whole crazy chain of events. But seeing the huge old man approach his fallen comrade, one of the soldiers fired a shot over Nidas' shoulder, warning him off. By Tommy's reckoning he wouldn't be getting his hands on that particular Pen for about another fifty years. Tommy stumbled over the debris before he looked back again. Two soldiers were comforting Grandpa, helping him to his feet, whilst the others secured the rest of the church.

They'd done it! They'd actually managed to save Grandpa *and* get the Pen back! But that was only phase one of the plan complete. They still had to find a way of getting the Pen out of the memory before it was too late. If Nidas *had* been telling the truth, if he had already summoned that evil army, then they had to get back to reality before it had a chance of escaping to wreak its havoc.

Sprinting for all they were worth, they left Nidas behind and made for the town square. But they were too late. Nidas *had* been telling the truth! They were forced to skid to a halt. In front of them was a sight so frightening they could barely comprehend it.

It was *The Creperum.*

— CHAPTER TWENTY-FOUR —

The Creperum

The clear night sky had misted and not a single star could be seen; the moon was shrouded by the dark clouds that had formed over the town. The rain came first. Heavy raindrops that fell hard onto the ground, bouncing off the dirt at their feet, quickly turning into a torrential downpour. Then came the thunder! The loudest clap of thunder imaginable, making all three of them jump a foot into the air. Art clutched onto Tommy's arm as flashes of lightning illuminated the gloomy square. The wind howled, tearing at the windows and shutters of the surrounding buildings. But there were forces at work far worse than this storm. *The Creperum.*

Tommy hadn't had a clue what to expect – Mr Wiseman hadn't told them too much about it – but this *had* to be it. A huge cloud of black smoke billowed towards them, a furnace of orange flame behind it, moving as if it were alive. Just looking at it filled him with terror.

'What *is* that?!' Ben yelled above the noise of the storm.

'It's that thing! It's gotta be!' said Tommy. 'Gimme the Pen,' he added, grabbing it off him and shoving it deep into his pocket. *He* was the Guardian; the Pen was his responsibility, and he wasn't about to give it up without a fight. They heard a voice from behind that caused them to spin around. The voice of a person that this cloud of evil had somehow managed to make them forget – Nidas. He'd followed them out of the church and was now approaching, a sickening grin on his face.

'I told you it was too late!' he chided. 'I've already summoned it. Soon it will consume you, and the Pen will be mine!'

But rather than confront them as Tommy had expected, Nidas walked calmly to one side, seemingly content to watch as the cloud of darkness approached them. Turning his attentions to the thick wall of smoke, Tommy stood in horrified wonder as it began to form shapes. Just a few at first, but then more and more, spewing from the main body of the cloud and growing even bigger. An unnaturally loud crack of thunder split the air, forcing them to cover their ears, the pain making their eardrums feel fit to burst. Then a fork of lightning struck one of the buildings, setting it on fire. They watched as the wisps of smoke began to change, transforming themselves into more definite, solid shapes. This was impossible! The smoke was actually turning into real, living things! Some of the shapes had morphed into rats. Actual, real life rats! Dozens of them with huge teeth and even bigger noses and with long, thick, hairy tails. Then more of the smoke changed into different shapes – spiders this time – spiders larger than dogs, their pincers clicking furiously as they climbed up the buildings, over the fountain and even up to the bell tower, surrounding the square completely.

'I get it!' Art exclaimed. 'I know what's happening! I know what this is! It's just like Mr Wiseman said. He *couldn't* warn us about what we'd be facing, because he didn't know. This *Creperum* thing, it transforms itself into *our* own worst fears.'

Tommy and Ben looked horrified.

'See, look!' Art continued, pointing at the storm clouds and then at the rats. 'I hate thunderstorms *and* I hate rats! That's why they're here!'

'And *I* hate spiders!' Tommy added.

Tommy then noticed something leaning against the fountain in the middle of the square. One of the last things he expected to see there.

'Ben, is that your old mattress?'

'What?' Ben replied, flushing a deep crimson. 'Nah, it can't be.'

'Yeah it is, look,' Tommy insisted. 'That's your old *He-Man* duvet cover. What's it doing here?'

Ben shot him an angry look.

'So I had a bed-wetting problem, alright?!' he admitted with no small amount of embarrassment. 'Y'know what,' he then added confidently, 'this isn't too bad actually. We can handle a few rats and spiders, that's noth…' He was cut off mid-sentence by a loud roar, louder even than the deafening drum of the storm. It seemed to echo and vibrate throughout the town, threatening to smash what remained of the glass in the windows and doors. They followed the noise and looked skyward. Standing even taller than the rooftops was a Tyrannosaurus Rex. A proper, man-eating, bloodthirsty T-Rex! It glared down at them before letting out another almighty roar, baring all of its ridiculously huge teeth, its breath warming them against the storm. Tommy and Ben looked accusingly at Art.

'Sorry, guys,' he said, trembling. 'That one's my fault too. I was always afraid of them!'

The Creperum had stepped up a level. It had just become *very* dangerous indeed.

'Can we get outta here!' Ben demanded, his it's-only-rats-and-spiders confidence fading rapidly.

Tommy wanted nothing more. Art was right. This was all of their worst memories, their worst fears, any nightmare that they'd ever had, everything coming for them all at once. *But how did they get out of here now?* They were surrounded. Tommy knew that they had to get the Pen out of the memory before this *Creperum* thing escaped, but the question was *how?* There was only one thing he could think of. One place that seemed like the most sensible place to start.

'C'mon,' he said, 'let's get to the café – that's gotta be our way back! And try not to think of anything scary!'

They made a break for it across the square. Tommy's fear intensified as he saw that dozens of the creatures he'd seen in his memory had also surrounded the square, crawling cat-like across the rooftops and fixing them with their own hungry stares. And yet they had no choice but to run straight towards the evil cloud – it was their only way to the café. Behind them they could just hear Nidas shouting, his voice reduced to a faint whisper in the storm.

'Your resistance is useless, Guardian! *The Creperum* has

gathered. You cannot run!'

But run they did. And faster than they'd ever run before, none of them daring to take their eyes off the constantly changing black cloud, shapes forming and figures dropping from it and morphing into horrible memories from their past. Another roar from the T-Rex told them that it was chasing them, cantering at a frightening pace, its large yellow eyes following them as they ran; the heavy footsteps shaking the ground like an earthquake. Then another monster appeared; one that dwarfed even the T-Rex; one that could only possibly exist in the world they were now in – a gigantic version of Barbarus! The huge henchman was poised menacingly behind the building that was ablaze, his arms as big as tree trunks and folded across his gargantuan chest. On his shoulder was the sinister Styx, holding onto the giant's neck and directing him forwards.

'Jeez!' Ben shouted. 'Look at the size of him now!'

But Tommy didn't want to look. He just kept running as more and more things began to appear out of thin air. To their right, a ghost train appeared; the ghost train from the Little Millbrook carnival. Tommy was certainly to blame for that one. Then another thing appeared in front of them, blocking their path. A sight that simultaneously made the hair on the back of Tommy's neck stand on end and his blood boil. It was a vision of the doctor who'd treated Grandpa at hospital. The one who'd broken the news. Except this doctor was different. This one just stood there staring at him, a horrible smile on his face and an evil, red glint in his eye. Next to him was a dark, hooded figure holding a tall scythe.

'NO!' Tommy yelled, the pain from Grandpa's death angering him. 'Go away! You're not real! None of this is real!'

'Oh but it *is* real,' Nidas' voice said from behind them.

They spun round to find themselves face-to-face with him again. He'd followed them and had somehow managed to get hold of another gun. He pointed it at Tommy's chest.

'*The Creperum* is *very* real. And once I have the Pen the whole world will see just how real it is!'

He was right. If this thing got out into the real world then the consequences would be terrible. A world where everybody's fears and nightmares became a reality; it would be utter chaos. He couldn't let him get his hands on it.

Then, even as they looked at him, wisps of black smoke slowly started to drift towards Nidas from the dark cloud, surrounding him completely and swirling around him like a mini tornado. Then from within him, like his own spirit was leaving his body, a different Nidas rose into the air. A darker and, if possible, more malevolent Nidas, hovering above the normal one, at least four times larger in size. The real Nidas laughed at them, his gun still pointed at Tommy as he gave a signal. The larger, shadowy figure of Nidas stretched its arms out, reaching out for the Pen. The facial scar on this supernatural Nidas writhed like it were alive and then, before their very eyes, transformed into a snake and dropped to the floor, hissing threateningly at their feet. There was nothing they could do. They were done for. *Or were they?*

'Quick!' Ben shouted, 'the ghost train!'

They darted to the train, and all three crammed themselves into the nearest carriage. Thankfully, miraculously, it started to move. Only slowly at first, painfully slowly, but metre by metre it began to gather pace, picking up speed as it rolled along its imaginary track. It took them on a ride through the war-torn square, with different horrors in every direction. The train took them past Nidas, around the fountain and in and out of the buildings, a terrifying mystery tour of the entire area. And still they gathered speed. It moved more like a rollercoaster as it took them up and over the church, streaking past the bell-tower at break-neck speed and then down again, through the legs of the angry T-Rex and close to the flailing fist of the supernaturally mammoth Barbarus. All the time, they could hear the screams of Nidas as he encouraged his army to take them – dinosaurs, goblins, werewolves, anything horrible that they'd ever imagined. They whipped past the buildings, most of it a blur, but Tommy could still see that dozens of those memory creatures were there too.

'Wooo hooo!' Ben yelled, the three of them holding on for all they were worth in the cramped carriage. 'This is AWESOME!'

As they sped past the fountain for the second time, Ben leaned out of the car and swept something up in his hand.

'Look, Tom, a grenade!'

Great! Tommy thought. As if things weren't dangerous enough – now Ben had a live grenade.

'Be careful with that thing!' Art yelled back at him, a

little green from the ride. Tommy, holding tightly to the bar in front of him, tried hard to focus, the wind making his eyes water so that tears streamed down his cheeks. In the distance he could see the café, its door open invitingly. And they were heading in the right direction! Still though, between themselves and the café was the thick wall of black smoke – the entity that spewed all of this evil. It had grown even larger now and stretched high into the night sky, merging with the dark storm clouds above. And the train's path was leading them right to it. Tommy suddenly had an idea.

'Throw it!' he shouted.

'What?'

'Throw the grenade!' he shouted again. 'Chuck it at that!' he added, pointing at the cloud.

'Really?' Ben asked, looking like all of his Christmases had come at once.

He didn't need to be told twice. Pulling the pin from the grenade, he threw it as hard as he could, straight into the heart of the dark cloud. Seconds later, and with them still hurtling towards it, there was a great explosion, a large patch of orange and red flame erupting from the centre of the cloud. A gaping hole momentarily appeared in the belly of the great beast just long enough to allow their carriage to fly right through it. Tommy could feel the heat of the fire on his face as they came life-threateningly close to its flames.

'YES!' they all screamed in unison, seeing the café drawing near. But this part of the ride was over. The ghost train came to a sudden, grinding halt, throwing them forward and dumping them unceremoniously onto the hard gravel floor.

'Quick!' Tommy said, looking behind him at Nidas and the mass of approaching creatures. 'Let's go!'

The race was on as they ran to the café, Ben out in front and Art lagging behind. It was only twenty or so yards ahead of them now. They were almost there.

Ben, noticing the creatures on the roof of the café, called back to them. 'Tommy!' he screamed, pointing upwards. 'There's one of those things!'

They were sat on the roof waiting for them. Another creature had joined the first one, then another; each one looked as vicious as the last, their wide eyes glowing red in the night, and their razor-sharp teeth bared. There were three of them up there, lined at the edge of the roof, ready to pounce. Tommy turned to check on Art and warn him of the new threat, but he'd already seen them.

'Just keep going,' he called, 'and hold the door for me!'

More of the creatures cropped up all over the square, swelling the ranks of the supernatural army of *The Creperum*. They were on top of the church, behind a burnt-out truck – everywhere. All scurrying around on all fours like a pack of angry primates, closing in on their intended prey. The door to the café was almost within reach now. Even if it wasn't the portal back to reality, then at least it would provide them with temporary safety from the horrors that stalked the town square. In the hope that it would help them get home, Tommy fumbled around in his pocket and pulled out the Pen, holding it in front of him like a relay baton, optimistically willing the café to transform itself into Mr

Wiseman's house.

But nothing happened.

He and Ben hit the steps to the café at the same time, stopping in the doorway to turn and encourage Art onward. Nearest to them, running for all he was worth, was Art. Tommy could see the tears rolling down his cheeks as he ran for his very life. The backdrop of the square looked like Hell itself, swarming with the evil of *The Creperum* and also Nidas, who had now given chase and was only a few short metres behind Art, his gun raised.

With Art just yards from them, one of the creatures leapt down from the roof and into his path, blocking his way to the café. He had no choice but to stop as the creature reared up onto his hind legs, towering over him. It snarled as gloopy saliva dripped from its fangs, and then it leaned in towards him, dangerously close, bringing its face even closer to his. Art was frozen with fright, and the whole square seemed to stop in order to watch the exchange. Tommy, Ben, Nidas, even *The Creperum* appeared to pause momentarily, as the creature sized up its prey, staring deeply into Art's eyes, evaluating him. Whether it was fear or something more supernatural, Art couldn't move. He was held there, suspended by the hypnotic gaze. He was surely done for.

Tommy felt useless. There was nothing he could do. Nothing but watch, as one of his best friends was mauled by this... this *thing*. Momentarily, he looked into the night sky. As he did so, he saw something as it flew, spinning, through the air, sailing in a direct collision course with the creature, and then Tommy beamed in glorious amazement as the missile came down squarely on the back of the creature's head with a heavy thud. It was Ben's chair leg! The beast let out a painful howl before scampering off like a wounded dog. *What a shot!*

'Better than a rifle, eh?' Ben exclaimed proudly.

Genius! How many more times did Ben have to save them?!

'Art! Run!' they screamed in unison.

The race was back on again, as Art came to his senses, snapping out of whatever terrifying spell the creature had put him under.

What happened next seemed to take place in slow motion. Art dived for the doorway of the café at the same time as Nidas took aim. Simultaneously, another of the creatures pounced down from the roof. Tommy stretched out his arm, Ben grabbing hold of him for support, ready to reel Art back into safety, reaching for his hand as he dived through the air towards them. Then three things happened at once: Tommy heard a gunshot, was blinded by a flash of brilliant white light, and then he felt a tremendous amount of pain. And then there was nothing.

CHAPTER TWENTY-FIVE

Harbour View

Tommy had no idea how long he'd been unconscious, but when he came to he felt immediate pain in his arm. He breathed a sigh of relief when he saw that the source of the discomfort wasn't from a gunshot wound, as he'd first feared, but from Ben who was still gripping his arm so tightly that it was beginning to stop the flow of blood. Ben just stared at him with a glazed, fearful expression, clearly hanging onto him for dear life. Tommy managed to free himself from his grasp and then checked himself over, only satisfied when he couldn't find any bullet holes. He was even more relieved to find that he still had the Pen of Destiny.

'Ben? Are you OK? Ben? Are you hurt?'

'Huh?'

'Have you been shot?'

'Umm... no, I'm fine.'

'Good, get up then!'

Tommy stood and looked around him, fearful that Nidas or one of the other evil creatures had followed them into the café. He was surprised to find, though, that they weren't in the café at all – they were back in Mr Wiseman's basement. They'd made it home! The magic of the Pen had somehow taken them out of the memory and back to safety.

Away from the perils of war, the monstrous Nidas and away from *The Creperum.*

'Art, come on, get up,' he said, noticing his friend lying face down at his feet. 'Art? Art? You OK?'

He shook him hard, fearing the worst. He didn't respond.

'Ben, quick! I think Art's hurt!'

They both seized him and as they did he let out a panicked gasp like coming up for air. He sprang to his feet, and backed himself against the nearest wall, looking about him fearfully.

'Art it's OK,' Tommy assured him. 'We're safe. We're home. Those things have gone. We did it! We're out! We've got the Pen! We can save Grandpa!'

It was at that point that Tommy noticed Mr Wiseman standing in a shadowy corner of the basement.

'Mr Wiseman! Look! We've got it!' he said proudly, showing him the Pen. 'We stopped *The Creperum*, right? We stopped it from breaking through! Now we can rescue Grandpa. What do we do?'

Before the curious little man could answer him, somebody else ran into view. Somebody soaked to the skin and boasting a shocking bush of frizzy hair.

'Ben!'

'Jennifer! What are you doing here?'

For a brief moment she just stared at him, and from the look on her face, Ben couldn't tell whether she was pleased to see him or whether she was about to unleash another of her furious attacks.

'This young lady has been very keen to see you,' Mr

Wiseman announced. 'Very insistent she was. Wouldn't take no for an answer.'

An uncomfortable silence followed until Ben finally said, 'Jen... your hair...'

At that remark her bottom lip quivered and tears welled in her eyes. Ben thrust his hands up to protect himself as she rushed at him, but, rather than slap him as he'd feared, she instead threw her arms around him and hugged tightly.

'Oh, I don't care about my hair!' she replied. 'I've been so worried about you, Benny! I'm so glad you're OK.' She then peppered his face with sloppy kisses. Tommy had to fight the overwhelming urge to heave.

'Worried? I thought you were cross with me,' Ben commented, relieved that he was no longer in her bad books.

'I couldn't stay angry with you,' she insisted, throwing her arms around him again as he smiled smugly.

Had Tommy been presented with this scene a week ago, he may well have been a little jealous – but not now. Now he was pleased for him. Ben's bravery certainly deserved a bit of recognition, and if it meant that he was the one who ended up getting the girl, then so be it. That particular green-eyed monster had died. Besides, at least it meant that Tommy didn't have to hug Ben himself. He had more important things to do now. Like saving Grandpa.

Ben couldn't pass up the opportunity to show off a little.

'You should've seen me, Jen,' he announced proudly. 'I saved Tommy again, didn't I, mate? I had to jump off a church roof to do it too! I slammed into that big baddy and got the Pen back. And I threw a grenade!' he added, impressing the starry-eyed Jennifer. 'Tell her, Tom. Tell her how good I was.'

When Tommy refused to add fuel to his ever-growing ego, he moved on to the next witness.

'You tell her, Art. Art?'

But Art didn't answer him either. He just stood there with a dazed, vacant expression on his face. He still hadn't spoken since coming out of the memory. The confrontation with that monster was clearly having a profound and lasting effect on him.

Tommy thrust the Pen towards Mr Wiseman.

'So, what do we do now?' he asked. 'How do I change it? Can I use it to stop the Cult from attacking Grandpa?'

'Well, do you know,' he replied, 'that after all of that it may not be necessary.'

The little man smiled. 'If my calculations are correct, and you'll be pleased to know that they always are, then I do believe that your actions tonight would have already altered the timeline.'

'Huh?'

Tommy concentrated hard for a moment. Could their actions in France have changed the present already?

'Are you telling me that Grandpa's alive?!' he blurted. 'That he hasn't died?'

The others, equally confused, also waited for the response. Mr Wiseman opened the door to the basement and stood to one side.

'Why don't you see for yourself?'

Ben nodded his encouragement, and without wasting

another second Tommy made for the stairs. Suddenly he found himself running across Harbour View, past Art's house and towards Grandpa's. Could it really have worked? Could he really allow himself to hope that Grandpa was now at home, alive and well?

He arrived at Grandpa's in such a rush that he barely slowed in time to stop himself colliding with the gate. There were no obvious signs that anyone was at home; the house was in complete darkness. He took a moment to gather his thoughts as he caught his breath, finding it difficult to muster the courage to even ring the doorbell. This was it: the moment of truth. Everything he'd been through up until now had led him to this.

Yet against everything that he'd faced up to now – Nidas, Barbarus, even *The Creperum* – against all of that, he'd at least always been able to hold onto the *hope* of succeeding and of seeing him again. To hear his familiar greeting and to see him once more in that ridiculous gardening vest. But if Mr Wiseman was wrong, if history hadn't been changed, then all of that hope would be lost. It sounded silly now, after everything he'd encountered, but he almost didn't want to know. At least then there'd be no chance of his dreams being shattered.

He steadied himself and shook away the negativity. It had to have worked. It just had to. He pressed the bell, hearing its familiar tone sounding inside. An eternity passed with no sign of activity. Not a light came on or a single noise was made. He waited longer, but still there was nothing. He cursed Mr Wiseman loudly. It hadn't worked.

Why had he let himself believe that it had? Now he felt like he'd lost Grandpa all over again.

Dejected, Tommy turned to leave but was stopped by a loud 'clicking' noise – the clicking of a lock. That was followed by a bolt sliding back from the top of the door. He turned eagerly, waiting impatiently for it to open. But wait is what he had to do. For there was then the coded beep of an alarm being deactivated and the turning of yet another key. What was going on? Grandpa hadn't had that many locks before. The place had been turned into Fort Knox!

With the anticipation building, Tommy braced himself for the door opening, hoping beyond hope that he found Grandpa on the other side. He watched on as the door was pulled from the inside, but it still remained closed. He then heard the muffled mutterings of annoyance from a familiar voice and then the sliding of a second bolt, this time at the bottom of the door. Only then did it finally open.

Standing before him was a sight so welcome that Tommy almost had to rub his eyes like they did in the cartoons; he had to be sure that he wasn't dreaming.

It was Grandpa! Standing in the doorway. And he looked very much alive and well!

'Hello, stranger,' he said fondly.

Tommy loved that phrase.

'Grandpa!' he cried, throwing his arms around him. 'You're alive!'

'Of course I am,' he beamed. 'You didn't think that I'd let them get rid of me that easily did you?'

'But what happened?' Tommy asked, still not really

understanding it all. 'How much do you know?'

'Enough, Tommy. I know enough. More than I knew the last time we spoke, that's for sure.'

Tommy began to notice a few changes in him. Nothing major, but certainly big enough changes for Tommy to see. He seemed different to how he remembered: less fragile, that was for sure. He dressed younger too. Gone was the usual lounge attire – shirt and tank top – replaced now with a much younger and more practical outfit. He looked like he was ready to go paintballing, either that or storm the beaches all over again. And if Tommy wasn't very much mistaken, he could even see a few muscles under his top! Things certainly had changed. It looked as though Grandpa had led a completely different life.

'You mean you actually know what happened to you?' Tommy asked him. 'First time round I mean?' By Tommy's reckoning, if the timeline had been altered like Mr Wiseman had said, then surely Grandpa would have no memory of that alternate reality at all – it would never have even happened to him. 'I thought I'd lost you.'

'Now now,' Grandpa comforted, as Tommy's emotions threatened to bubble over. 'It's all OK now. I'm fine. Much has changed since you embarked on your little adventure. And I know most of it. Well, what I've been told anyway. I know that you've saved me, Tommy, and that you've saved the whole family. And for that I can't thank you enough.'

'But who told you?' Tommy asked, already knowing the answer.

'Why, Mr Wiseman, of course. He's been quite the mentor over the years, I can tell you. Speaks very highly of you too. And do you know he's not aged a bit since I first met him either,' he added, that familiar glint of youthful mischief in his eyes.

'Hey, where'd you get that from?' Tommy asked, noticing a mark on Grandpa's head. It hadn't been there before.

'Oh this?' he replied, rubbing a scar just below his hairline. 'You know precisely how I got it. You were there when it happened!'

Tommy stared at him, puzzled.

'Those bricks, remember? In the church? This is the scar that it left. I remember it as if it were yesterday, for you I suppose it was!'

This was incredible. Tommy had literally just seen that happening, yet to Grandpa it had happened half a century ago.

'And with that everything changed, Tom,' Grandpa continued. 'That confrontation and the warning I had from your friend. Even those bricks. All of it is the very reason that I'm alive today.'

'How'd you mean?'

They were so wrapped up in their reunion that they hadn't even made it over the doorstep.

'That incident during the War – when Nidas tried to take the Pen from me – it actually saved my life. His attack made me immediately aware of the importance of the Pen and of all the dangers I would come to face. Before, I just thought that it was some crazy man handing me a worthless old pen, but since Nidas saw fit to interfere, well, then I realised its true value. And it was that knowledge that led to vigilance, Tom. It led to caution. And ultimately, it led to me becoming a true Guardian of the Pen of Destiny.'

'So you really do know all about it then? About being a Guardian and all?'

Tommy couldn't help but feel a fair amount of pride. Both him *and* Grandpa joining that illustrious list of protectors. He was startled, though, by a female voice that came from the kitchen.

'Who is it, dear?' the voice called. 'Is it him?'

Who could that be? It certainly wasn't his mum's voice, but then, who else would Grandpa have in there?

'Who was that?' Tommy asked, feeling slightly uneasy. That voice had caught him off guard. In fact, it had freaked him right out. It almost sounded like it was... but no, that was silly. It couldn't be her, could it?

'Grandpa? That sounded like...'

Grandpa smiled excitedly.

'Yes, love,' he called back down the hall, 'it's him. It's Tommy.'

'What's going on?' Tommy demanded, scared all of a sudden. His stomach did an involuntary somersault as he attempted to process what he'd just heard – that voice from the past.

'Are you ready for this, son?' Grandpa asked him.

'Ready for what? What's going on?'

Before Tommy could finish, another person came into

view, wiping soap suds from her hands with a tea towel as she walked excitedly from the kitchen.

'Well, don't leave him standing out there in the cold, Len, bring him in!'

It *was*. Tommy couldn't believe it. It was Nan!

A lump formed in his throat.

'Nan!'

'Tommy!'

He ran into her arms and buried his head into her shoulder. There he just stood, squeezing her tightly, too afraid to let go in case it all turned out to be a dream and he ended up losing her again; he'd been without her for so long.

Grandpa, no doubt feeling like a spare part, realised that this reunion wasn't going to end anytime soon, so he did the only thing he could do and joined them. Together they hugged for the longest time, Tommy lost in feelings of pure happiness – so lost in fact that he even thought he could hear the ringing of bells and blaring of sirens; and there he was thinking that all that soppy stuff had just been a figure of speech. *What did he know?* He couldn't believe his luck. He'd set out in the hope of using the Pen to change what had happened to Grandpa – he'd no idea that his actions might be able to get Nan back too. Never in his wildest dreams did he think he'd get to see her again, at least not outside of one of his memories anyway. He'd got two for the price of one, and he couldn't be happier.

When Grandpa finally managed to prise them apart, Tommy remained lost for words.

'But... how?' he managed.

'Now that,' Nan answered softly, tears welling in her eyes, 'is a very long story.' She looked at him lovingly, still holding tightly to his hand. 'Oh, my brave grandson! You've been through so much.'

'And so much has changed since we last spoke, Tom,' Grandpa intervened. 'What you and your friends did changed everything. Because of you, your nan and I have known all about the Pen, about Nidas, everything. And we've been working with Mr Wiseman to protect it from the Cult. He told us all about your role in its story too. You've been magnificent, Tommy. We're so proud of you, but until today we couldn't tell you how much. You see, even as a baby we knew how special you'd become, what you would turn out to be. We just couldn't talk to you about it. It was your actions that saved us my boy. Not just back in France but now too. *The Butterfly Effect*. Like I said, ever since you and your friends warned me of Nidas we've become more security conscious. We had to be. You've seen our locks, Tommy. Those scoundrels would never get the chance to burgle here. And even if they did, then we'd have a surprise or two in store for them, I can tell you.'

He smiled happily and rubbed Tommy's shoulder.

'We've been waiting to tell you all this since before your father was born.'

Tommy shook his head in disbelief.

'All of that from Nidas attacking you?' he commented, in awe of the knock-on effects of that single act.

'Yes. He changed the entire course of things. He's not

as clever as he likes to think, you know. Turned me into a proper Guardian you see. And when us Parkers guard something, we *really* guard it.'

Tommy thought for a moment. 'So does that mean you want it back then?' he asked. 'The Pen, I mean. Now that you're Guardian?'

'Oh no. It's yours now. Yours by right. Mr Wiseman tells me there are important times ahead. The battle. The dangers of the despicable *Creperum*. It's all just around the corner. At least now we can face it together.'

Tommy felt tired all of a sudden. He'd done what he'd set out to do. He'd not only managed to save Grandpa but Nan too. And he'd stopped *The Creperum* once already, surely that was enough? All he wanted to do was spend time with Nan and Grandad, and go and see Mum and Dad again. He wanted to settle back into his normal, quiet life and leave all the danger behind him. Maybe he'd even find the courage to ask Helena Lundy out; he'd certainly done scarier things in the past week. All of that wasn't too much to ask, was it? He'd even do some homework if it meant that he didn't have to see Nidas again.

'I still don't get it though,' Tommy said, putting those protests to one side for a moment. 'Nan, how did you... I mean.... what happened with you and the...'

'Well let's just say that Ben wasn't the only one to benefit from changing history a little,' Grandpa interrupted, winking at his nan.

She smiled broadly.

'Since your grandpa brought that little pen home,' she

said, 'we've had a lifetime of adventure together.'

It was only as she spoke that Tommy began to notice the physical changes in her too. Like Grandpa, she'd altered. Rather than the neat little perm that she'd always had, she now had straight hair tied back in a ponytail. And the flour-covered apron she'd always worn was replaced by a dark jumpsuit. Forget the blue rinse brigade, Tommy thought, she now looked more like a cross between a grandmother and Rambo. He smiled to himself. *Gran-bo*.

But Tommy didn't care. She was back with them, and that's all that mattered to him.

'And we can't wait to tell you all about it,' Grandpa said. 'You'll need to know it all anyway, for what's to come.' He ushered them along the hallway. 'Go on. You two go in there, I'll put the kettle on.'

Tommy and Nan then disappeared into the living room, and even though he knew he'd have to face all of those dangers in the future, he'd never felt safer.

Also available from Candy Jar Books

THE LIARS' AND FIBBERS' ACADEMY
by Laura Foakes

Danny Quinn isn't exactly lying when he announces that his sister has been reincarnated as a dog.

No one believes him though, and he is quickly sent off to The Liars' and Fibbers' Academy – a special place for deceitful children only to learn how to tell whoppers more convincingly.

Aided and abetted by a girl who insists she's a mermaid named Derek, and Inigus Jowly, the school's mysterious caretaker, Danny is able to hoodwink his family until he finally learns the truth.

But this turns out to be more outrageous than any fib he could come up with...

ISBN: 978-0-9928607-3-8

Also available from Candy Jar Books

SILENT MOUNTAIN
by Michelle Briscombe

Jack Jupiter is not cool, he is not brave and he is altogether unremarkable. With constant bullying at school, Jack buries himself in a wildlife book given to him by his father.

When his gran predicts that 'the freeze' is going to happen, Jack cannot resist the urge to test her prophecy.

At the frozen lake he finds much more than he expected. He is drawn into a thrilling and dangerous adventure, where fantastical creatures and unrelenting enemies lead Jack to discover the truth about his father and the mythical Silent Mountain.

ISBN: 978-0-9571548-1-0

Also available from Candy Jar Books

Beware of the Mirror Man
by Benjamin Burford-Jones

Gathering dust in a deserted attic is an ancient black and white television set. Beyond the cobwebs and old bits of furniture, the TV serves as a refuge, home and working TV studio for strange little creatures, known as mimics, who perform 'live' to anybody who switches on the set.

When 12-year-old Sophie moves into the house she stumbles across the attic's secret inhabitants. But all is not well. She is shocked to discover a dark force is lurking at the edge of all mirrors that will do anything in its power to destroy her likeable new friends.

Even more worrying, she receives a mysterious note of warning... Beware the Mirror Man!

A fantastical and heart-warming tale of curses and mirrors, ancient foes and the fluffy little creatures living in your attic.

ISBN: 978-0-9566826-3-5